The Windsurf Boy

Bel Mooney has worked as a journalist for a wide variety of publications, appears regularly on television and radio and now writes for *The Times*. Her previous books are *The Year of the Child - Portraits of British Children*, and *Liza's Yellow Boat*, a picture book for children. *The Windsurf Boy* is her first novel and her second, *The Anderson Question* is also available in Pavanne. She is currently working on another novel.

She is married to Jonathan Dimbleby, and they live near Bath with their son and daughter.

Bel Mooney

The Windsurf Boy

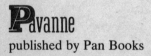
Pavanne
published by Pan Books

The author and publishers are grateful to The Carcanet Press
for permission to reproduce lines from 'The Usk', from *In the
Trojan Ditch* by C. H. Sisson; and to Faber & Faber for
permission to reproduce lines from 'Usk', from *Collected Poems,
1909–1962* by T. S. Eliot.

First published 1983 by Jonathan Cape Ltd
First Pavanne edition published 1984 by Pan Books Ltd
This revised Pavanne edition published 1987 by Pan Books Ltd
Cavaye Place, London SW10 9PG
© Bel Mooney 1983
ISBN 0 330 29734 1

Phototypeset by
Datasolve Information, London
Printed and bound in Great Britain by
Cox & Wyman Ltd, Reading

For Jonathan

Do not suddenly break the branch, or
Hope to find
The white hart behind the white well.
Glance aside, not for lance, do not spell
Old enchantments. Let them sleep.

T. S. ELIOT, 'USK'

Nothing is in my own voice because I have not
Any. Nothing in my own name
Here inscribed on water, nothing but flow
A ripple, outwards. Standing beside the Usk
You flow like truth, river, I will get in
Over me, through me perhaps, river let me be
   crystalline
As I shall not be, shivering upon the bank.
A swan passed. So it is, the surface, sometimes
Benign like a mirror, but not I passing, the bird.

C. H. SISSON, 'THE USK'

—

One

That house had always smelt slightly of damp sweaters put
too soon in drawers, old gymshoes, sand and oilskins. Anna
Lewis breathed it even before she put the key in the lock.
She knew what the rooms would look like, and how the dust
would have arranged itself upon the silent clocks. Nothing
changed; the rooms led off a small, square hall, its linoleum
floor the colour of dried mud and its walls hung about with
ancient anoraks and unravelling straw hats. In the tiny
sitting-room was a window seat (made from draped orange
boxes fitted neatly into the square bay window), a couple of
basket chairs, a battered brown sofa whose cover sagged
upon the rush-matting floor, and a cheap, light-oak coffee
table, which had been given to Hilda as a wedding present
and which had found its way, with countless other family
rejects, into the holiday house on the water's edge.

Behind the sitting-room, the kitchen was cloaked in Formica of a particularly virulent blue, and in mistaken mitiga-
tion someone had once painted the woodwork scarlet. The
pantry was by the back door. There was an efficient notice
pinned to it with rusty drawing pins, which said, 'BEFORE
YOU GO – make sure that basic stocks like tea, coffee, sugar
and tinned food are replaced. Electricity and water *off*.
Always leave the house as you would like to find it. PLEASE!'
Once, years ago, Anna's mother had been angered by the
second cousins and their friends who had borrowed the
cottage, but failed to understand the nature of the place.

It was impossible, thought Anna with the key still poised,
even to approach this unprepossessing pile of bricks and
mortar without her mind shooting into reverse gear, skit-
tering backwards through time beyond her control. It was
like the old pop song which wails that there is 'always
something there to remind me' – something obvious, like

7

the house and the river, but something intangible too, like a smell which hints at a long-forgotten solution to these fragments.

She turned at the door and called out to the small boy who was struggling down the hill, around the corner of the house and out of her vision.

'Hurry up, Tom! Don't you want to see the cottage again?'

'This bag's too heavy,' he complained.

'Well, leave it there and come on!'

He dropped the nylon hold-all on the path and ran to her anxiously, tossing the fair hair from his eyes.

Laughing, Anna caught him, and covered his eyes with her hands, whispering that he must not look at the view, not yet. She pushed open the door and they walked into the hall, tiptoeing and not speaking – as if to disturb the silence were to miss something. Tom whispered at last, 'When were we last here, Mum?'

'Three years ago, when you were four. Do you remember?'

He hesitated. 'Yes. I ... think there used to be a teddy in that room. Was there?'

'Go and see.'

They walked into the small back bedroom and saw the twin beds with polished bed-ends, the tall chest-of-drawers, the little wall-lights with their dusty parchment shades, and the old brown teddy bear leaning on one of the pillows. Hilda had carried him there the year after their parents had bought the cottage, saying that she felt sorry for the place, empty, in the long months when they were in London. She and Anna had imagined the cold air penetrating the brickwork, the summer flies dying soundlessly on damp sills, and spiders spinning secure webs throughout the winter. A lonely house, the laughter gone. It needed a guardian, they decided, placing the bear upon his throne. All three children left old toys in the cupboards, things they rarely used, to keep company with books their father thought he might read on holiday: old-fashioned anthologies on war economy paper, dog-eared thrillers, and a set of Sir Walter Scott with foxed pages.

Tom snatched the battered bear from the bed, tender as

always to small furry objects. Idly, Anna pulled open the middle drawer. The sweaters were still there: navy oiled wool and thick brown double-knit with darned elbows, and the off-white polo-neck she had given her father the Christmas before he died. In one of the small top drawers was an assortment of folded tee-shirts, one broadly striped navy and white, like a matelot's, the others pale and faded in comparison. Tom came and peered, on tiptoe, into this drawer.

'Isn't that Dad's – that blue and white shirt? Why does everybody leave clothes here – don't you want them?'

'Well, when people come here for their holidays and they know they'll be coming back, they leave some useful bits and pieces to save carrying them next time.'

'But Dad won't be coming, will he? So why don't we take his shirt and give it to him?'

Anna saw the worry in his pale eyes and stroked his head. 'We'll do that, darling. We've got four lovely weeks here to look forward to, and when Dad phones you, you can ask if he wants that tee-shirt. Anyway, do you want to sleep in here, or in the dorm upstairs?'

He said, 'Here, near you.'

Anna's parents, William and Barbara Lewis, had bought the bungalow (for that is what it really was, despite the flight of stairs which led to the attic, giving it claim to the title 'house') when Anna was ten, Hilda eight, and their brother Richard twelve. They decided that the plain cottage (which they chose to call it, although Barbara laughed that it was neither old nor pretty enough) standing square on the edge of the river, would be ideal for holidays until the children had grown up and then, improved a little, a good place for retirement. Anna could still recall the quality of her first impression, as the family stood on the shingle beach and stared through the large, open black gates at the squat building, washed pink like so many houses in that area. It was constructed like a child's drawing, with a little window each side of the front door, two dormers in the grey slate roof and a chimney right in the middle. 'Well kids, it's ours,' their father had chuckled, waving the bunch of keys with the estate agent's tag still attached; then Anna had walked straight up to the house and all round it, as if to claim it as her own.

Behind (she discovered then with even more delight) a steep path led up through a wild orchard of unpruned plum and apple trees. Every year they produced an abundance of fruit that fell and rotted on the ground because the family had gone. In the winter the grass was starred with clumps of snowdrops and, later, wild daffodils nodded around the gnarled tree-trunks. The orchard was mysterious and beautiful. On a summer evening anyone who walked down that steep path towards the house became indistinct, as the low sunlight filtered through the tattered heads of tall cow-parsley – flickering on the tips of waving grasses and gilding even the plainest human head.

To Anna it had seemed like a Wendy House magically grown, and she heard with disbelief her parents laughing at the hideous colour scheme in the kitchen. They complained that the real yacht's mast, 'planted' in the garden by the previous owner (who presumably thought that a love of boats had to be advertised thus) bordered on vulgarity, and they wondered if they should change the name from 'Ahoy' to something less hearty. 'It's a lovely name,' she had protested, dancing a spiky hornpipe around the offending mast. 'And it's a super mast too,' Richard had added, encircling it with his arms as if to protect it from their parents' notions of acceptable taste.

So the mast and the name had stayed, together with the scarlet woodwork, blue Formica and yellow Belling stove, and the inconvenient, triangular basin in the corner of the narrow bathroom. Barbara Lewis had furnished cheaply, buying old furniture from the woman at the pub, who was amazed that people 'like that' should pay five pounds for what she had rejected in favour of black vinyl. Then everything that was not wanted found its way into 'Ahoy': odd cups and saucers, a gilt clock, the primary-coloured cushions that had gone out of fashion, some Impressionist prints in mock Old Master frames, and a clumsy little bureau where they kept curling Basildon Bond and information about the tides. There were too many ashtrays and china ornaments. The old barometer in the hall did not work, and the wooden wall clocks remained unwound, as William said that he did not need to be reminded, by their ticking, that the holidays would soon be over.

Indeed Anna's father used sometimes to shake his head, when returning after a long absence, at the lack of choice, of touch, about their holiday home, and say that he yearned for a pretty Chesterfield, or at least a decent rug. But, thrown together in that way the ugly and rejected things settled beside each other, their colours and shapes fading somehow within that delicate atmosphere, until as the years passed they attained the beauty and inevitability of objects used in a ritual. When Richard, Anna and Hilda grew up, adding their own store of disliked presents or 'joke' purchases to the cottage, they had begun to understand how such offerings could become transformed, gaining dignity as part of the pattern.

'This is where I'm going to sleep. Don't you think it's a nice room? Now you can go and look at that view from the window. I think it's the prettiest sight in the whole world.'

Anna stood with Tom in the front bedroom. It had a square bay window which matched the sitting-room window on the other side of the front door. Faded cotton curtains, with an indeterminate floral pattern in pale blue, drooped to within three inches of the sill. One summer, when Anna was fifteen, her father had painted the dark oak furniture white, lightening the room and throwing the old crimson carpet into relief. A double bed faced the window; on summer mornings you woke early and pulled aside the curtains to see the river spreading its pellucid grey, and the gulls squawking in search of breakfast.

'It's so hard to imagine', thought Anna, glancing at the bed, 'lying there with John, making love again and again, and watching, that spring, the rain stream down the window whilst we laughed, deep within our warmth ... and yet it was true, it was all true.'

'Your Dad and I came here for a holiday after we were married,' she said, half to herself.

11

Tom looked up, interested. 'Here? Why?'

She had told him before, she knew, but he loved to hear the smallest details of family history repeated again and again. 'You have a holiday after you're married, called a honeymoon. Dad wanted ours to be here because he liked it, and we couldn't afford anywhere else.'

'Was it before I was born?'

'Of course, Tom! You have babies after you get married – well, usually. Anyway, we did.'

'Why?'

She knelt and hugged him. 'What a funny question. If you're asking me why people have children the answer is I don't know. If you're asking me why we had you, I'll say because we loved you.'

He frowned. 'But you didn't know me then. Mum – did you and Dad love each other then?'

Anna looked into his face and nodded. He was silent, as she expected, his habitual questioning stilled by the vast mystery of what she had just admitted, contrasted with what he knew to be the current truth. He kneaded the teddy bear, holding it in front of him like a shield.

'Poor little boy,' thought Anna instinctively, feeling, at the same time, irritated with herself for such automatic sentimentality. She rose to her feet, briskly. 'Look, we've got a lot to do. We'll get the rest of the stuff from the car – all your toys, remember? Then there'll just be time for you to run to the village shop along the lane. Or do you want me to come too?'

He shook his head; doing things alone meant growing up. 'Good boy.'

By six-thirty they were sitting outside on the wall, eating sausages wrapped in slices of bread and watching the pink light on the water.

'I always used to sit here with my father, you know. It was our favourite thing – to stare at the water and feel peaceful. I love the river.'

Tom agreed, mumbling through the food, but Anna did not hear. 'It's as if I've always been coming here, ever since before I was born, and the river is a part of me. None of the others felt the same . . .'

Mouth empty, Tom interrupted. 'What are we going to do on our holiday? Will we have adventures?'

Gaily, Anna turned to him, 'Yes, we will. Lots of lovely things are going to happen and we'll meet people and go on the ferry, and . . . eat ice-creams.'

'Is it true?' she wondered gloomily to herself. 'The only trouble is, it could all be true, for Tom, if I make the effort. It's all up to me. Nobody else.'

She sighed.

'Mum – why is the cottage so dirty? I don't like it.'

There had been mouse droppings in the frying pan, and Tom had shuddered with distaste, a city child. Now she reached out and patted him, saying that he must not mind such evidence of the tiny lives that were lived on, making 'Ahoy' a home when nobody human was there. Mice weren't dirty, she said, only alive like us. He nodded, the idea suddenly pleasing to him.

Two

As she drifted into sleep, early, after the sausages and chocolate and a brief argument with Tom about whether or not he should go to sleep in his clothes, Anna heard the pinging. She had forgotten it until then, although the sound was deeply ingrained into her memories of the place, so that hearing it again, after a gap of three or four years, was like a gentle electric shock. It transported her back to those nights when, as a child, a teenager, a young woman, a wife, she had lain awake and heard each halyard, stirred by the breeze, hit its mast with a clear metallic ping.

Her father had loved that sound. Sometimes at supper he would hold up his hand, quelling their noise and saying, 'Listen . . .', and he had a private fantasy with Anna that the boats, cold, were complaining to each other like a bunch of tinkling old ladies.

William Lewis had been an armchair sailor, buying *Yachting World* whenever they came to the village, though never during the rest of the year. He took his children on trips to boatyards to ponder the purchase of this sailing boat or that fishing boat, or even once a huge, ramshackle Dutch barge. But he never did buy a 'real' boat for his young family, only a stout rubber dinghy with an unreliable outboard and a small wooden rowing boat. The three children learnt to handle both, although Anna never lost her terror that the rubber dinghy would hiss slowly to oblivion beneath her, plunging her into the cold and slimy reality of her fairytale river.

As they rowed in circles in the shallows their father would sit on the little terrace in front of the house, watching the river through his binoculars and occasionally drawing their attention to the beauties of a passing ketch with tan sails. He dismissed as beneath contempt the elaborate launches trailing arrogant wakes which came to dominate the river traffic as the years went by. In those days there were only a handful of boats moored out in front of 'Ahoy', in the bay formed by a wide bend in the river. Now it was impossible for any newcomer to rent a mooring from the Harbourmaster; countless boats bobbed in front of the cottage as visible proof of affluence.

It was not until she was an adult that Anna had realised that her father had been, in a strange, undefinable way, as afraid of that river as she was herself. The hand which grasps the tiller or rope, or takes the wheel, must have confidence, must know that it has the right to control the water and the weather. For William there were too many questions perhaps, and when at last he hit upon his first positive plan to buy a boat it was too late.

He decided on a chugging fishing boat that could go up river or out to sea, for 'days out', he said, though his children had long grown up – as if he could return them to the vivid past by talk of family picnics. William had taken Barbara, indulgent as always, around the boatyards and chosen the type with great care. He made lists, worked out his budget, and was delighted when George the ferryman telephoned to say that his brother-in-law's cousin had the very boat, a real bargain too. William told Barbara that it would transform their retirement in two years' time – when he would be able to buy *Yachting World* for ever, forget conveyancing and the Magistrates' Courts, and be lulled at night by that insistent pinging on the wind from the water. And later, they told each other with a smile, there would be grandchildren, and holidays and picnics with them, so that the whole cycle could be repeated, their old age full of hidden laughter.

But William Lewis had a massive coronary the week before he was due to journey down to view that fishing boat. Four years passed very slowly before Anna's mother could even glance at *Yachting World* on the shelf of W. H. Smith without tears of anger coming to her eyes.

The next morning was fine. Anna woke very early, even before Tom first stirred beside the unfamiliar teddy bear, and walked to the window to pull back the flimsy curtains. It was high tide. The river was as full as she remembered, brimming (it seemed) almost to the wall of the garden, held in place by an act of unseen will – like the tears in the eyes of someone deeply moved who proudly forbears to cry. Already the indistinctness of the dawn had disappeared, although the thick trees on the opposite bank of the river still wore wreaths of mist. The water was gold and silver-blue; the boats showed starkly against its light. For a long time Anna stood looking.

Later, she went into the kitchen in her dressing gown and searched for food. 'We'll have to go shopping today. Stock up,' she said to Tom, who had already dressed himself. Apart from dozens of ancient bottles, packets and tins, all afflicted by damp, the pantry contained some tins of soup, a tin of minced beef, an unopened packet of crispbread in a tin, and a bottle of good dry sherry, barely touched. For that Anna thanked her sister under her breath.

'Hilda was here at Easter and left some odds and ends.'
'Who's Hilda?'
'Your aunt, silly. We only know one Hilda, Tom.'

15

'Did she bring Simon and Christopher?'

'Yes, they had their Easter holiday here. Must have been jolly cold this year.'

Tom was silent at that. A resentful expression settled upon his features as he hauled himself up on the old blue and red table and kicked at it with his dangling feet. 'I wish they could've taken me. They have more fun than we do.'

'What do you mean?' asked Anna, although she knew.

'Well, because you and Dad don't live together any more it . . . it isn't nice any more. Simon and Chris go fishing with their Dad. Aunt Hilda goes too. They all go. Simon and Chris got fishing rods last Christmas and I bet they brought them. I bet they caught lots of fish. I bet their Mum cooked it and they had it for their tea.'

Helplessly she murmured, 'But you don't like fish much.'

'I'd like that fish. It wouldn't be like the sort we have at school with all that white stuff on. Last year Simon said his Mum had said they were going to take me with them. It's not fair.'

The note of resentment had changed to wistfulness, and Anna's irritation subsided. She felt sorry for him. 'Look,' she said, 'we'll do it next year. We'll have a big family holiday here with Hilda and Alan and the boys, and I'll get you a fishing rod and it will be lovely – just like when I was a little girl and we all came as a family, for all the holidays.'

'Was my Grandad alive then?'

'Yes, he was, darling. And he tried fishing, but never caught very much. He just liked sitting in the boat and daydreaming.'

There was silence for a few minutes whilst Tom spooned baked beans into his mouth. Then he asked, 'Mum, if we come to this cottage next year, with all of them, will Granny be better?'

Anna felt relieved, since she had thought he was about to ask, yet again, about his father. She dreaded having to explain, once more, that when John left their home in April the parting had been permanent. At first Tom had thought it was a game, only seeing Daddy at the weekend, meeting him in the park with strange pretty ladies who hid Mars bars in their handbags. Then he had started to complain, and absorbed his mother's anger like a sponge, without knowing where it should be directed. One day, just before the school holidays started, Anna had found him crying, yet that was not the worst thing. This time he attempted to stifle his tears, his small face growing red in the process, because he said he was much too old to cry. 'By that token,' thought Anna, 'the passing of the years should insure us against our own pain, so that we face old age and death with perfect, grown-up equanimity.' So she had knelt and cried with him, to show that it was acceptable, and realised, when he cried out, 'Why did Daddy leave me?' that hers was not the only rejection.

For the last three summers John had been restless. Like a schoolboy (Anna thought at the time) he complained about his job, bored with computers and reminiscing about his days at Cambridge when he was last (he said) free. Anna had asked him helplessly what freedom means, only to be accused of pedantry. Then, throwing his large-boned frame upon the creaking sofa he had announced that he was bored with taking turns in 'Ahoy', and wanted sun. So they had tried packages in Portugal, Corfu and Spain, waiting in queues at Gatwick, forgetting some essential item of clothing like a striped tee-shirt, and suffering from stomach-ache and heat. Tom complained all the time, because they had not brought enough toys, or brought the wrong toys, and why could they not fit his giant box of Lego into the hold-all? John had slouched drinking each night, watching morosely as the orange sun sank behind the vivid blue swimming pool, and they both sat in silence, listening to the shrieking disco. He called for double brandies whilst Anna, sipping her first Campari, watched him nervously and made him worse. He criticised her appearance and told her she should 'make more of herself', while girls with brown shoulders slid by, to and fro, with John not troubling to conceal his stares. They had been nightmares, those holidays. Sometimes Anna had wandered off alone, staring over a foreign bay and hearing, faintly, a mast somewhere giving off its familiar tinkling sound.

Whilst they were miserable elsewhere Hilda and her family used 'Ahoy' as if it were their own, which Anna resented. Richard came back from America with his second wife, a tall, well-dressed woman who spoke a lot about her feelings, and who exclaimed loudly when Anna first met her that the 'darling little house' was 'terrifically quaint' and that there was something 'really, really British' about it. Anna supposed that Lisa was right. A plain Wendy House, crumbling at the corners and stuffed with a hotch-potch of ill-matched objects given individual value by collective pride and by nostalgia – well, she thought, it was as adequate a metaphor as any for England.

Richard had taken her out to dinner with Lisa to an expensive restaurant just north of Notting Hill Gate, and had started the meal by apologising that the friend – a man of course – he had also invited could not come. Lisa had warned him openly at that point that 'people in a divorce situation feel very negative about attempts to pair them off', and he had retorted that he had been in the divorce situation himself. When he sent the wine back because it was corked Anna decided that the evening was not promising, and so she launched into a long history of the family, for Lisa's benefit. 'And yet,' she thought at the time, as she spooned the ice-cold soup and told anecdotes about their childhood holidays, 'I'm doing this for Richard, my brother, to see if even now he might reveal, by a smile or a laugh of embarrassment, the little boy in putty-coloured shorts who saved his pocket money to spend at the village shop.'

There was just one brief period (she explained to her new sister-in-law) when 'Ahoy' had risen from its status as holiday home. When the time came (two years after the flowers had withered upon the gravel of the 'Garden of Remembrance') that would have marked William Lewis's retirement to a newly refurbished cottage, Barbara astonished her family by saying that she would move there alone. 'It's what your father would have wanted.' They protested that it certainly was not, that never would he have wished her to live alone in such a place, with its memories. 'I know everyone in the village by now. I'll have lots of company, as well as the fresh air,' she protested obtusely – as if loneliness could be staved off by a chat in the village shop and a monthly glass of medium sherry with the vicar.

So their mother sold her spacious Victorian villa in Fulham, but put her furniture into store. She explained that she was going to give her experiment a six-month trial. If her children were wrong, and she liked living in the cottage, the decorators would move in, the kitchen would be redesigned, a furniture van would carry south her pretty rugs and furniture – and the name of the place would be changed to 'Orchard Cottage', as she and William had decided before he died.

Anna felt outraged, particularly at the last idea, as if a government decree had forced a change of name upon her. 'I hate changing things,' she said to John as she poured his coffee. He had chuckled that it was about time; 'Whoever heard of a place called "*Ahoy*"?' She was disappointed that he did not share her reverence for names, for identity.

She need not have worried. As anyone might have predicted, Barbara's plan did not work. She had walked from room to room feeling, not grief or loneliness, but rage. Alone in 'Ahoy' she forced the passion of twenty-eight years of married life into those five small rooms, and they could not stand the strain. Barbara would pick up a glazed ashtray or stare at the garish reproductions on the walls, and try to imagine the place transformed by her own delicate watercolours and Royal Doulton, and yet she could not. She did not weep because William was not there; she gazed with hard, dry eyes at the river he had loved, and hated it for its indifferent perpetuity, whilst she and her husband were cheated of what they had a right to expect.

'It still makes me angry to remember how much Dad looked forward to retirement,' she wrote to Anna in her precise hand, 'because after all those years of hard work he did deserve it, didn't he?'

Anna wanted to write back and say that not one of us has the right to expect and that perhaps it might be better to try and accept . . . something along those lines. But she tossed

19

the pen aside, time after time, furious at the emptiness, the inevitability.

Her plan a failure, Barbara frustrated her children still further by declining to return to London, deciding instead to buy a flat in the near-by town of Synemouth and to make some money by letting the cottage all year round.

'Our mother's gone mad,' said Hilda at the family council, called by Anna to deal with this new evidence of their mother's perversity.

'Well – she has a point in that it would make some money,' said Richard thoughtfully, sucking on a small cigar, 'and are we going to use the place enough to justify keeping it up?'

Hilda leaned forward possessively, '*We* use it – Alan and I use it. When this baby comes we'll have all our hols there. Of course, if she wants to pay for it to be done up, and let it for part of the time – when we're not there – that would be all right. You couldn't let it as it is.'

Richard pointed out that decorating and refurnishing the cottage would be expensive, 'Though I agree, it's a shambles as it is.'

Hilda was looking decisive. 'If Anna and John don't want to go much, and you're away in the States, Richard, Alan and I could go for just the last two weeks in August, and we could let it for £100 a week during the first part of the summer. Easter too. There'd have to be a meter . . .'

At that point Anna pointed out that the cottage belonged to their mother. Her dryness was lost on Richard. 'That's what I was thinking last night. It does raise the question of inheritance . . .' he said, countering Anna's small noise of protest by the observation that realities have to be faced. Seeing them both look pugnacious Hilda settled the matter, 'Don't bring in red herrings, Richard. For heaven's sake let mother do as she likes for the moment, or there'll be a scene. You know what she's like.' They continued to talk about house prices, assessing the profit their mother had made by exchanging a large house in London for a small flat in Synemouth, and of course there was the small income their father had left her . . .

Anna listened in silence, wondering how it came about that adult family life revolved so often around questions of property. Their toys had been shared, and their sweets ... but even then she knew that her recollections were a closely woven mat upon which she had embroidered her own design. Now Richard talked like a businessman and Hilda like a practical housewife, which is what they were. Anna sat, resolving stubbornly that the holiday home would remain with its face, name and nature unchanged, that no tawdry transactions with strangers would mar her memories.

She volunteered to visit Barbara, and report the outcome to the others. A plan was taking shape.

It was a four-and-a-half hour train journey from London to Synemouth, cutting across England's southern counties. Anna noticed how villages were sprawling, and how new hotels loomed near roundabouts, convenient for businessmen on their way to conferences. She caught her breath at the curve of hills and the veil of green in the trees. Sometimes, framed for a second in the speeding window she would notice an old man in one garden bending to the soil, whilst next door a woman pinned out billowing sheets, oblivious of his presence, and close to her a child bowled a little toy along a concrete path. Anna stared. She wanted to seize such moments, and to understand what lodestone drew all such people (and herself) to nest in rows and take part in the same rituals, though separated by the strips of lath and plaster. All the small dramas of babies being born, and girls setting off to be married in odd, uncomfortable clothes, and old men hearing the doctors' grave, evasive words with loosening terror – all the fascination of the humdrum held Anna transfixed, when she thought about it dreamily – as on a train you do, when the book has fallen aside.

Synemouth was a small holiday and fishing town at the mouth of the river, built higgledy-piggledy around steep narrow streets. Two years after Anna's visit that spring it was to boom with tourists and new hotels and the kind of shop that sells the work of local craftsmen as well as home-made pâté. Barbara's flat overlooked the harbour, whilst 'Ahoy' was six miles away upstream. Both were about to become extremely valuable properties – a fact about which Richard Lewis was repetitive, confirming Anna's disappointment with the mind which sought the numinous in the business pages.

Barbara greeted her daughter effusively, giving kisses and sherry in the well-proportioned sitting-room, with its pale green carpet and scattered Victorian bric-à-brac. Only her eyes betrayed her, roving here and there as if something had been lost in a corner and never found.

After a plain lunch of mackerel with brown bread and salad, and more sherry, Anna took a breath and raised the subject of the cottage.

'Mother, can we talk about . . . you know . . . your plan? You asked us what we thought . . . and we had a sort of meeting.'

Barbara laughed nervously, 'Sounds dreadfully formal, my love.'

'Well, not a meeting. A talk, about it all.'

Whilst Anna cursed herself inwardly for falling into her mother's own evasive habits of speech, Barbara interrupted. 'Anna, darling, you know I don't want to do anything you children don't approve of. I know I should have listened to you about trying to live there on my own. I was silly, wasn't I? But that's all over now. I'm so nicely settled here . . . and oh, I haven't told you about my new friends. Harry and Molly Black, they're called. Retired. They've opened the sweetest little antique shop in Stall Street. By the old Market. Harry and I are going to go to painting lessons together. And Molly says she won't be jealous!' She giggled girlishly.

Anna said that she was glad it was all working out. She watched the progress of a large old oyster-catcher, whose tan sails carried it slowly towards the sea.

'You know, when Daddy died I felt so cross that we weren't going to get the chance to do all the things we'd planned to do, that I made up my mind to jolly well show him.'

Anna looked back, puzzled. 'Show who?'

'Why, God, of course! I know it sounds silly to you, dear, because you don't believe in those things, but still . . .'

'God?'

'Yes, I said to him – just because you've spoilt it for us doesn't mean you're going to spoil it for me. But I went through a time when I didn't really believe in it either. It seemed so cruel. Then I realised that I was lying awake at night blaming somebody, and so it must be God. So I decided that I'd prove to him that I could stand up for myself, even without Daddy to lean on. That was really why I moved away from London, where I'd have had you all . . .'

With a quick gesture Anna pushed back her hair. There were no questions needing such answers.

'You don't have to upset yourself by talking like this, Mummy,' she said.

'It doesn't upset me,' Barbara replied, mildly.

'Well, we were going to talk about the cottage.' Anna injected jocularity into her voice. 'You want to let it, but not if any of us really object, is that it? Well, I don't really know how to tell you . . . but Richard and Hilda were terribly upset. They couldn't bear the idea.'

Barbara looked surprised, and asked why.

'Richard said it was awful to think of strangers in the old place, and Hilda was practically in tears at the thought. You remember that old teddy bear she took – it's been there all these years?' Barbara nodded, a sentimental smile on her face. 'Well, she said she couldn't imagine leaving him there to be destroyed by strange children.' She too fixed a smile on her face, as if indulging this myth.

'Is this really true, darling, or are you exaggerating?' Barbara asked.

'Honestly,' said Anna quickly, taking advantage of the doubt, 'that's how they feel. But they both asked me not to tell you. Of course, they said that if you really *need* the money then that's different. But if not, we'll all make sure it gets used. We'll do it up. Look after the place.'

'It's not a question of need, and you know that Anna,' Barbara said. 'Daddy left me . . . well . . . all right, as you know. I just felt, when I lived there, that the house was abandoned. All the past, all gone, and nobody caring now. Things go that way. But still, if that's how you all feel. If you all care that much . . .'

Anna widened her eyes. 'Not me, Mummy. I didn't mind too much – and it's not for us to tell you what to do. But if you think Richard and Hilda are right, then I do too. But you mustn't ever tell them I told you about the fuss they made. I promised them. So you've got to keep it quiet.'

Her mother enjoyed the idea of a secret, especially one that gave her the advantage of knowing that at least two of her children were sentimental under the surface. 'I won't say a word. I'll write and tell them I've changed my mind. But I'm not going anywhere near the place, you know. It will have to get dusty and you'll all have to spring clean it when you go. It makes me sad to be there when it's all quiet, with the river outside the window and the seagulls crying . . . it's too sad.'

The nine years Barbara spent in her flat in Synemouth were, all the family agreed, a success. She hardly ever mentioned William. She joined clubs and did good works and even enjoyed a brief flirtation with a retired Brigadier whose wife had died the same year as William. But William's habits were too deeply ingrained upon her life for her to consider another adjustment, and the Brigadier felt secretly that it would be wrong to entrust his wife's china to other hands. So the unspoken need receded, and when he became too frail to manage for himself he moved to Sussex to be near his daughter, and wrote to Barbara for a while from the private old people's home.

Barbara gazed upon the river a lot; too much, she thought at times. The small things happened to her that happen to everybody, the shopping, eating and drinking, the meetings with people known as friends and evenings with the comforting television set – and there were the Christmas cards to be written again, fresh bills, the death of a pet. Three grandsons were born, and her daughters assumed that this would transform the old woman's life, although from a distance. Richard got divorced and remarried, and he too believed that these events would reverberate through his mother's days with the significance of an earthquake, not knowing that the movement of the river outside her window, grey in the winter or coldly green in early sunlight, could wrench his mother's gaze in mid-sentence, so that the flimsy air-mail letter would flutter to the floor.

Then this year, in March, Barbara wrote a letter to each of her children. She had spent the Christmas with friends in the town, but had been sure to write and thank them for their useful gifts. Then – nothing, until these missives. She had broken her leg, and was in hospital for two weeks. Anna rushed down to see her (a cheap-day return) and closed her mind to the dreary hospital ward in which her mother lay. A couple of weeks later another letter said that she would be moving into a nursing home and that the flat was already in the hands of the agent, who guaranteed a good price. Barbara's neat handwriting communicated the fact that she would, of course, like to see them all, but only when they were next visiting 'Ahoy', for they were not to make a special journey. It was a formal note, identical to all three, and its tone effectively placed each one of them outside a fence, suddenly set in once-familiar soil.

This time Hilda made the visit. It happened that she was indeed taking an Easter holiday in the cottage with her family. With concern she reported back that the leg was still not right, that there was a mysterious back pain too, and that their mother was evasive on all questions about her health.

Anna felt guilty at the time, but she could not make the journey down. John was in the process of leaving, and she felt sure her mother would be upset at the news; in any case her energy was spent. Then despite herself she was forced to become involved after the resentment Richard caused. He wrote from New York asking if Barbara was sure that her will was in order, and it took the combined efforts of Hilda and two friends in Synemouth, plus a cashmere bedjacket from Anna, before Barbara would forgive him.

When finally she did, Anna was annoyed at the long, fulsome letter that landed on her mat and praised 'their little boy' for his cleverness at being made deputy managing director at the age of thirty-seven. Now Richard sent flowers once a month and wrote long letters about Lisa's pregnancy, and between his visits to America crammed in flying visits to the nursing home. Hilda was just as assiduous in her attentions from afar, with her weekly letters telling how well the boys were succeeding at school and how Alan's practice was flourishing, and the small gifts in padded envelopes. 'They flap around, as if they don't want to know anything that might stop all their activity,' Anna would think sourly. She felt guilty because John had told her that she did nothing to keep him in their marriage, and guilty because it was therefore her fault that Tom was so confused and worried about his father; and furious with her mother for adding to this burden.

But at last she had written to Barbara and said that she was bringing Tom to spend the whole of August in the cottage, that they were looking forward to seeing much of her, and helping her to get better.

Three

After breakfast Tom wanted to explore the village. They walked up through the orchard, holding on to the little, broken wooden fence that edged the stepped path. At the top of the orchard was a white gate which led out into a wide lane bordered with thick clumps of red campion and celandine, ragged robin and cow-parsley. Just off this lane was the village car park, where Anna had left her car.

The village sprawled in humps and bumps, accommodating the curves of the land and the bends in the river. Its geographical centre was the little church with its squat Norman tower, but this was lost behind the crest of the hill from 'Ahoy', and could only be glimpsed if you walked along the beach and over a field – a long walk Anna had taken less and less as an adult, although as a child she had often accompanied her father through the lych gate and learned from him the names (now forgotten) of pieces of old stone.

The social hub of the village was at the opposite end, the busy cluster of pub, shop and pier, and the pontoon which made the fantasy of messing about in boats become a reality for the scores of summer visitors. Except at an exceptionally low tide you could not walk from the front of 'Ahoy' along the beach to this centre of activity. For most of the time this lent an air of exclusivity to the strip of shingle outside the Lewis's gates; on a hot day it was a nuisance, for a long climb back up the orchard, along a lane and down the village street was necessary to reach what was, after all, only a couple of hundred yards away.

Tom danced upon his shadow. A cabbage white flitted across Anna's path, to lose itself amongst the feathery cow-parsley in a hedge that seemed to crackle with life. As they walked along the lane Anna breathed deeply, and allowed herself to feel a content of sorts, for the first time for months, as if already this place, this river air, was weaving its old enchantment. And half-unconsciously she breathed to herself, 'It's all going to be all right,' without knowing why; without knowing.

At the end of the lane was the village shop, its window filled with a jumble of tins and packets and fading postcards of the church. Mary Treadle kept the shop, George the ferryman was her husband; together they knew everything that was going on in the village, and most of what happened within a radius of five miles as well. When Anna had first brought John to the cottage, for their week's honeymoon, Mary had left flowers by the back door to greet them, though no one in the family had thought to tell her of the event. Anna remembered too how George had stomped through the garden on his bad leg that first morning and grinned at them through the kitchen window. 'How's 'e shapin' up, then?' he had asked her, with a knowing grin at John. The childhood rituals, the visits to the shop for sweets and the ferry rides, had shifted; Anna had not minded that

George, an essential participant, felt thus privileged to acknowledge this other, adult, rite.

They saw him now, as they approached the shop, limping along the lane to meet them. After ruffling Tom's hair, and giving him a Cellophane-wrapped sweet, George looked at Anna. 'All right then, my dear? Mary said the boy was in last night. No husband then, I see.'

It was not a statement, it was a question, and once again Anna wondered at the advance intelligence. She decided not to be evasive. George had been in on the beginning, she thought, so he might as well know about the end. 'No, George. He's not coming down. Matter of fact, we're not living together any more.'

He looked grave and shook his head, staring at the ground. 'Now that's bad, that's bad. My mother, she do say – anyways, she did when she were with us, like – she'd say, when God puts the peas in the pod they'm to stay in that pod.'

She forced a smile. 'Well, John decided he didn't like our pod, George, so that's that.'

He wagged a finger at her. 'You mark my words, he'll be back, that boy. You remember what owd George do say, your John'll come back.'

'John's not a boy any more. He's nearly a middle-aged man now – though he doesn't like the idea. We've all grown older, except you.'

George smiled at her, tenderness creasing his battered face. 'When I think of what a little skinny thing you was, comin' up the shop to buy your sweeties. How many year be it, now?'

'Twenty-five – don't remind me,' said Anna.

'Well, well . . . but look at you, you look as pretty as that time you brought them two boyfriends down at once, and them Selway girls at the pub was jealous. Said you was greedy, like!' He chuckled, and she joined in.

'It's nice of you to pay me compliments, George, but I am getting old. I had a birthday the other week.'

'Well, it's not for a gennulman to ask a lady's age, is it? But I'll tell'ee summat for nothing. Them Selway girls 'baint a patch on you. They'm both fat now, 'cos they've had so many buns in their ovens they've risen like the dough theirselves!'

Anna threw back her head and laughed. 'You're just as wicked as ever, George.'

They heard the sound of a bell, and George looked round. 'I better be goin' now,' he said, and hobbled away at speed. There was no car ferry at that point of the River Syne. Only George's big old wooden boat, with its smelly outboard, could ferry picnickers across to the densely covered bank on the other side, with its mysterious creeks and dells. At any time you could stand on the village 'front' and pull the thick rope to sound the old brass bell, summoning the ferryman – even at night, when the water slipped black beneath the bows, as cold and threatening as the river of the Underworld.

Anna and Tom wandered round the village, greeting one or two old residents who remembered her well, and exclaiming at the smart new houses that filled every available gap between the cottages. They were uniformly blue and white, with an occasional pale turquoise diluting the self-consciously nautical air, and all bore names like 'Sea Spray' or 'Ferry View' – names, Anna reflected with affection, that were at least a little better than 'Ahoy'.

One of the new buildings was a Spanish-style concoction which had the name 'Hacienda' blazoned in gothic poker-work on a varnished section of wood. Its shutters were varnished too, and matched the carved gateposts in orna-mentation. It looked as out of place in that little street as a mantilla on a Devon cow, and Anna wondered aloud how the owners had ever managed to obtain the necessary planning permission. Where the new houses had been built close between the old thatched cottages the effect was like that of a mouth in which some of the teeth were fitted with sparkling new crowns, whilst the old ones had the natural flaws and patina of age.

Anna did not like it, though she held the feeling in check. Why should she object if people chose to retire to the village she thought of as her own – to meet the architect and builder, and to construct for themselves a dream home, a brilliant vision in plasterboard and glass, with louvred cupboard doors and permanently bright brass knobs? Why should they not give their rejoicing visible shape – even if it took the form of a mock ranch? In this sunlight, at least, she was prepared to be generous. The village was changing faster than ever, she thought – but it had always changed: the young people growing and leaving, the city-dwellers (like her parents) buying up the cottages when the old people died. Out of season the place had a ghostly air; few children played in these village streets.

'What do people do here in the winter?' asked Tom, as if picking up the thread of her thought.

'They just live.'

'No, I mean what do they DO? Have they got jobs?'

Anna thought, 'Some have, some haven't. Mr Treadle, who we were talking to, he and his wife have the shop and the ferry, so they work like that. Some people work on the farms round about, and some go into Synemouth, I suppose. On the bus – to work in the shops, maybe. But a lot of teenagers have left because there aren't any jobs for them. And a lot of old people come here to live when they retire.'

'What's retire?'

'It means that when you get to a certain age you don't do your job any more.'

'So do you have a holiday then?'

Anna looked down at his face, noticing the still unformed delicacy of the line from his forehead to his nose – a line that was imperceptibly setting into John's profile. His skin was soft and glowing. She said, 'I suppose it is like a holiday. Your life is one long holiday when you retire, and so people do their gardens and hobbies ... and things.'

She hated the thought. Twenty-five years since William and Barbara had first brought them to 'Ahoy'; twenty-five years until the time when (presumably) she would retire from the Redmond Press for ever. 'Twenty-five years each way, and I'm standing here thinking about it,' she reflected – and the mind buzzes back and forth, trying to understand the idea, like a trapped fly trying to find a way out of the closed room into which it was born and in which it will surely die, dried out upon the sill. 'Twenty-five years each way . . . and here am I in the middle way,' she quoted to herself, 'trying to . . . what was it again? Trying to learn . . . something or other.' She could not remember the lines, but it was something beyond them that Anna's mind chased, jagging to and fro like the butterfly she had watched earlier.

At the foot of the hill was the river, and a cluster of boats that had been pulled up on to the strip of beach outside 'The First Mate's Arms'. There was a small quay; from it led a long pontoon formed by floating platforms linked by railed walkways, the whole thing miraculously held in place by an assortment of ropes and anchors. Men fished and children hunted crabs from this pontoon. On an August day it hummed with the noise of outboards, laughter, and the too-loud instructions of tentative holiday sailors. George's ferry chugged across the river and back, and people on holiday for two weeks felt a sense of importance if they gained first-name terms with him. When he hobbled along the quay small children stood aside with instinctive respect for the man who knew this river as well as he had once known the faces of two sons – drowned while they were fishing early one stormy morning years ago, when the Syne decided to claim her traditional quota.

It was almost lunchtime. A warm breeze blew Tom's hair back as they walked down the steep road, then stood looking out at the river. Girls were lying in swimsuits on the small patch of stony beach; groups of people already stood outside the pub balancing plates of sandwiches and brimming glasses.

'Mum, I'm really hungry,' said Tom.

'We'd better go back to the cottage.'

'Why can't we have lunch here? A sort of picnic. Go on, please,' he pleaded.

The crowded pub deterred her. 'Still,' admitted Anna to herself, 'I haven't come to terms with being alone. It would be John who would go and get the drinks – always. And now I feel nervous about going in there, and organising everything.' A few men stared, or she imagined that they did, putting her arm around Tom's shoulders so that she

31

should feel less alone. 'All right,' she said, briskly, 'wait here and I'll go and get us a picnic.'

She fought her way to the bar, and then to the food counter, and finally carried crisps, crab sandwiches, a cornish pasty, a can of lemonade and a glass of wine outside. Tom stood, scanning the doorway, a worried expression upon his face. 'He's afraid of being left alone too,' thought Anna, as she negotiated the small flight of stone .steps down to the beach, spilling a little of her wine.

Settling uncomfortably upon the pebbles they ate in silence, watching the water. From this low angle the river looked impossibly crowded with boats, as if nothing that ventured out could move without becoming entangled in someone's lines, or bumping into an orange buoy. Around Tom and Anna people were talking in loud voices; a girl laughed harshly, and the screams of the children sounded close. Anna sat trying to remember something – the thought that had eluded her earlier – but failed. 'It's too noisy and too hot, and maybe I just feel depressed suddenly because I want it all to be as it was. Or I want myself to be as I was,' she thought, and sighed.

Suddenly Tom stood up, shading his eyes and pointing out at the water. 'Look, Mum, what's that?' he called. She could see nothing, even though she stared hard in the direction of his pointing finger.

'Look there, look!' he cried impatiently, and Anna screwed up her eyes against the light which, shimmering off the water, dazzled her. Then in the distance, through a gap between two boats, she saw what appeared to be a bird's wing, sweeping low upon the water. She stood up too, seeing what Tom had seen and smiling down at him.

In the distance, floating effortlessly amongst the moored boats and gliding out and away from the shore with perfect freedom, was a small blue and white sail. It caught the sunlight, glittering. At times it seemed to become part of the river itself, breaking its dancing surface, and Anna caught her breath at the silence, the beauty. She could see a tiny figure, like a black speck against the light yet clearly defined, which appeared and reappeared as the little windsurf board cut to and fro in the bay; and they stood watching, quietly.

Four

'The Park' was a Victorian gothic building on the outskirts of Synemouth, looming over a quiet road of Edwardian redbrick villas. Tall gateposts, each surmounted by a carved stone lion, flanked a gravel drive that curved between well-kept lawns. The place had been a hospital once, with forbidding corridors and high, echoing rooms, painted in that ghastly green which hospital administrators so often choose to heal the sick. But in the 'seventies a spacious new hospital had been constructed on the other side of the town, with a well-equipped obstetric unit and (this the pride of the Regional Health Authority) a forward-looking department of gerontological research – to take account of the presence of Barbara Lewis, Molly and Harry Black, and so many others on that part of the coast. All the Synemouth Hospital had in common with the old building were walls of eau-de-nil.

Bought, gutted and completely transformed, 'The Park' became a nursing home, with beige-carpeted corridors and magnolia paintwork, and copies of *Ideal Home* on the waiting-room tables, to suggest to a casual observer that this could well be home.

In the front hall, an auburn-haired woman in her late forties sat behind a reproduction antique desk, which might have passed for the real thing but for the fact that the mock-drawers, finished with dainty brass handles, concealed enormous and efficient filing systems. When Anna approached, clutching Tom's hand, the receptionist was riffling through one of these with one hand and holding the phone with the other. She spoke in a low voice; Anna had a sense of secrets kept, with none of the promise of

Christmas. She smelt the woman's perfume and noticed how the hair, clearly visible down to the roots upon that bent head, was in its natural state dull and grey.

The phone clicked down. 'Mrs Lewis was it you wanted? Just a moment, please.' With a bright smile the woman consulted the book before her on the leather surface, then directed them to the second floor and room twenty-four. 'The lift is down the corridor and through the swing doors.'

'Not the lift,' thought Anna, feeling afraid, suddenly – as if it had not occurred to her until that moment that she would actually come face to face with her mother here at last. 'We'll walk up, Tom, it'll do us good. Exercise.'

The nineteenth-century staircase curved around its polished rosewood banister; their feet were silent upon the carpet. Tom whispered, 'Mum, I feel shy – because I haven't seen Granny for a long time. I feel all funny in my tummy.'

'Oh no, don't be so silly,' Anna replied, her voice high and bright in the quietness, as they crossed a patch of variegated light thrown through a tall blue, gold and red stained-glass window upon the landing, as if upon a church floor.

'Darlings!' Barbara called out in her old theatrical way, walking stiffly across the floor in a pink cotton dressing gown and holding out both her hands. Anna kissed her mother. She smelt of Bronnley lemon soap, and her hands were cold. 'Look, here's Tom,' said Anna in a voice she hardly recognised as her own, 'hasn't he grown? Isn't he big now?' As her mother bent to fuss over the child Anna stared at her; the wrists poking from the frilly sleeves, the neck, the curve of the back. She was shocked at Barbara's thinness; it was as if someone had peeled away the soft and fleshy woman Anna remembered. Revealed was a frail and bent stick creature, whose bones strained as if to burst from beneath the skin.

'You look really wonderful, Mummy,' Anna said.

It was true in a way. Barbara's hair was set back from her forehead in soft grey waves, and it was as thick as ever. Her face was made up, with just a touch of pale blue upon her eyelids, and her nails were carefully varnished, as ever, a pearly pink. Nevertheless there was something odd and unnatural about the smile, the near-gaiety of her expression, as if someone had mistakenly painted a new picture upon a canvas that was thin, papery and vulnerable.

'It's wonderful to see you both again. It seems . . .'

'Yes, I know,' broke in Anna, too quickly. 'It's extraordinary how quickly the time goes.'

'I suppose it does, darling. When you're so busy. And of course things have been hard on you, haven't they?'

'Never mind about me, Mummy, tell us about you. How are you? You look wonderful.'

'It's sweet of you to say so, darling. I'm fine. Fine.'

'Well . . .' Anna looked around the room, 'this is nice. Are you comfortable?'

'Very comfortable. You can do what you like with your room.'

'It's lovely.'

The room was about twelve foot square, the mullioned window looking out upon a quiet garden, with a glimpse of the sea glistening between the tree-tops. It contained a small armchair, covered with beige linen, facing the view, and another, without arms, upholstered in cream vinyl, next to a light-wood coffee table. A small fridge and a television set completed the furniture. Barbara's old transistor radio stood upon the table, and next to it was the tapestry on which she had been working, flung down carelessly when they arrived.

With prints of Degas ballet dancers on the walls, and a muted brown and gold rug, the room had an air of miniature completeness, of stasis, that Anna found disturbing. It was as if her mother had been suddenly transformed into a little doll, placed carefully in the dolls' house drawing-room by its small owner, who had forgotten to return.

It was the bed that shocked Anna most – the more so because of the contrast with the rest of the room, and the silver-framed family photograph (the five of them sitting on the wall outside 'Ahoy', years ago) that stood upon the television set. High, enamelled in white, with wheels and pulleys, it was unequivocally a hospital bed, and jutted out into the apologetic room like a broken spar.

'Now tell me what you've been doing, tell me everything,' said Barbara, drawing the seven-year-old boy upon her lap as if he were an infant. 'There ... are you having a lovely holiday?'

Anna held her breath, but he did not squirm or seek to escape. 'Well, we only got here yesterday, so I don't know yet,' Tom replied.

Barbara let him slip off her lap. 'Of course you did! And you came right away to see your silly old Granny, bless you.'

Anna picked up the photograph and put it down again. She wondered, through her tight smile, why her mother had to talk in that way, foolishly, and with no sense of who it was in the room with her. Apparently Tom did not notice, for he stood in front of Barbara, not pulling his hand from hers, and asked, 'Granny ... why are you living here now? Is this a proper hospital?' Anna walked quickly to the other chair and sat down facing them, but her mother avoided her gaze.

'Well, I've just come here to have a little rest, my love. You tell me – do you think it looks like a proper hospital?'

He looked around the pleasant room, taking in the picture and the flowers and the fruit. Anna had taken him to visit friends in various London hospitals, and he remembered the wards, the smells, the huge expanses of mopped floors, and flimsy curtains drawn around this bed or that.

'Not really,' he said. 'Can I have a grape?'

Barbara pushed him in the direction of the fruit bowl.

'Eat as many as you like, my love. I'm getting old now, Tom, and it's nice to have lots of people to look after me. This is like my holiday home!'

'Is it really nice, Mummy?' Anna asked, quietly.

'Wonderful. The nurses are nice and the food is really good – much to my surprise. Do you know, we had the most delicious mackerel last night. I know they were fresh. They even mash the potatoes well. I don't think even Hilda could find something to complain about!'

Anna felt the familiar resistance against being drawn into a conspiratorial joke about her sister, even though she shared her mother's irritation with Hilda's immutable certainties.

Barbara had fallen into the habit soon after her husband's death, as if by criticising each of her children in turn to the others she could demonstrate both her knowledge and her rights.

'I suppose it should be good – since you're paying for it,' said Anna.

'True.'

Tom was playing with two small metal cars he had brought in his pockets, making them crash noisily to an accompaniment of guttural sounds. The little din seemed harsh and out of place in that room. Anna said, 'Oh Tom, do hush,' sharply, and in the moment's silence that followed she could hear a radio somewhere in the distance, playing light music.

'Mummy, I wish to God you'd tell me how you are,' whispered Anna, suddenly. 'What's going on?'

Barbara motioned towards Tom. 'Not now, dear. Don't let's do that now. Anyway, I want to hear all about you.'

Anna felt as if someone were slowly tightening the red kerchief she wore around her neck. She swallowed. 'Well, there's not much to tell. I'm still plodding along with the firm. I was going to leave, for a change, but they made me a senior editor. It means more money. It's all right. Sitting round all day reading other people's books isn't a bad way of making a living.'

'And is Tom all right – with that woman?'

'Yes, she collects him from school every day and I pick him up at six-thirty. She's nice.'

'Oh . . . yes, well, children need security, don't they?'

'Of course.'

Barbara looked down for a moment, then across to where Tom was dropping orange peel into the waste-paper basket. Anna thought, 'I know what's coming.'

'And how is . . . John, these days? It's so dreadful, Anna. I can't believe it.'

'Why not? It's perfectly believable to me.'

'But you two seemed so suited . . . and so happy. I always thought you were like Daddy and I, when we were first married.'

'Did you? Well, it just shows how you can take the world in.' Anna made her voice as flippant as possible. From the corner of her eye she saw that Tom was listening, staring at his dirty knee and picking an old scab. Lowering her voice she added, 'Don't let's bring all that up now, please. It's upsetting ... pour le petit.'

Her mother poured herself a glass of water from a cut-glass jug Anna recognised. She had given it as a present when William and Barbara had celebrated their twenty-fifth wedding anniversary with a family party. They had played the old games partly from habit, and partly to distract attention from the perpetual bickering between Richard and Susie, his first wife. William had loved the Waterford crystal, which matched his whiskey decanter, and the heavy glasses – taking a pleasure in the accessories of his life that Anna could not understand.

Barbara noticed her daughter's gaze, and said, 'You can have some of your own things around you here. It makes it more like home.'

This time, when she looked round, Anna noticed things which had escaped her before: the pretty antique sewing box William had bought Barbara the day he became a partner, the leatherbound *Oxford Book of English Verse* he had chosen one Christmas, the green-glass fruit bowl with a silver stand his partner had given him one year – though why, Anna could not recall. Two small Staffordshire figures stood upon the window sill, with a little silver mirror, and the old red leather photograph frame that had contained William and Barbara's stiff wedding photograph for as long as she could remember.

The familiar pretty objects, as much a part of the scenery of Anna's childhood as the ugly ones in 'Ahoy', seemed like fragments, isolated pieces of Roman mosaic from which the archaeologist tries to deduce a past glory. 'I'm glad,' she said.

There was a short silence, then Barbara rummaged in the bedside cupboard and produced a bar of chocolate for Tom. 'There's a little shop-trolley that comes round each day. We can buy all sorts of things. But Molly comes every day and brings me what I want. Molly and Harry are both so good to me, dear. The other day they reminded me that they'd never met you. They've seen Richard and Hilda once, when they were down, but never you. I'd love it if you'd go and visit them. Why don't you give them a ring?'

Absent-mindedly Anna nodded, and so Barbara scribbled the telephone number on a piece of paper and handed it to her daughter. Anna felt helpless. So Molly visited and was good; and so was Harry; and so (surely) were other individuals in her mother's world, who nevertheless had no place in that life as she knew it, and none in her own. She resented them: their solicitude, and the time, the long vacant hours of old age, that enabled them to display it.

Without noticing, she had pushed the scrap of paper roughly into her jacket pocket, so that her mother's voice sounded pained. 'Look, you'll lose it. Haven't you got a nice note case? Do phone them. It would please them so much, because they don't get many visitors, unless . . .' The voice tailed off, and became apologetic. 'But you must only do it if you have the time. The main thing is for you to have a lovely holiday.'

Anna heard it, and thought, 'One day, perhaps, I shall be in a flat somewhere by the sea, watching the trees shed their leaves, and waiting. Hilda will ask her boys to visit their aunt, and they will groan inwardly at being forced to accommodate themselves to age and its desperation. Will they come? Will Tom come, with his children, or will I feel too ashamed to ask them?' It was imminent self-pity, not guilt, which made her store the paper carefully inside her wallet, saying, 'I'm sorry, I wasn't thinking. Of course we'll visit them.'

Barbara was satisfied. They spent the next ten minutes talking of people they knew, and which old friends or relatives Anna had seen. Barbara asked questions about theatres and dinner parties, but usually interrupted before the description she had requested was finished, so that their talk was like a series of short stories with the crucial pages missing, cut short before the dénouements.

'It wasn't like this when I talked to my father,' she

thought. After school, or when she came home from college in the holidays, William would sit in the Windsor chair at one end of the long kitchen table and fire questions at her, brushing aside the inadequate, short replies of the daughter who thought it too much trouble to tell. 'Now I want all the details,' he would say, settling his elbows upon the table. Barbara used to joke that it was all part of their father's training: he was forced to extract the smallest details of approximate truth from strangers who sought justice or property, and were horrified at the price. William Lewis was a good solicitor and had never wanted to be anything else, despite his distaste for divorce, with all its bitterness.

But Anna knew that his persistence meant more than that. It was because he was interested. He had the rare capacity to reach right out towards those he loved, and enter even into the changes within them, instead of keeping them fixed neatly, wings spread in the most flattering position, in his collection of desirable objects. He understood Richard's ambition (though it was scarcely fledged when he died), listened patiently to Hilda's boyfriend troubles, and bore Anna's silences. When he had pressed her gently, wanting to know her, Anna had often brushed him aside; and she could remember the hurt that drooped at the corner of his mouth. A burly man, not tall, with a fleshy jaw and oddly small, sensitive hands, reaching out to her with, 'What did you think when he said that . . .' or, 'Did you wonder whether . . .' Remembering, with a catch of love in her chest, Anna listened to her mother discussing the price of clothes with sudden irritation.

'Mummy, there's too much to talk about now, and I want to talk properly,' she said, shutting the flow. 'I'll come in two day's time, and I won't bring Tom. Is that all right?'

'But darling.'

'No, I've decided. I'll bring him the time after that. It's not fair to . . . No, I don't mean that, I mean that I want to sort things out with you. I'll find someone to take care of him for the afternoon. Perhaps George Treadle will take him to and fro on the ferry.'

Tom's eyes lit up at this prospect, and he started to whoop

with delight, but then he looked across to his grandmother. 'I'll come and see you lots of times, Granny.'

'Of course, my pet.'

'Granny . . . ? Mum didn't tell me what's the matter with you. Are you sick?'

'Oh, don't you worry about me. I've just got a bad leg and a bit of a pain in my chest sometimes. That's all. Now you run along, and be a good boy for your Mummy.'

As they were about to get into the car, which was parked at the side of the building, Tom asked, 'Where is Granny's room? Can you see it from here?'

Anna judged that it must be at the back, and so they walked a hundred yards until they turned the corner of the building and were standing at the edge of the long wide lawn they had viewed from Barbara's window. In the distance a nurse pushed a tiny woman in a wheelchair. Under a tree, on a long teak seat, a group of people sat in the shade, a family (Anna guessed) visiting that man in the dressing gown. The sun was hot and high in the sky. The people were dappled in a sharp white light, like deer poised still in jungle grass, camouflaged, yet not protected by the light from sudden death.

They studied the rows of windows, each with its own graceful point, until at last Anna stretched out her arm and said, 'Look!' Her mother was standing by the window, looking out; a slight figure in pale pink, with grey hair. They waved, but she did not see. Tom shouted, 'Granny!' but his voice was lost upon the air. Barbara stared ahead, wearing the look of expectation mixed with resignation that you see in the faces of those who wait in a queue for a late bus.

Five

'I'm going to sunbathe.'

'Why?'

'Because I want to.'

'Why do grown-ups always want to get burnt? If you run around and play the sun hasn't the time to burn you, not like when you're sitting still.'

Anna laughed, pulling the old deckchairs from the little garden shed and brushing off the accumulation of cobwebs and mouse droppings. 'Ugh,' said Tom. One of the chairs was slightly more presentable than the others, so Anna singled it out for her struggle, feeling rather as she did when changing Tom's nappy for the first time and the limbs would not go where she wanted. 'I never could get a deckchair up,' she said; then, 'Oh, blast and bugger it!' when the fleshy part of her thumb was pinched between two bits of the wood.

The chair erected, she looked at it with distaste, thought of fetching a damp cloth, then changed her mind, flopping down on the grubby canvas. Tom was looking at her expectantly.

'I want to go out,' he said.

'You went out this morning.'

'But that was only to see Granny.'

'Charming,' said Anna, opening her book. Why was it that children were able to penetrate, in one sentence, to the heart of one's own guilty feelings? Tom did not really care about seeing his grandmother, but why should he? They had not spent years together; she had not retrieved the toys he threw from his pram, because London had been too far from Synemouth and in any case (thought Anna) Barbara had not sought such involvement. 'And yet she did all those things for me, for years, and she was what approving people would call a proper mother, there at night with a warm

42

drink; but still I recognise the distance between them, and like him, I already dread the next visit.'

Tom was talking – or rather complaining, to himself. She said firmly, 'Now listen, young man. I'm going to have a quiet sit down here, with my book, and you are jolly well going to leave me alone. Do you hear? You go and play with your toys, and when I've been sitting here for half an hour, if you haven't disturbed me, we'll go and eat ice-creams and watch the boats down on the front. OK?'

He nodded and ran into the house, as Anna slid down in the old chair and stretched out her bare legs in the sun. They were pale and she noticed with disgust how her thighs spread out upon the canvas, the flesh pitted like the skin of an orange. 'That's the trouble with reaching thirty-five,' she muttered aloud, prodding her limbs with a finger, 'your body goes completely to pieces. It breaks up on you. God, how depressing.' She spread out both her hands, palms upper-most, and stared at them. There too – a complex web of tiny criss-crosses: enough for the least percipient fortune teller to conclude (for a price) that you are getting older.

'What does it matter anyway?' she thought, picking up her paperback from the grass. Anna had always been amused by women she knew who spent longer and longer at the hairdresser or beauty salon, to compensate for the gradual erosion of their looks. She had worn the same, scant amount of make-up and kept her hair in the same brown bob for years now, even though, from time to time, John would complain that she ought to 'make more' of herself. The women he liked all did, but even when he was leaving Anna scorned to make the kind of 'effort' he suggested. But her birthday, spent for the first time alone, had been a gruelling experience. With Tom in bed, Anna had opened a half bottle of Moët, and cooked herself a veal escalope, sloshing too much lemon juice into the pan so that the meat tasted sharp. Slightly drunk, she had stared for a long time into the mirror, then cried in bed at ten o'clock, because John had gone and because she had not dared to ring a single friend to tell them of her need.

'It's funny, but I think about him less and less,' she

thought, opening *The End of the Affair*, and gazing at the print without reading, her eyes catching odd words like 'love' and 'hope' then moving on. 'And all the passion, all the agony Greene portrays here – what does it amount to but the single act of sex I've done without for months now, and could do without for ever? When I think how I cried and cried, just like someone in a novel, and now I'm sitting here looking at my own legs and thinking how hard it is to believe in all this renunciation, this great drama of the soul. You forget it, after a while.'

Tom approached with a chunk of Lego, asking her to separate two tiny pieces that were stuck together beyond the power of his small fingers. Tetchily, she did as he asked, then waved him away, holding the book in front of her face.

'Mum . . .!'

'No.'

'I can't understand how to make this digger.'

'Then make something easier.'

'But all the easy models are boring. I . . .'

'For God's sake, TOM!' she shouted, her voice harsh.

There was a silence for some minutes. Anna turned a page, dissatisfied with what she read, her mind wandering. She hated the character Sarah in Greene's novel, infected as she was with God and choosing to renounce, in that name, what most people never find. 'I just don't believe any of it, that's the trouble,' Anna thought, flipping the book shut. 'People don't give things up like that. They don't choose pain just because they are tainted with religion – and they don't die for it either. It's what's wrong with the book . . .' She kicked at the grass and wished she had brought out one of the ordinary whodunnits that lay around the house.

Tom was standing by the lichen-covered wall that separated 'Ahoy's' garden from the beach. Too small to see over, he had raised himself on the old log that had lain there for ever, and was looking intently out at the water. The sun gleamed on his pale hair and skin; she let her eyes travel over his little body, with its bony knees and slightly hunched shoulders, feeling a rush of pity flood her eyes. Then, as if

44

he knew she was watching him he turned, his mouth open with excitement, all memory of her shout erased.

'Mum – I can see him! I can see him!'

'Who?'

'It's the windsurf boy. Out there!'

'It's *who*?'

'That boy. That windsurf boy we saw yesterday.'

Anna rose and strolled towards the wall, leaning upon it at his side. She followed his pointing finger, and saw the same blue and white sail out in the bay. It was closer this time, so that they could see the brown figure, arms spread out, leaning sharply back towards the water as the white platform cut through the little waves. He caught a passing breeze; a few seconds later it dropped and the sail wobbled for a moment or two, before the young man shifted his position, so that the sail filled again and he set off in a different direction.

'I wish I could do that,' Tom said, wistfully.

'It's pretty hard I should think,' she replied. 'You must have to be strong.'

'I am strong. I could be a windsurf boy. Will you buy me one?'

Anna laughed. 'You must be joking. And by the way, I think the word is "windsurfer", not "windsurf boy". You can't do that until you're grown-up, I'm afraid.'

Later, when a Lego boat was satisfactorily built and sank like a stone in the washing-up bowl, Tom and Anna climbed the orchard hill and walked the long way round to the village 'front'. The place was busy, as usual, with little boats bustling to and fro, carrying boys in lifejackets and old men in yachting caps. The sound of outboards made a background noise like the hum of a hive. Anna imagined how a space invader might come and lift the lid off this particular piece of sky, and wonder at the tiny creatures dashing hither and thither, with no apparent pattern or purpose, around the amorphous wet stuff, drawn by some extraordinary compulsion to set themselves upon it in fragile floating shells.

They walked along the pontoon, and Tom stopped to watch a group of four children, all about his own age, catching crabs. Each child had a bucket; two of them held proper crabbing lines over the water, and the others made do with a piece of fine cord wound around a wire coat-hanger, with a safety pin on the end. On the boards beside them their bait stank – a sweet smell of old meat and fish and bacon rind, exposed to the afternoon sun.

'Why do they catch the crabs?' Tom asked.

'We used to do it – just for fun,' she replied.

'Do they mind?'

'I don't know. They see the bait and have a nibble, so that can't be bad. They don't get hurt. I don't see how they can mind.'

In the children's buckets, the crabs struggled furiously on top of each other, waving pincers in the eddying murky water and clunking shells against the orange or blue plastic. Tom watched, fascinated. Suddenly one of the boys called, 'Hey, look at him, he's the biggest yet,' and winding his line around its holder he pulled the unyielding creature from the darkness of its natural element into the light, so that it hung, claws flailing, as if drowning in the air. The boy dropped this crab into his bucket to join its fellows, but it fought against capture and imprisonment and safety, crashing against the side of the bucket, where the water level had risen almost to the top. Its captor flinched nervously as the pincers sliced the air, clutching the side for a moment before falling back into the bucket.

'Help, he's going to get out,' cried Tom.

The boy looked around and explained, 'I don't know why he's fighting. We always let them go in the end.'

'He wants to let himself go. He wants to be in charge,' grinned Tom.

They jumped back in alarm. The crab had managed to hurl itself over the side of the bucket, to hit the boards with a thud. The five children squealed and danced with excitement as the creature started its sideways flight, claws rasping on the dry wood. Instead of instinctively heading for the water, it scuttled, in its frenzy, into the middle of the pontoon, where people were walking. It stopped, sensing the vibrations, and squatted there like a terrified, ugly alien; yet a small soft creature under its slimy shell.

Anna stared. She hated such things – all insects, even little fish. The children were laughing. The crab did not move, and she noticed how its shell was mottled, beautifully, in browns and greens.

'It's cruel,' she said to the boy with the crabbing line.

'We aren't going to hurt it,' he said.

'But it doesn't know. You never do,' she said, and quickly bent to pick up the thing, not minding its claws. For a second she looked into the waving, furious eyes, then turned to drop it, with a plop, back into the water.

'Why did you do that, Mum? We wanted to see what it would do next.'

'Poor crab,' was all she said, pleased that he had used that 'we', and could stand now, as part of the group, to catch more crabs.

After a few minutes Anna sat down upon an upturned dinghy, spread her legs out in front, and let her gaze drift up and away over the boats, to the trees on the other side of the river. She remembered how they used to take picnics to that bank, across on George's ferry or else chugging across in their own rubber dinghy, with their father at the outboard. They would play hide and seek amongst the gnarled trees which strained back against the steep lie of the land, and dipped to touch the water itself.

Barbara used to wrap lettuce sandwiches in greaseproof paper, and pack them into an old, unravelling basket ... But another image superimposed itself upon that one, an unwelcome vision of a frail figure at a window, wearing a too-young, baby-pink frilly dressing gown and staring out at the world. Anna screwed up her face and banished it. No, something else ... then, not now. There were secrets in those trees and dangers for any child. Cowboys and Indians, baddies and goodies, even fairies and witches when Richard was prepared to be babyish, whilst the smoke from their picnic fire drifted gauzily through the trees a few yards off, and Barbara cooked sausages in the old frying pan. Fear was far away ... but once Hilda had jumped sideways to avoid her brother in a game of Touch, and had fallen heavily into a shallow pit, disguised by spreading bushes. Anna could feel her own helplessness now, as Hilda screamed and Richard ran for their parents, who came running to soothe the sobbing child with hugs and Elastoplast. It was easily done.

A noise disturbed her. She dropped her gaze from the distant trees to the river, where George Treadle's ferryboat was swinging across in a wide curve, bringing passengers from the opposite shore. There were about five people on board, but one of them was clearly impatient, for he stood in the bows with one foot on the gunwale, ready to jump ashore. As the boat drew nearer Anna saw that he was not a man, as she had at first supposed, but a teenage boy.

With about fourteen inches of water between the ferry and the landing-stage he leapt off, calling 'See you, George,' over his shoulder and striding off up the gangplank in battered trainers. Anna watched, wondering why he seemed familiar. She had not seen him before, she was sure; he had the kind of face that would be easy to remember. Almost arrogant in expression, it was still beautiful, rather as a starkly modern piece of furniture has its own angular beauty. It was the kind of face (Anna thought, with some amusement) that you associate with Californian beaches, not villages in the south-west of England. The boy had short brown hair and wore a denim shirt flapping loose over blue shorts. He looked about sixteen or seventeen, she guessed, although he lacked the gangling awkwardness of most boys that age and moved with compact grace.

Her pale legs were spread in the path he must take in his rapid, jaunty progress along the pontoon. Anna saw how tanned and muscular his own legs were, and quickly pulled hers back out of the way, with some shame. There was such a careless speed and assurance about his manner that she felt annoyed, and wanted him at least to look down and say, 'Excuse me.' But he did not.

The boy strode past her and the children without looking to left or right, and once he was past them he hoisted himself along one of the narrow gangplanks by taking his weight upon his arms and letting his body swing, like a gymnast. 'He really thinks he's good – cocky little sod,' thought Anna, smiling to herself. And it was then that she realised where she had seen him before. Something in the compactness of size and shape; something seen in the distance balancing wind and water – he was the one they had watched upon the river, windsurfing with such skill.

Six

Barbara turned from the window after standing there for so long that her leg became numb, and the sight of the patients under the trees had dissolved into the whiteness that was becoming so familiar. Everything swam together before her eyes, the corners softening, the individual colours merging and diluting with a generosity of light from the sky. Yet there were no tears, although the first time this had happened she had raised a hand to her eyes to wipe away whatever moisture made all external things glitter so. She discovered that her eyes were dry. It was as if by staring at the world, with its leaves and grass and flowers and sounds and people moving, by staring long and hard enough, she could see through it, passing beyond into the heart of things.

She blinked and rubbed her eyes. The room came into focus, lit from behind her, the bed casting its shadow upon the floor. Orange peel littered the area around the waste-paper basket, where Tom had thrown and missed, and he had left grape pips upon her coverlet. Mechanically she picked them up, the pain incising when she straightened again, so that her hand trembled, poised above the detritus within the basket. Barbara stared at the crumpled tissues, the papers and the pips, and thought how squalid, how pathetic was this excrement of her existence.

'But there I go again, wallowing in the sort of feeble self-pity I thought I'd got rid of for ever,' she thought, checking herself and hobbling away from the ordinary little waste bin with its perfectly harmless, untragic contents. After William's death she had allowed herself to invest every single object around her with pathos, so that even the bread knife became a symbol for the cutting short of shared breakfasts and drew her irrational hatred. The house, the furniture, the rugs, the ornaments, the books – all of it was dusty suddenly with a fine drifting of memory; and yet solid, for all that, unarguably there. And Barbara had noticed, for the first time, the space between objects, as an artist pays attention to the necessary spaces in his composition; except that she had nothing to create, now that the frame was empty of William.

'Any moment now Nurse Anderson will come in and glare around at the mess. She'll ask me how "we" are, as if all she wants is to become the Siamese twin of an old wreck of a thing like me. What an idea! One day I'll scream and throw my tray at her when she says "we". How I hate her cosy, lower-middle-class way of muffling everything with cotton wool, so that it's all nice and sweet, and so that even my horrible dimpled lump becomes "our breast", and she has the cheek to call my smelly urine "our waterworks". One day I'll throw "our little sample" in her silly made-up face.'

Barbara thought about lying on the bed, then changed her mind, although she was breathing painfully again, something catching in her chest, so that even a small cough was difficult. In the armchair she let her head loll back, exhausted, and stared at the smooth white ceiling. They had come and they had gone, and this room bore no trace (now that the pips and the peel had been cleared away) of the arrival she had longed for. 'But did I, really?' she asked herself, falling into her habit, grown in the last ten years, of correcting and questioning herself, as a partner or a close friend might do. 'How much do I really want to see my children, and how much is that sort of habit too, an assumption, like love?'

Yet before Anna and Tom had arrived she had bathed carefully, soaping herself, dusting liberally with her favourite lemon fragrance, and even sprinkling the matching cologne upon the clean bedlinen as well as upon herself, terrified of the stale and decaying smells she sometimes detected in the atmosphere when she returned from the bathroom at night. She had secreted the chocolate for Tom, and debated a long time about whether to buy him a colouring book and some crayons, or, rather, whether to give Molly the money for such a purchase. 'Better wait until you know him a bit better,' Molly had finally suggested, 'then you'll know what kind of thing he likes.' She had agreed; but waited nervously, ready a whole hour before they came, and worried that she had no gift for either of them, to reward them for the visit.

'Anyway,' Barbara thought, 'typical of Anna not to bring anything for me, not even a bunch of flowers. I didn't expect it, of course, and I don't really mind. It's not that. It's just that she never did think of things like that; normal things, like taking flowers to a hospital. Or to a nursing home. Perhaps she didn't because this is a nursing home and she didn't want me to think she thought she was visiting a hospital. Maybe she was being tactful. What a strange girl, Anna is, even if she is my daughter and I do love her. Maybe it's the clothes. When I was young you always dressed smartly in your thirties, to go anywhere. A dress, or a suit, that sort of thing. And now they all wear jeans and tee-shirts and those shapeless jackets, and even the ones in their thirties try to look like teenagers, with things written across their chests. It can't be done. We realised it, so they should realise it.'

So often now she felt irritable, although no one had said or done anything to annoy her. It was not what they did; it was simply that they were. No human being could cross her path without conjuring up images of other human beings, from a former life, who surpassed them; or spectres of early hopes disappointed. 'That's why the old are always testy or full of grudges. You imagine that you will sit remembering all the happy times, and yet what is left to you is resentment. You resent your children for not being as you hoped they would be; your friends for growing old or dying too, so that they can't serve your needs; and people around you – like

Nurse Anderson – for being so young and alive and yet so dead, full of empty clichés and magazine emotions and horrible common sense. And suddenly, when you're doing nothing as you are nearly always doing nothing, you remember somebody who annoyed you, years ago, and you still feel a prick of anger, even now. Oh dear God, I wish you would take all this spite away from me, so that I could accept the people around me, as I expect them to accept me.'

She closed her eyes and breathed deeply, feeling some of the tightness vanish from her chest. Her arms flopped, open-palmed, upon the supporting chair; she allowed her still knees to relax and fall apart. Sunlight from the window was pale gold, to blue, to red, to white upon her eyelids; time suspended and the bright neutrality returning. Then there was a brief knock and the door opened.

Barbara looked round, expecting to see one of the nurses, but young Dr Elkins stood in the doorway, fiddling with his moustache.

'Sorry to disturb you, Mrs Lewis. I just wondered if everything was all right?'

He was still learning, this doctor, she thought. Probably guilty about private medicine too, and partly despising us all, so that even the politest inquiry sounded cool.

'Oh, I'm fine.'

'Dr Jacobs would like to come and see you this afternoon.'

'Oh – today?'

'Yes . . . er . . . it will be convenient; it's not your treatment day?' He made as if to glance at the notes he was carrying, but did not open the file, waiting for her to tell him.

'I don't go today. I'm here all day.'

'Good . . . er, so that will be fine. I might see you later then. Goodbye.'

He closed the door behind him and Barbara settled back, closing her eyes again. Another knock. This time she refused to open them, clenching tightly so that the colours became blackness.

'Mrs Lewis? Are you all right, Mrs Lewis?'

The voice was gentle, and Barbara smiled, looking up.

'Hallo Sandra. Just having a rest after my visit.'

Sandra Massey was the only nurse Barbara called by her Christian name, although she had not invited a reciprocal intimacy. The large patient woman in her forties, who had returned to nursing now that her children were grown, occasionally reminded Barbara of a milky ruminant creature which necessarily accepts its own usefulness.

'Why don't you make yourself nice and comfy on the bed?'

'No, I'll have to be in there soon enough. Might as well make the most of my time outside it.'

'I wish you wouldn't always say things like that, Mrs Lewis. You sound so . . . so . . . er . . .'

'Bitter?'

The woman looked confused. 'No, I wasn't going to say that. Sad, I was going to say. Didn't you enjoy your visit? Wasn't it your daughter who was coming today?'

'You've got a good memory, Sandra, after two days off. Yes, it was Anna, the older one, with her little boy.'

'Oooh, that's nice. How old is he? What's his name?'

Sandra's face lit up as if the imagined pleasure were her own: real, experienced.

'Tom. He's seven, I think. Or is he still six? You forget, with grandchildren.'

'Of course you do. I said to my three, don't you be too quick about making me a grandmother. But our Susan's is due in a month's time now, so I'll soon be a granny like you!'

'Oh, but a very young granny.'

The nurse sighed. 'Not so young now, I'm afraid. I can't do as much as I used to. You get tired. Backache – things like that.'

Drily Barbara murmured, 'Yes, indeed you do. I know,' deliberately, to see Sandra's cheeks grow pinker with consternation. 'Oh I'm sorry, Mrs Lewis. I wasn't moaning. I'm lucky to have health and strength, and not a poor back like yours.'

'Don't worry, Sandra, I don't mind at all. I don't mind anything.'

The nurse shook her head slightly and looked cowed, without reason, as she walked across to the washbasin and took the thermometer from its glass. 'Oh well, let's get on with the routines.'

Barbara said, 'It's funny you know, with one's children ... You'll find it too, one day, if not now. There comes a time when they suddenly seem strange, like creatures on another planet ... as if you're looking at them through a telescope. There's Richard, so successful, and by the way did I tell you they're expecting a baby too? Oh yes, I did. And there's Hilda who's so happy with her husband and her two boys – she's good at nearly everything. But Anna ...'

'It must be awful for her, left alone with Tom.'

'Do you think so? I suppose.'

Sandra Massey looked up sharply, not prepared to tolerate such questioning of the obvious. 'Well, of course!'

'Anna always adored her father. That was the worst thing, when he died, for her I mean. I think so. It's hard to know.'

Sandra agreed, 'No, you never know, with people,' and held out the thermometer. Obediently Barbara opened her mouth. The thing felt hard, almost painful, under her tongue, and yet she was used to its coldness.

'Being here is never as I thought it would be,' she thought, as Sandra stared down at the watch that was pinned to her plump bosom. 'I imagined long, quiet days reading, and visits, and little sleeps, but mainly all the time left, to catch up on the books I saved to read until I had the time. I thought there'd be lots of time to think, too, embroidering and listening to the radio. And yet they come in and out, wrapping that rubber thing around my arm, and sticking the thermometer in my mouth, and marking my visits to the lavatory on the graph – as if all that made any difference! Endless cups of tea, with two dry biscuits on the green plate, and the menus to be filled in, and Dr Elkins knocking on the door, and Sandra coming in to tell me that the ambulance is waiting for me so can I come downstairs. Who would have thought that all the time would be spent making sure I'm keeping alive?'

Without knocking Nurse Anderson bounced into the room, smiling her pink smile, her pearl studs in place.

'Oh, I didn't realise you were already doing all that, Nurse Massey.'

'Yes, I'll manage, don't worry,' Sandra replied.

'Did you enjoy your visit, dear? Your daughter, wasn't it?'

'Auuuh,' said Barbara, the thermometer in place.

'That was nice for you.'

Statements, people always made statements, telling you what you needed, what you wanted, and what you must think about all that happened in their little world that had become yours too. Barbara wanted to tear the thing from her mouth and shout that it was not nice, that there was nothing to say, that they should all get out of her room and leave her to contemplate the white light in the sky. But she nodded again and assented. 'Auuug.'

'Waterworks all right today?'

She nodded.

'Bowels open?'

She shook her head.

'Oh dear, would you like to take something for it?'

Sandra's pencil was poised; she looked concerned. Barbara took the thermometer from her mouth and held it out, 'I wish you wouldn't leave that thing in for so long. I feel a fool with it stuck in my mouth. And do stop fussing about my bowels. There's all the rest of the day to get through yet, and I might put my mind to making something happen, just to pass the time. Visits to the loo are something to look forward to. And now for heaven's sake, stop fiddling with me!'

She made an ineffectual brushing-away gesture with her left hand, but knocked her knuckles against the table, so that tears stood in her eyes. Sandra was staring down, looking rueful. But Barbara caught Nurse Anderson's reflection in the mirror, where she had turned to pat her glossy fringe, and the blue-shadowed eyes turned briefly to heaven in supplication. Then the nurse turned to say coldly, 'Now, now, Mrs Lewis, don't let's get ourselves worked up. Nurse

Massey has to go through the routine, and you know that as well as I do. Now then, would you like me to get you out a fresh nightie? We're having a visit from Dr Jacobs, aren't we?'

'This was clean on this morning, because we were having a visit from our daughter.'

'Well then, you'll be fine.'

Nurse Anderson's smile was as soft as neon light; Barbara hated her and sulked. Sandra was looking worried again. 'Why is he coming this afternoon? It's not his usual afternoon, is it?'

'I don't know why,' Barbara muttered, 'Dr Elkins just told me.'

Nurse Anderson was clearing away, clattering briskly, as Sandra never did. 'Oh, I know what it's about. He just wants to have a little talk.' She looked across to Sandra with an expression full of conspiracy, but any significance eluded the other nurse, who smiled in a puzzled fashion and said, 'That'll be nice.'

'What does he want to talk to me about? I know everything he has to tell me.'

Nurse Anderson looked at her coldly. 'Well, it's not for me to say, Mrs Lewis, but I think he wants to have a proper talk with you about your plans.'

They had gone at last. Barbara picked up her tapestry, then let it fall. Her body was aching, yet she felt determined not to lie upon the bed, not today. Plans! You would laugh, if it were a laughing matter, she thought, stretching out a foot and regarding the twisted blue veins that stood out like lumps of grapes from her feet. 'Plans? A Caribbean cruise, a flight across the Andes, a run in a marathon, with feet like that?' She knew what it was, what he wanted to say, and said, 'I won't do what they want, I won't,' as she heaved herself to her feet, and decided, through the twinges and stabs of real pain, that other movements inside her body made the promised visit to the lavatory urgent.

'And won't they be pleased,' she said.

Seven

Mary Treadle was not the kind of person who could easily allow the lives of others to meander along, with the slow, steady movement of the Syne, without her intervention. From her shop she felt that she ruled the village; the village (which could not do without her expensive but convenient wares) felt, at times, unconvinced of the benevolence of the dictatorship.

When old Mrs Selway went blind it was Mary who organised a group of willing ladies to go and sit with her, when her son and daughter-in-law were busy in the pub. Equally effective was her dislike of those she described as 'hippies'. When a shambling young man, with 'sixties hair fifteen years out of date, took 'Rose Cottage' on a long let, and brought a girl, a baby and another shaggy young man to live there, Mary Treadle's imagination revolved around nameless iniquity. When the hapless girl in her trailing skirts and multi-coloured knits tried, in the shop, to make conversation about the healthiness of stone-ground flour (which the Treadles did not stock) she felt the ice close around her heart. Conversations would stop when the trio entered shop or pub, and Mary would hiss to horrified old ladies that she wouldn't like to say which of them fathered that poor baby. In the end the three young people left the village, taking their earthenware pots and wickerwork and books on yoga and rosy, well-kept baby, and returned to their friends in Stoke Newington, shaking their heads because the virtues of love and peace and stone-ground had not penetrated the idyllic riverside village they had seen as a retreat.

George Treadle kept apart from all such tittle-tattle. He allowed the wife who stood behind the counter with rolled-up sleeves to rule his life, as she ruled the nervous young men who brought supplies to the shop. With the memory of two coffins laid out in their low sitting-room, and Mary sobbing upon one and then the other, the strong woman beating upon his chest in her rage, he allowed her to mother him as well. But sometimes he would interrupt as Mary imparted a particularly scandalous piece of news to a friend, with a mild, 'Now, Mary, now. You don' rightly know if that be true.'

His wife would reply by addressing her confidante, as if he were elsewhere. 'Oh owd George, he do live in a world of his own, like a babby! Like I was saying, Pat, I just happened to be leaning out the window and I saw her with that bikini top right off, for all to see!' Then George would hear the ferry bell, and hobble away from their O-mouths of alarm.

He did agree, however, when Mary said to him at breakfast that she was 'worried about that poor little Anna Lewis'. Anna had reverted to her maiden name, a decision which normally would have met with Treadle disapproval, were it not for the fact that they saw her as a victim; besides which habit had made that name, not the other one, natural. The Treadles liked Anna, accepting her as a part of their own past, before the village sprouted holiday homes from every nook and cranny, so that it was impossible to get to know the changing owners and tenants. The Lewises, said George, were 'one of the old families', conveying in that phrase his own nostalgia for the village of the 'fifties and 'sixties, a proper village, with children (including his own) playing in the streets, and the arrival of the few summer visitors a genuine excitement.

It was because George thoroughly approved of his wife's plan that he stomped down the orchard path one grey morning, pushed his head around the kitchen door, and invited Anna to pop up to the shop there and then because Mary had a melon and a couple of fresh chops in, that would be sold soon, 'but she do want you to 'ave um'. The summons touched Anna, as evidence of their concern.

When she reached the shop, ducking her head as second nature to enter the small room, it seemed as if the floor space was filled by a woman who was stacking groceries into a box. It was not that she was large, although she was in fact slightly taller than Anna herself. But she was dressed as if for lunch in London, in a floral dress that poured forth frills from every seam, and delicate high-heeled sandals. Since everyone in the village wore jeans, tan cotton smocks, or rough sweaters, this apparition with elaborately curled chestnut hair seemed out of place, filling the shop as inappropriately as a piece of bejewelled Renaissance enamel work stuck in a carpenter's wooden frame.

'Anna, I want you to meet Valerie Paul,' said Mary Treadle quickly, seeing that Anna was about to withdraw and wait outside. 'Mrs Paul, this is Anna Lewis. I was telling you about her.'

The last words were emphasised. The woman turned to Anna with a bright smile. 'Hello. You have a holiday cottage here too, don't you?'

'Yes, it's along this lane, but down a bit, by the river. It's the pink one, called "Ahoy", with the mast in the front garden. Have you just come to live here?'

Valerie Paul pushed a hand through her hair and laughed, 'Oh no, we couldn't live here all year round. Bit too quiet. We live in Bristol, but we've had a house here for two years.'

'Really? Whose house did you buy? I know the village very well, though I haven't been down for three summers.'

The other woman looked down at her sleeve, and fiddled with the thick gold bracelet on her wrist. 'Oh, we didn't buy anywhere old. We had a house built. We found the place first and decided that it would be good for holidays. More for them than for me, it must be said! First we rented a cottage, a broken-down old place full of the most awful junk. So Adrian bought a plot of land . . . and here we are.'

Anna asked again which house they owned, and had to be severe with the corners of her mouth when Valerie said proudly, 'It's up the road and off to the left, down Church Lane. We've got brown shutters, have you seen it? It's called "Hacienda" because Adrian loves Spain. We used to go there every year before it got so common.'

When the shop was empty Anna looked at Mary Treadle

and grinned. 'Gosh, Mary, this village is getting very glamorous.'

'Well, I do like to see a woman make the best of herself.'

'Oh, definitely.'

'It'll be nice for you to go up there for a drink tonight, won't it, Anna? I thought it 'ud do you good to meet someone your own age, instead of sittin' all alone in that cottage, and your mother so sick, and all.'

'She's not alone, she's got me,' said Tom, who had been peering into the frozen-food cabinet, where multi-coloured lollies lay covered in delicate frost.

Mary Treadle handed him a bar of toffee and said, 'Yes, my dearie, but I wanted your mum to meet some grownups.'

'Oh, I see,' said Anna, who had not, until then.

She looked gloomily into the small white wardrobe. Two pairs of blue jeans, one pair of rust cotton trousers, an old flowered cotton skirt and a blue cheesecloth dress – that was all she had brought, except for an assortment of tee-shirts, one cardigan and her cotton jacket. There was nothing fit to clink glasses with crisp frills. What on earth was the woman doing, walking round like an advertisement for *Vogue*? Anna stared out of the window at the grey water, working out all the permutations she could have worn, had she imported her London clothes to 'Ahoy'. It was futile.

Music drifted from the sitting-room. She had allowed Tom to sprawl and watch an old film, a Terry Thomas comedy, countering his complaint about the old black-and-white set with the observation that the film was monochrome too.

Sitting at the little dressing-table, Anna rested her chin upon her hands and studied her reflection. A thin face, overshadowed by her heavy fringe and ear-length bob; brown eyes; full mouth – Anna imagined that she looked exactly as she had at twenty-five, and she was not displeased.

She smiled at the reflection, mimicking vivacity, and said, 'You must be Adrian! How lovely to meet you. I hear you are a Hispanophile. And what a lovely Spanish-style hacienda you've built here!' She giggled, showing her teeth; then stopped, leaning forward to examine them more closely.

It starts with the gums, retreating from the enamel like vulnerable, pink sea-flesh from any probing harshness, and bleeding slightly upon the brush. Around the eyes appears a web of fine lines, more subtle than the feet of any crow, resembling rather the tracery of veins in the tail of a tropical fish, or the work of a demented spider. Smile lines carve a passage down from nose to corner of mouth, and the edges of the lips lose their definition, breaking up into invisible channels. Anna had once read of a model who, knowing this, decided to smile less to preserve her looks. She had wondered at the time what on earth that girl could be saving her face for. Old age?

'It was all very well,' she thought now, frowning at the glass, 'to sneer at vanity when I was thirty, but now when I'm faced with a sexy woman of about thirty in the village shop, I sit here wishing I had smiled less when John came home late for the fourth night in a row with long hairs on his suit, and refrained from laughing aloud when that twenty-year-old girl rang hysterically to say she was in love with him. Just think how I might have saved my face, in more ways than one.'

She pinched her own forearm. As age creeps upon you the pinch stays there, just for a second, the skin losing its elasticity and retaining the touch, just as the thighs relax into puckers of mirth. 'God, it's disgusting,' thought Anna, all humour gone, and picturing for a second those muscular brown legs that had walked past her without a pause, throwing her own white limbs into dreadful contrast. She waved a mocking finger at her own reflection and said aloud, 'Lady, you are getting old, and that's all there is to say. Next thing, you'll be lusting after younger men, to try to recapture your lost youth.'

She had not noticed Tom standing in the doorway.

'What are you doing, Mum? Why are you talking to yourself? What does "loosting" mean?'

She felt foolish. 'Oh, I'm just telling my face in the mirror how pretty it is. Now go back to your film!'

At six Anna dragged an unwilling Tom up the hill. When he complained that he hated going to see people he did not know, she assured him that she hated taking him, but had no choice. She felt tense, uncomfortable. The blue cheesecloth, John's matelot sweater knotted round her neck in the current style, and a good mask of make-up (by her own modest standards) gave her confidence. At the gate of 'Hacienda' they paused. Anna warned Tom not to say that she had laughed when they had first seen the house.

'Why not?'

'Because they'll be hurt.'

'Why?'

'Oh, for God's sake, Tom!'

Valerie Paul opened the door and held out an arm in a theatrical gesture of welcome. Anna observed the tight, white jeans and purple silk blouse, adorned with a heavy-weight amount of gold chain. Then she looked over Valerie's shoulder.

The house was open-plan, so that from the front door she could see immediately that there were only two or three people in the room. It was a long space, with sliding patio doors along one side, and a low ceiling, intersected by the sort of track lighting Anna always expected to move on its own, pursuing its prey. The floor was covered with a thick gold carpet; split ranch-style doors led into what Anna assumed must be the kitchen. The long sofa was covered in material the same colour as the carpet, with the subtle, shiny finish of good synthetic pretending to be velvet. The low back of this sofa was punctuated by hard little cushions, patterned in brown zig-zags; their colour was picked up by the huge leather armchairs with arms the shape of saddles. An elaborate brick-and-copper fireplace was filled with an arrangement of orange dried flowers; glass shelves each side held an assortment of chrome objects and sea shells. In the centre of the room a large square coffee table, smoked glass supported upon chrome legs, displayed a fanned arrangement of *Yachting World*.

'How old are you?' asked Valerie, patting Tom's head. He ducked. Without waiting for a reply she went on, 'You'll be able to talk to my little boy in a minute, though he's not so little now! He doesn't like his mum's friends.'

A tall fleshy man in a crumpled, cream lightweight suit was advancing across the room towards them, shirt buttons straining across his stomach. The hand that held Anna's was damp, and clasped for just a moment too long. 'Hello, I'm Adrian. Heard about you from Val. Now, before I introduce you, let me get you a drink. What'll it be? G and T?'

Anna asked if she might have some wine.

'Of course! Red or white? Sweet or dry? You name it.'

Valerie steered her to where three people stood; two men in well-pressed denims that looked as if they might have been bought yesterday, and a woman in a clinging dress of pink cotton jersey. The shorter man wore a red cotton neckerchief; the other, whose face was pale and thin, had a yellow golfing sweater over a white shirt.

'Anna, this is Jasper and Susan Herbert, who've got a holiday cottage here too. And Tony Keene, who's an old friend down for the week. This is Anna – she's been coming here for absolutely yonks.'

Jasper, the one with the jaunty neckerchief, looked at her with interest. 'Super spot, isn't it? I came on business to Synemouth, drove out here, fell for the place, bought a cottage. We bought at just the right time too, and converted the old place for a song. 'Course it pays to be in the know.'

'What do you do?'

'He's an estate agent, of course, wouldn't you know!' laughed Susan, looking at her husband with some pride and fingering her silver chains.

'Did you buy a house here yourself?' asked Tony, offering Anna a cigarette, which she refused.

'Well, no. It was my parents. They bought a cottage here when I was ten.'

Jasper whistled, 'Must have been dirt cheap then. When would that have been, the 'sixties?'

'Jas!' said his wife, frowning, and he covered his mouth in mock confusion. 'Oops sorry! Wasn't meaning to guess a lady's age.'

'Did you have a lot to do to the place, like we did?' asked Susan, when Anna said nothing.

'Not really, though I suppose it needed it badly. We liked it as it was. It's terribly scruffy.' Anna was surprised at how much she resented 'Ahoy' being brought into the conversation, as if an old and intimate friend's faults were being discussed.

'We gutted ours,' Jasper said with relish. 'You know, knocked through, new kitchen, proper bathroom, downstairs toilet, shower, the lot.'

'It's very smart now,' said Valerie. 'Oh, and I meant to ask you, Sue, do you have a proper cleaner?'

Susan frowned, 'Well, Mrs Edwards is supposed to come in once a month whilst we're at home, just to keep it nice. But honestly, dear, when we arrived this time it was in an awful state. The dust! I had to tell her.'

'I know the feeling. The hours you spend standing over them, when it would be quicker to do it yourself.'

'And cheaper, Val!'

'Right! But I asked you because that old lady from the little green house on the front won't come any more. Says it's too much for her. And I can't find anybody to come in. Honestly, they go on about the unemployed . . .'

Tony was waggling his glass. 'Hey Adrian, what is this, a dry house?'

'Sorry. G and T again?'

'Now Anna, tell us all what you do.'

'I work in publishing.'

'Gosh, that sounds intellectual,' said Susan, with a nervous laugh.

Anna knew that her face was set into that acutely interested expression she could always assume when her heart was sinking and her feet telling her to leave. She heard herself asking fatuous questions about the price of land and the state of interest rates (Tony was a bank manager) and she altered the mask to one of frank disbelief and concern when Adrian, who was a dentist, informed them that his private practice had started to slacken off because of the economy. 'When it comes to the crunch, people put their

64

teeth last,' he said with disgust. Anna thought she was supposed to laugh, started, then changed her mind.

John would have left, she thought, with a sudden searing regret. In the politest, smoothest way imaginable he would extricate them both from boring parties, and they would collapse with laughter outside the door, then find the pub. 'Alone, I'm hopeless – I'll stay here and get drunk because there's nothing else to do.'

At that moment she felt Tom (who up till then had been staring from the window at the patio, sipping his orange juice) pulling at her dress.

'Oh good, here's Matthew,' said Valerie.

Anna bent down. Tom's face was radiant, as he pointed behind her and whispered, 'Look, Mum – it's that windsurf boy. He must live here! This is his house!'

The boy Anna had seen on the pontoon shuffled into the room, and scowled when Valerie flung an arm around him. 'Here's my little boy, Anna. Shake hands, Matthew.'

The hand that held hers was dry and hard, clasping for a fraction of a second, before it dropped.

Anna was astonished. Her covert calculations about Valerie's age must be wrong, she thought, if this huge teenager was her son. As if she could read the thought Valerie giggled with selfconscious pleasure. 'Don't be taken in by him, Anna. I know he looks about seventeen, but he's still only a fifteen-year-old baby, aren't you?'

'Must you, Mum?' He was scowling.

Anna said, 'I've seen you windsurfing. At least, Tom saw you first. You're very good at it.'

Tom was looking up with open hero-worship. The boy said, 'Yeah, I go out most days, even if there's only a bit of wind.'

Adrian clapped his son upon the shoulder, spilling some of his gin upon the carpet, where it was soon absorbed. 'I should think you do go out most days, sonny Jim. Do y'know, Tony, he pestered me and pestered me to get that thing, and guess how much I had to pay for it?'

'Oh, Dad.'

'There he goes again! If I pay good money for your

windsurf board I don't know why I can't tell my own friends about it. Five hundred, it was, give or take a pound or two. So I told him, you make sure you get my money's worth or I'il sell the damn thing!'

The bank manager nodded, turning to Matthew. He looked reproachful and the boy scowled all the more. 'You kids have got it made. When I was your age I thought I was lucky to get a bike, no kidding.'

Jasper nodded, whilst Adrian beamed. 'That's right. Me too. This one – he's got a TV in his bedroom, and the new music centre we gave him last Christmas. Millions of tapes. The lot. And his school fees will have me bankrupt before long.'

'I hate it.' The boy was sullen, his face crimson. Anna felt sorry for him.

'The trouble is, somebody I know spends more time doing sport than concentrating on his school work. It's O levels next year and all he thinks about is windsurfing.' Valerie wagged a finger at him.

Abruptly Matthew turned to Tom, who had been gazing at him all this time. 'Wanna come and play a TV game?' Tom nodded, speechless at the honour, and the tall boy led the small one across the room, as if he were leading his own army safely away from the enemy.

For ten minutes more Anna bore the renewed chat, but when Susan and Valerie were absorbed in a conversation about a new range of make-up, she turned away and followed the boys into an alcove off the main room, in which there stood an enormous teak television set. Tom was happily missing the flying white shapes, and yelping now and then when he gained a point.

'Seems a good game,' she said, sitting next to Matthew.

'You always say you hate them, Mum,' said Tom.

'You seem really good at windsurfing. Did it take you long to learn?'

Matthew looked at her, directly, in a way she found discomfiting. Then he grinned, all trace of the sullenness gone. 'Do you know much about it?'

'No.'

'Well, how do you know I'm good at it?'

'Good question. Well . . . you don't fall off.'

'I do if there's a high wind and I don't gybe fast enough.'

'What does that mean?'

'Turn the thing round. You have to swap sides. What happens is – you go forward on a beam reach, rake the sail forward sharply and bear off. If you don't spill wind by sheeting out you can be thrown off balance by a sudden gust. So you pull on the boom to drive the stern around, then let go so's the wind can flip the clew the opposite way. Then you pull the sail round, grab the boom, and get under way.'

She smiled. 'Clear as daylight.'

'Don't you sail?'

'No – I've been coming here for years, but I was never very keen on messing about on the river. I was nervous, I suppose, and all those ropes confused me. I just like watching.'

'But it's easy.'

'Easy for you, not for me. You look at home on the water.'

'Yeah, I am really. More at home there than anywhere else.'

When he smiled she noticed that his teeth were even and healthy.

Tom stood up, placing himself between them to regain Matthew's attention. 'Will you teach me? I'll be good at it. Then I could teach Mum!'

It was easy for Matthew Paul to condescend to one so much his junior, so he gave Tom a soft rabbit-punch and said, 'Oh, I might. If you behave yourself. But only on dry land.' Then he looked at Anna with level confidence, wrinkling his eyes in faint mockery, 'I'd like to teach you. It's about time you learnt about the river.'

Absurdly pleased, she looked away across the room to where the others still stood talking and laughing. By now, the voices of Valerie and Susan were shrill; Anna felt the wine working in her, too, and longed for some food. In that bare, golden room, with all the objects suspended, as in aspic, Adrian and Valerie, Jasper, Susan and Tony looked like models placed in a room-set for an advertisement, one that would be dismantled afterwards; the glasses washed, the lights turned off. Already there was a sense of finality in the air, and the voices faded into longer silences as the pleasantries ran out, and each became dimly aware of the emptiness in the stomach and beyond. Anna watched them, beckoning her, offering 'one for the walk home'. They seemed puffy and insubstantial in comparison with the boy Matthew who stood beside her, just taller, with his hard, clean lines and that honesty of expression which refuses to smile when a scowl is more natural.

'Look at them all – they're pissed,' he said.

'I'd better go. I hope we'll see you, Matthew,' said Anna.

'Course you will, stoopid. You'll see me on the river.'

She joined the others, suffered Adrian's heavy arm around her shoulders and smelt his sweat, faintly. Tony recounted an interminable joke, and glanced at her from time to time with that sidelong predatory look which announces that, since there are two 'singles' in the room, they must be destined for each other. Adrian saw. 'Now then, Tony, you're not to go paying midnight visits to her cottage. You might bump into me!'

'You are awful, Ade,' said Valerie, smiling.

Jasper held out his hand. 'We'll keep in touch Anna. Nice to meet you. Come round for a meal, or something.'

'That would be wonderful,' she said, and called Tom.

Looking back for Matthew she saw that he had slumped upon the sofa, watching the television, and did not observe their departure.

Eight

Anna approached the telephone as if it were an enemy, feeling as she had long ago, when her parents insisted that she arrange a visit to her elderly aunts. She dialled the number quickly, in case she should change her mind.

Molly Black's voice sounded fragile and distant, but her pleasure was unmistakable. Anne winced at the word 'kind', because it was not, she well knew, kind of her to telephone, nor was it kind of her to promise to visit that morning, before going to 'The Park'. Old people delight in twisting a knife, very gently, in your wounds, she thought, only half-listening to the fluttering sounds down the line. They choose to imagine kindness and abase themselves before it, so that you will drown in their tears of gratitude. There was a sour taste in her mouth.

'You have an antique shop, don't you?'

'Goodness me, no, not now. Not for ages. It was too much for us to manage in the end, so we sold it. Didn't Barbara tell you? Now we're at 26 'The Batch'. It's that row of cottages on the left as you drive down Cove Road. Do you know it? Don't worry about time. We'll be pottering about, as usual.'

Afterwards, still feeling the unaccountable anger, Anna decided that her mother must have told her about her friends' sale of their shop. But when? Two weeks in the summer, perhaps – until those packages abroad; a day or two at the end of December, with Tom to look after and John to appease; a phone call here and there . . . what time had there been to absorb the little details of her mother's life, still less remember what happened to her friends? The phone calls had been functional: did Anna know what Hilda might like for a birthday present, or could she discover when Richard was due back because he had not written, or else

Barbara was 'just wondering how Tom likes school?' and Anna consciously closed her ears to the quietness behind her mother's every word, its crackling emptiness carried quite clearly by the GPO. So, in this way, months passed and then years, and Anna slowly realised that her mother meant far less to her without her father, but shied away from the truth by refusing to involve herself in the life that was lived, as it had to be, without that centrifugal spirit.

Anna left Tom with George, both of them happy at the prospect of a morning chugging to and fro across the river, which sparkled in the morning sunlight. She drove off to Synemouth along narrow lanes fringed with tall, tangled hedgerows which hid the view of the river and, later, the distant sea. They were like tunnels, some of those lanes, with the trees linking overhead and the road curving downhill, as if you could drive on and on, through the soft warmth into the centre of the earth, and wait there defying autumn and winter, ready to burst upwards and outwards in the spring.

Anna amused herself by distinguishing between those passing drivers who lived in the area and those who were strangers. The first group (with whom she identified, as her father used to do) backed up without hesitation when there was only room for one car to take the road, and waved confidently at another driver who gave the same courtesy. But the strangers were nervous, hating to back and back to find a passing place, driving with hands high upon the wheel and gripping too tight with concentration to be able to wave a thank you. Little signs from time to time promised a 'Passing Place' ahead, and Anna smiled to herself at the ambiguity. 'It's not the places that pass, but the people, and yet the skin of the world is flaking too, passing and changing with us.'

'The Batch' was easy to find. A tiny woman, with white hair fluffed around her plump face, and a summer dress of mauve and blue flowers, took Anna's hand and showed her into the sitting-room.

'So kind of you to come. We've heard so much . . .' she was murmuring, as Harry Black rose quickly and eagerly to his feet and held out his hand. He was tall and slightly stooped, with receding grey hair and mottled spectacles, held together in one corner of the frame by black masking tape.

Two wing chairs with white antimacassars, a round gate-legged table which had been polished until it shone, and a small velvet sofa for two people – that was the room complete, except for the rows of books with well-worn jackets that lined the fireplace recesses, and the clutter of little objects (silver-topped scent bottles, old pipes in leather cases, china figures, silver egg-cups) upon the mantelpiece. A tray was laid for morning coffee, with china cups and a plate of sugary biscuits. On the windowsill lay a pair of powerful binoculars, ready to view the harbour.

The pleasantries over, Anna chatted about Tom and described the ferryboat, then fell silent, biscuit in hand. She looked across to them with an air of expectation.

'Er . . . well, now, tell us how you find your mother.'

'She's terribly thin. She doesn't eat enough.'

Molly hesitated. 'But she keeps herself looking well, don't you think?'

'You mean her hair, her make-up? Oh yes, she always did.'

For a fraction of a second Molly looked at her husband, and catching her eye he looked down.

Anna said, 'I don't understand. I wish I knew what's the matter.'

'Oh dear,' said Molly, leaning across to pat Anna's hand. 'It's not for me . . . I do wish she would . . . well, I know how difficult it is. Barbara will talk to you soon, she promised me that. But you must realise . . . I want to warn you that she is really quite ill.'

'But how can she be?' Anna felt that the expression on her own face was stupid.

The old lady pulled a handkerchief from her pocket and played with it, twisting the fabric in her lap. There was silence. Outside seagulls screamed in the clear, sunlit air. Inside the room Harry sighed and stretched his legs out in front of him, settling back into his chair with an air of resignation. 'How can any of us be?' he asked. 'It just comes,

71

that's all. You're going to see Barbara now, after here?' Anna nodded. 'Well, talk to her. *Talk* to her. She's an independent and strong-minded woman, your mother. She knows exactly what she wants in life.'

'Yes, she does.'

Anna knew that her voice sounded dubious; inside she seethed, hating them for all this knowledge of her mother's character, and the assumption that she did not know. She fell silent and stared around the room, her wandering gaze falling upon a framed colour photograph on the wall at Harry's shoulder. It showed a man and a woman, standing with three teenage children amidst lush vegetation.

'That's our son Christopher, with his wife Sally and their children. Lee and Kane, the boys. Terry is the girl. Odd name for a girl, isn't it? Christopher went out to Queensland fifteen years ago and he has made quite a success of it. Farming. We've always lived in the country.'

'Where?'

'Hampshire, before.'

'Do you ever visit them?'

'We went last year,' said Harry. 'Didn't Barbara tell you? We went for six weeks and she said she missed us a lot, poor dear. When we sold the business we had some money put by so we decided on a good long holiday in the sun. Of course, they'd been over here before that. We had a good time, didn't we, old girl?'

His wife looked wistful. The handkerchief twisted and twisted in her lap. 'Oh yes, we certainly did. But coming back was terrible, Anna. I thought I'd never get over it. When you get to our age you can't help feeling that, well, you know, it might be the last time. It's so far away, and he is our only child. You can imagine . . .'

Anna, who could not, looked at them helplessly and nodded. Harry had been watching his wife closely, and rose to stand by her chair. 'Pooh, stuff and nonsense, Moll! If I know you, you'll be drawing the rest out of the Abbey National next time there's a real frost, and getting your bikini out for those beaches!'

She reached up and her hand closed around the one that

rested upon her shoulder. She smiled at Anna, the trembling gone from her mouth. 'You see how he teases me? But I don't know what I'd do without him.' Anna stared at their hands – hers pale and blue-veined, his browner, with the prominent veins standing up in knots, still touching, reluctant to part.

They showed her their remaining collection of bric-à-brac: pretty things shored up against the days when there would be time to wear out the engraving with constant care. A little later Anna turned, as she walked along the road towards her car, and saw them standing at their front door, arm in arm, watching her gravely. Molly waved and called, 'Give your mother our love. Tell her I'll pop in in the morning as usual.'

The voice that cried out, 'Come in', was weak, so that Anna barely heard it. This time Barbara was lying on the bed with hair in damp wisps upon her forehead. The radio was silent. Outside a seagull perched upon the sill and stared insolently into the room, flying off as Anna entered. The room smelt stale. Barbara tried to raise herself upon one elbow, but abandoned the attempt and lay puffing, as if she had just climbed a long staircase.

'I'm sorry, darling, I must look an awful mess.'

Awkwardly Anna stood by the bed looking down at her. Her arms were like the useless appendages of a broken robot, hanging at her sides.

'Are you feeling worse today?'

'Yes, just a bit.' Barbara turned her head towards her daughter, and her weak smile bore a trace of apology.

'Oh, please tell me what's the matter. You must explain!'

There was panic in Anna's voice, and Barbara heard it.

She folded her arms across her breast as if to protect herself, and stared at the ceiling. 'Sit down here, by the bed. That's right. Oh, I didn't want to worry you, even though that sounds silly. You can't keep your family out of things, can you?' She sighed. 'I will tell you everything, Anna, though I'm afraid it isn't very cheering. You remember I told you about my fall – I wrote to you? You came down, but it didn't seem serious then, even at my age. They took me to the new hospital and it was ghastly. I was in a ward full of old women, dribbling, some of them wetting the bed, not able to get things for themselves.' She shuddered. 'I think half of them were, you know, not right in the head, but if not that place would have sent them mad. One of them used to cry at night, scream and scream, and her voice used to echo down the ward. It made me cry too. That was all there was to do.'

'Tell me what the doctors said to you,' Anna interrupted.

There was a long pause, then Barbara whispered, 'I don't want you to be upset Anna dear, because it won't help. I was told by the orthopaedic man that I would have to see Dr Jacobs.'

'Who is Dr Jacobs?'

'He's the cancer doctor, and he is very good, very kind.'

Anna felt she was hearing something she had heard before, in a universal dream, and could only utter the responses made up by someone else at an earlier time. She started to protest that it could not be true, but faltered immediately, because Barbara went on talking in her matter-of-fact tone. 'Actually, I told Dr Jacobs you were down here on holiday and he said he'd like to see you. You could make an appointment at the desk. You'll like him.' She turned her head to stare at Anna. 'Darling, don't look like that. You must be brave about it. I have to be.'

'But I don't understand. How can just a broken leg ... cause that?'

'Oh, it doesn't. It's quite complicated, and so I can only tell you very simply, in a sort of childish way. But what they actually discovered was breast cancer. You see I knew there was a lump, but you pretend these things aren't happening, and don't do anything about them because you think they'll go away. Of course, they don't. Evidently the cancer spread to my leg, which is why it broke easily when I tripped over the rug. It's quite common, apparently.'

'Breast cancer? Cancer of the breast?' repeated Anna, foolishly, her eyes filling with tears. 'Are you sure? Are you positive?'

There was just a suggestion of dryness as Barbara replied, 'Well, I'd hardly be likely to get it wrong, would I?'

'Well, at least they can cure that. I've read about it, Mummy, and I'm sure it's the one form of cancer that's easy to control. You'll be all right, I know you will.'

Barbara said nothing.

Her voice even brisker, Anna said, 'Now, I'll make an appointment with this doctor, and have a long talk with him. I want to find out what treatment you're getting. I want to ask him . . .'

'But you can ask me, dear. I'm on anti-hormone drugs at the moment, which are quite good because they don't have side effects. Awful things can happen if they put you on stronger ones. Your hair can fall out, things like that. Anyway, three times a week I'm taken to the hospital for radiotherapy. They shine rays at me. But sometimes, afterwards, it makes me sick.'

Suddenly Barbara's voice sounded plaintive, and she let her hands fall into their former position on her chest. Anna stared at her mother's face, then at those hands, helplessly. She imagined beneath that thin, papery skin collapse and decay, the substance of nightmare. She felt a dull ache in one of her own breasts, from which Tom had drawn his milk seven years ago, just as she, thirty-five years ago, had taken nourishment from this woman, in a similar bed. Anna's throat contracted with nausea.

'I meant to ask you yesterday, how are the Treadles?' asked Barbara.

'Just the same.'

'Still gossiping?'

'I don't know. I suppose so. Oh Mummy, why are you changing the subject?'

'It seems a good idea, darling. We've got plenty of time to talk. Did you ring Molly and Harry Black?'

'I went to see them, before coming here.'

'Did you? Oh, that was kind of you, Anna.'

'It wasn't kind, Mummy. They're nice people.'

'Don't get cross with me. It was kind of you to take the

time to visit my friends. You didn't have to. They so love seeing people.'

Anna thought, desperately, that she did have to, that she was no match for coercion by guilt. 'Molly said she'll visit you in the morning, as usual.'

'She does so much for me.'

Anna nodded, too quickly, then asked, 'Did you sell your flat so that you could afford this?'

'Yes, I couldn't bear that hospital. It's what Daddy would have wanted.' There was a note of defiance in her voice.

'But what about when you leave here, will you get another flat?'

Barbara's eyes grew opaque, and she looked away, across the room to the window. Her chest moved rhythmically. 'Anna, dear, would you mind if I had a little rest now? I so want to sleep. I feel very tired today, I'm sorry. Will you bring Tom when you come next?' She hesitated, 'When will you come next?'

Anna thought of all Barbara's days in the flat she had sold, her soul ranged with the bric-à-brac upon the shelf. The months when Richard was in America, and Hilda absorbed with her family and that rambling house, and Anna herself ... meeting John, having Tom, working, enjoying drinks and dinners, quarrelling, watching John leave, and more drinks and dinners and work. That was her own life and it had had to be lived, but in another country; with her mother here by the river and the sea, dying slowly minute by minute, even before that fall, even before the invasion of her cells.

Panicking, and stifling the sob that lurched in her throat, she said, 'I'll come tomorrow, first thing in the morning.'

Barbara's eyes were closing slowly, like those of a lizard in the sun. 'No,' she murmured, 'not tomorrow. Molly will come in the morning, and I have to have my treatment in the afternoon. Come the day after. And do bring Tom with you. I want to see him as much as ...'

There were no nurses in the corridors; Anna might have been finding her way down to the foyer of a discreet hotel. Only the slight smells in the atmosphere, a hint of disinfectant, gave away the secret. There was nobody to grab and ask the truth, that Barbara was dreaming or asking for attention, and that Anna could drive back along the lanes and wave at other drivers with that odd and welcome lightness of spirit she had felt just a couple of hours ago. There was nothing to do, it seemed, but walk warily, now that the universe had tilted, and wait until it could be restored, as it must be, to its proper axis.

'Can I make an appointment to see Dr Jacobs?' The receptionist reached for the large red appointment book, in which each segment of each hour was accounted for in blue ink, neatly.

'Any particular day?'

'Friday?'

'Yes ... now you're Mrs Lewis's daughter, aren't you? Let me see, what about Friday morning. The doctor is due to see Mrs Lewis at 11.30, so would you like to talk to him first? About 10.45?' Anna nodded.

'Your name is ... Mrs ...?'

'Miss Lewis,' she said, pleased for a second that at least John had left her with something. 'And yet I feel quite neutral,' she thought, 'as neutral as this nursing home, and this receptionist with clean fingernails.'

Nine

Nurse Anderson jerked the curtains aside with a rattle, revealing a pearly sky.

'Tea, dear.'

'At last, I've been awake for ages.'

Barbara raised herself on one elbow. The nurse looked down at her, noticing the thick hair matted, 'like a Brillo pad', she thought, with an inner smile.

'Those sleeping pills aren't strong enough,' said Barbara fretfully.

'Well, we can't go on taking stronger and stronger ones, can we?'

Barbara winced. 'I don't see why not. I could cease upon the midnight with no pain.'

'Whatever are you talking about, Mrs Lewis? Now – shall we get the routines done?'

'This early?'

'Waterworks all right?'

At exactly the same time, Anna stood staring from the bedroom window, at the river, in the grey light. She had woken at six with a churning feeling in her stomach, and could not stay in bed. For a long time she stood listening to the perpetual ping-ping-ping from the rigging, as a breeze ruffled the surface of the water and made the shrubs in the garden rustle. She shivered and tightened her old mauve candlewick dressing gown tightly at her waist, tucking both hands across her breasts and under her armpits for warmth.

She wondered how she could have considered that view beautiful. The river always looked the same, lacking all passion, all sympathy, as cool and neutral as the décor in 'The Park' nursing home. It was all right, she thought, for the likes of Matthew Paul to skim its surface, unthinking, and taking the sparkle of sun on the water at face value; as she had always done, especially when standing by the garden wall with her father and rejoicing in the fact that the view was unchanged, year after year. This morning the Syne looked dull and threatening; the familiar sound was maddening, pinging away at that portion of her skull that had been excavated and exposed for the river itself to view.

Anna had forced herself to seem cheerful, and listen to Tom's hero-worship of George and the boy Matthew, glad that he was so distracted. Matthew had given him a packet of crisps, and let him stand on the windsurf board, though out of the water of course, and George had said he could go on the ferry any time. So he rattled on.

She steeled herself later and went to see Valerie Paul, feeling not the ghost of a smile this time, when she visited 'Hacienda'.

'I don't like to ask, Valerie,' she said stiffly, once seated with a mug of coffee on her knee, 'but I wonder if, on Friday morning, do you think that Tom and Matthew ... ? Tom thinks Matthew's wonderful and it would be a great help. You see, my mother's terribly ill, I've discovered, and I don't want to take Tom because I have to see the doctor ...'

She stopped suddenly; Valerie saw the reason at once. She did not rush over uttering warm words of comfort, because people rarely do – shying instead away from grief because they know that the white cross will soon be chalked upon their own front door. Embarrassed, Valerie looked away. She blurted that of course Tom could come, and it would do Matthew good to take charge of him, and be better for the little boy than spending the morning with those dreary old people at the shop. She played with her large sapphire ring, twisting it round and round so that it caught the sunlight like a significant symbol. Anna had noticed that the fingernails were varnished a pearly pink to match the toes. Valerie fiddled with her fingers, buffing the nails with her own flesh, and twisted the strands of her hair as well – so that all her energy went into these acts of evasion, and there was none left for the messy, dying creatures beyond the ambit of her perfume.

'I'm ... I mean, it's awful for you,' she said.

'Yes, it is,' Anna replied.

'It's not serious though.'

There was nothing of the question about her statement, nothing so inviting; and so Anna rose to leave with a weary, 'No, she'll be all right.'

Ten minutes before the appointed time Anna sat in the foyer, letting the pages of a magazine riffle through her fingers. It seemed as if all her nerve endings were marching with stiletto heels upon the surface of her body. Upstairs, on the second floor her mother lay in bed perhaps, or walked about her room with that stiff gait, picking up a Staffordshire figurine or tidying her workbox, remembering the wholeness of which they were once a part. She was expecting the doctor, and then her daughter and grandson, who would look pleased to see her and avoid (the child's presence an insurance) all talk of disease, arrangements, treatment.

Anna felt almost angry again. She suspected that she might have taken Tom on thrice-weekly visits until their month was up, with her mother prattling about trivia while her life was slipping away.

At that thought, Anna checked herself. The life was not ebbing, because she, Anna, knew about breast cancer; that is, she had read perhaps a half-dozen articles on the subject, and so attributed to herself the collective wisdom of half-a-dozen journalists. On the surface of her mind were vague facts and generalised statistics, all combining to reinforce her faith in science, if not in miracles. But underneath that surface was a swamp of speechless terror which sought to bubble through the rational calm with inarticulate murmurings about 'the disease', and 'the worst' and 'a growth', and all the other misshapen fantasies.

Dr Jacobs's office was on the fourth floor. It had a distant view of the sea, sparkling between the trees, but lack of space had forced a large grey triple filing cabinet up against one corner of the window, so that a section of the vista was cut off by its ugly shape. Similarly, the room was spoiled; once larger, it had been divided, so that what was probably once a spacious board-room in the old hospital was now partitioned into areas without proportion, the cornices brutally chopped off.

'Miss Lewis, yes.' He walked forward, his arm outstretched, 'I am so pleased to meet you at last. Your mother has told me a lot about you. Do sit down.'

For some reason Anna had expected a small dark man, maybe foreign. Dr Jacobs was very tall, so that his shoulders hunched automatically, as if to disguise the height. He had an angular profile and grey, receding hair; his voice had the accent of a third generation successful in the profession.

When she was seated, he leaned forward, both elbows on his desk, hands clasped very precisely.

'How much do you ... er ... know about your mother's illness, Miss Lewis?'

'Not, not as much as I should. She only told me the day before yesterday. I live in London, you see.'

'You don't see Mrs Lewis very much then?'

'Oh yes. Well, no. I came down to see her just after she had her fall. She was in the new hospital then. She seemed fine then. She didn't write, or tell me.'

He nodded. 'That's not altogether surprising. We sometimes find that patients are reluctant to involve their families. It is as if they are afraid of being a burden. It's an interesting fact that we often ask old people if they have children – when filling in forms, you understand? – it is one of the first questions. Very often the answer is no. Then it emerges that they do in fact have children, but grown-up children, of course. They say no because the children have grown up and gone away, and so in that sense they do not have children. I think I can understand why your mother didn't want to tell you. But it would have helped if we had known sooner. Obviously from our point of view it would have been better had your mother gone to her doctor as soon as she noticed the lump. But like many patients, she simply hoped that it would go away. Unfortunately it never does.'

Anna buckled and unbuckled her watchstrap, digging her forefinger into its prong. 'Dr Jacobs, can you explain to me just how ill my mother is? I thought, for instance, that if someone had breast cancer, and had not gone to the doctor early enough, you could . . . take the breast off, and stop it?'

He held his fingertips together and shook his head. 'That's the way it used to be done. Now we very rarely perform such radical surgery, unless it is absolutely necessary. If by removing the breast we know that we are removing the primary, we do so, but – I emphasise – only if we are sure it will effect a cure. If there is evidence of a secondary, that is, a secondary cancer, then the patient is spared the trauma of a very unpleasant and psychologically disturbing operation.'

'Are you telling me that my mother has more cancer?'

'I'm afraid so, Miss Lewis.'

Anna looked down. There was a tiny spot of blood on the ball of her thumb, where she had applied too much pressure with the prong of the watch. 'She said, she said . . . it had spread to her leg. I thought she was getting it all wrong.'

He smiled faintly. 'Children never quite believe their old

parents, do they? No, she was quite right and it's a very common symptom. It's what we call a pathological fracture. You would be surprised how often it is a symptom of breast cancer, although a secondary – you see? It is an easy break through a part of the bone already eaten away with disease, and sometimes it can happen even with a very minor fall.'

His hands had not moved; still the cleanly manicured fingertips rested against their opposite numbers in perfect symmetry. His calm affected Anna, who took a deep breath and clasped her own restless hands in her lap.

'Is that all?'

He shook his head. 'Did you notice, Miss Lewis, that your mother was slightly out of breath?'

She nodded dumbly.

'Well ... I feel it's only fair that I should tell you everything, even if your mother has not. I know, she told me, that she finds it all very hard ... In fact, we have discovered a lung secondary. By that I mean, of course, another cancer. Again, it is not uncommon for all these symptoms to go together. The lining of the lung is infiltrated with tumour which secretes fluid. We can take the fluid off; it's what we call tapping. But it means there are days when Mrs Lewis finds it hard to breathe, as you have noticed. However, I can assure you that the treatment causes her no pain.'

Anna made her voice as flat as she was able. 'Can you tell me, Doctor, if everything you have said means that ... means my mother is bound to die?'

There was a pause while he looked across at her. Instead of answering, he rose, looked out of the window, then talked to the far-away sea.

'During these months I feel I have got to know your mother quite well, Miss Lewis. When people have cancer they often see their lives very clearly. They will sit in that chair and tell me things about their lives and their needs that they have never considered before. It is all in very sharp focus. And although I don't altogether subscribe to the currently fashionable theory that cancer is a purely psychological disease, I will say this – that one must place the

82

clinical notes alongside the knowledge one gains in those conversations, before one makes a prognosis. It is not for me to presume to tell you things about your own mother; there is no doubt that you know her much better than I do. But one thing I will say: very few old people willingly give up their homes, their whole lives, to go into a nursing home, when nobody has told them that they must, and when that action itself is likely to increase, rather than decrease, the probability of an early decease.'

Anna stared at his back. It was as if she had suddenly walked into a country where people spoke her own language yet abandoned the familiar sentence structure, so that words might be clear, but the meaning remained hidden. Several clauses behind him, she struggled to catch up. 'I'm sorry . . . do you mean to say that my mother shouldn't be here at all?'

He turned and sat down again. 'The nurses say that Mrs Lewis could manage if she wanted to. And they are right. To be frank, Miss Lewis, it can be exasperating for staff when a patient proves to be so negative.'

'Negative? How?'

Dr Jacobs sighed with an air of impatience, as if to say that he should not be telling Anna things she already ought to know. 'Your mother is a widow, and has been for about nine or ten years – is that right?'

Anna nodded. 'Ten.'

'Well, I can tell you that your mother's attitude to her illness is quite typical of many women in that situation. Widows. They are fine – often for many years – coping with life, alone. Then at the first sign of physical weakness, it all catches up with them. They never really wanted to manage on their own, you see. So, as I said, at the first sign of physical disability, it is as if their minds follow suit; they want – if you'll excuse the expression – to pack it all in.'

'Are you saying that my mother wants to die?'

He made a slight brushing movement with his hand, and shook his head. 'I don't think it helps to be as . . . well . . . blunt as that. It isn't as positive as that. Let me just say that she has a negative impulse where her own life is concerned. When someone has breast cancer we can safely predict that she will go through periods of recovery when she can lead an apparently full and normal life. There are ups and there are downs and this can continue for six months, a year – who knows? I had a woman in here, oh, about eighteen months ago. Breast cancer again. I gave her six months at the outside, and just last week my wife met her serving on the cake stall at the church fête. An amazing woman, full of determination and spirit. She told my wife that she has been kept alive by prayer ... but I would say it is her own will that's done it, not anyone else's. This is where the theorists come in to their own. Because so much of it does depend on the attitude of the patient. And of the patient's family.'

He looked at his watch. 'I'm so sorry to have had to tell you all this, Miss Lewis, it isn't something that one gets used to. Sometimes it's worse telling the families than the patients themselves. But I must be brief now, because I have to go down and see your mother. Are you staying to see her too?'

'I'll do something. I'll go for a walk and then come back.'

'Good.'

They hesitated, not looking at each other. Then Anna, conscious of a quiver in her voice, said, 'It's so hard to take in. I feel as if ... I don't know ... that I want you to tell me what to do. I don't know – on my own.'

His voice was kind. 'I know just what you mean, Miss Lewis. To put it in a nutshell, your mother could live at home and go to hospital two or three times a week for treatment, as long as she had someone, you know, on hand. You asked me how long, and I didn't answer. But although I don't like making predictions, I'll take the risk and say that your mother could enjoy perhaps six months or a year of life, perhaps more. Remember what I said about the cake-stall lady? But she has to have a purpose. Like so many patients of mine, she needs a real purpose for living. If you could persuade your mother to try to lead a normal life at home I know she would improve. If you allow her to stay here ... then I'm afraid that she will probably die by Christmas.'

Ten

Anna could not face a walk in the grounds of 'The Park'. The little figures in dressing gowns being pushed in wheelchairs or leaning on the arms of anxious relatives, the nurses flitting along under the mullioned windows like spirits from the hospital past, the dappled light beneath the trees – it would be intolerable, she felt, today. So she walked quickly from the front door of the building, out of the gates, and turned right along the road.

After about a hundred yards the quiet street in which 'The Park' was situated led out on to a main road. On the opposite side of this ring road that bypassed Synemouth was a new housing estate. Looking carefully to right and left Anna crossed this road, the noise of the passing cars buzzing loudly in her ears, yet not drowning the perpetual scream of seagulls overhead. Stranded on the island like a crab out of water, she heard a bus change gear, the intensity of its hum shifting into a higher key. Somewhere someone was using a chainsaw and that insistent whine separated itself crisply in her consciousness from the faint drone of an aeroplane, yet both united with all the other sounds into a murderous symphony inside her head.

It reminded Anna of when, just before John left, she would be attempting to persuade Tom into bed, and he would turn the chattering television louder to drown her instruction, reverting to crying babyhood when she snapped the button off, and then the shrill ring of the telephone would increase the din, until she wanted to beg for mercy. Later John would slam the front door, late as usual, and they would eat a meal in silence, punctuated by her anxious questions about his day, and who said what at his office, anything to draw him back, but then her husband would answer in monosyllables ('And did we answer our father in that way, all those years ago?' she wondered, picking at her food) and she would long for noise, to fill the empty air.

Quickly she left the road, striding down one of the many little streets that led off at right angles, lined with identical houses. Each house was red-brick, with grey-tiled roof and pale yellow windows and doors; they were pleasant, with decent proportions and no acres of unbroken brickwork as a whim of architectural style. Each had its own garden front and back, pocket handkerchiefs on which people had constructed miniature landscapes in grass, crazy paving and soil: the borders studded with gaily coloured bedding plants – pansies, primulas, wallflowers. Anna looked over the low brick walls as she walked past, noticing each flower, and the way in which the shadow of a red-hot poker made a small hard dot of darkness, with the sun at its height. In one garden five gnomes smirked at her from amongst the foliage, one of them standing in the middle of a cascading blue and white rockery, like a travesty of Venus in the waves. Next door, an elderly man bent over the central flowerbed, turning over the rich soil with a trowel and carefully removing impertinent weeds. He was in his late sixties she guessed, stopping for a moment and staring at him so that he looked up, nodded, then frowned slightly as the woman did not move, their eyes meeting in a sort of recognition, before dropping and shifting away. 'He is my mother's age, no older . . . Dad's age, what he would have been now if he had lived. Oh Dad, Dad, why did you have to die? Why did you fucking well die?' she thought, grinding her fingernails into her palm and turning from the man in his garden, all blurred before her eyes.

Gardening, like sailing, was something William had always talked of with enthusiasm. Walking on, not seeing the gardens any more, she recalled how he had allotted to each of his children a small patch of ground, saying that they must look after it well and grow whatever they liked. The Fulham garden was not large, a rectangle of lawn surrounded by herbaceous borders, with a shrubbery at the end. William had little time, except for weekends, and Barbara believed that gardens were to sit in, so their garden bore little resemblance to the tidy pictures in William's gardening books. Anna smiled. She had begged for a gnome to sit in her own little garden, but Barbara had refused. Her compromise was the purchase of two well-carved forms that sat mysteriously amidst the shrubs – a stone lion and stone elephant who silently guarded their patch of earth.

Hilda had edged her own garden with pebbles collected that summer from the beaches around Synemouth, and filled it with velvet pansies, purple, blue and yellow. Richard said that flowers were girls' things, and discovered that his mother liked fresh parsley, thyme and sage for her cookery. So, always wanting to please her, he grew them, and chives too, and mint which over-ran the lot. Anna had wanted to grow roses but her father had dissuaded her, and besides there were plenty of roses along the fence. Nothing he suggested pleased her. At last she tried to grow primroses from their tiny, tiny seeds, and when the patch of soil remained bare she cried because her seeds had failed. Then William had taken her to a garden shop, bought a little fuschia with its drooping ballerinas, and firmly packed the manure around its root with his boot, telling her that her garden was beautiful.

Now, behind the terraced house in Stockwell she and John had bought eight years ago, a garden showed itself as a patch of paving stones fifteen feet long, and five shrub roses in concrete pots with dirt upon their leaves. He had joked that it was his 'prison exercise yard'; Anna had hated the towering flats behind, with washing strung along each balcony. 'I must sell it,' she thought, 'I can't stay there any more. It's foul and ugly and unhealthy. I could move down here, live in the cottage, help Mummy . . .' Then she remembered, stopped; and in that instant it seemed as if all the houses in the road, neat and innocent though they were, stared and mocked, their flowery gardens a threat.

'Why does everything go wrong – for me?' she cried inside her head. 'And why are all these people so lucky?' Watching a hugely pregnant young mother half-walk and half-drag her screaming toddler up a garden path towards a yellow front-door that stood ajar, Anna hated her suddenly, resenting her presence, her fecundity, her pink cheeks, her crossed net curtains and orange tiger lilies. The old man in his faded jersey, weeding, had no right to be there. It seemed to her that none of these people – each one existing in a walled paradise not thinking of those outside nor caring to seek a key – not one of them should dig the earth, or listen to their children's breath, or relax at night with a cup of tea, the day's work over ... whilst all the time Barbara, her mother, was dying.

'My mother is dying,' thought Anna, and then she said it aloud to see if the words, hanging in the air in front of her mouth, would gain meaning from the ordinariness around them. And what if, illuminated with neon, those words had floated up above the rows of houses for all to read; would anybody rush to her, she wondered, with words of comfort and gestures of tenderness? Or would the shiny doors close silently, one by one, leaving her alone in the empty street, stared at by grinning gnomes? 'What else?' she thought, throwing back her head and looking at the cloudless sky.

Then she turned, shoving her hands in her pockets and retracing her steps. She thought that if Kindness did come along to offer her a cup of tea and words of sympathy and understanding – naturally because we all have mothers – she, Anna, would refuse. She would throw back her head and shout that her mother did not want to live because there was nothing to live for, nothing for anybody to live for; and so it was right and fitting to die, there in 'The Park' amidst neutral colours and an utter absence of hope for all – for each patient in a pleasant room, or each person hopefully planting seeds in the dry earth.

Barbara was sitting in the chair by the window, threading a needle with a long piece of crimson wool for the tapestry that lay on her knee. She was listening to a play on the radio, but switched it off as soon as Anna entered.

'Hello, Mummy. Don't let me interrupt what you're listening to,' said Anna, her voice unconsciously timid.

'Oh no, darling. It's a bit confusing. One of those plays

when all the characters sound the same so you don't really know what's happening to who! Not a bit realistic. Come and sit down and tell me how you are.'

'It's me that should be asking how you are.'

Anna felt shy, and glanced at her mother surreptitiously whilst picking up the tapestry, a pattern of full-blown crimson roses in a blue vase, to admire Barbara's neat work. Her mother looked serene; there was no evidence in her face of the exhaustion Anna had seen the other day, and none of the tension that might be expected following a visit from the consultant.

'I feel much better today, dear, much better. How's Tom enjoying himself? I wish you'd brought him.'

'Mummy, I . . .'

Barbara waved a hand. 'Don't explain. I understand. Dr Jacobs told me you'd been to see him. I suppose he told you everything?'

Anna nodded.

'I'm glad he did. I find it a bit hard.'

'Yes, I know.'

When Anna said nothing else Barbara looked worried, like someone on stage who has for a fraction of a second missed their cue, so that the disbelief is suspended and embarrassment imminent. She made some stitches, holding the tapestry close to her face, although her eyesight was good. She was creating the shadows at the heart of a rose, slowly, in crimson stitches, and held her head on one side to survey the effect.

Anna felt incapable of breaking the silence. She contemplated her mother, seeing her as it were for the first time, slight and frail, but with a face less lined than Molly Black's, and the indeterminate hair waving back from the almost-transparent forehead. Watching her thin hands, with the rings that had bound her to William loose upon her third finger as she fiddled with the wool, Anna had a sudden vision of them still for ever and consigned to earth. She shuddered.

'Anna, dear, are you cold?'

'No, I'm all right. I don't . . . I simply don't know what to say or do.'

Barbara's voice was infinitely sad, 'Darling, you don't have to say or do anything, anything at all. But I wish you would just try to tell me what you're thinking.'

Barbara watched her daughter's face suddenly lose its shape, collapse, as tears welled in her eyes and poured down contorted cheeks, but her own remained calm. Somewhere at the back of her mind she heard a voice say, 'She's crying,' as from a great distance – the voice of that part of her which viewed all external events with detachment, recollecting such emotion indeed, but already moving on to the exploration of new feelings. She stretched out her hand, which shook a little, and stroked Anna's bent head.

'You mustn't cry. I'm not crying. Everything will be all right.'

Anna choked. 'No, it won't! How can you say that? Dr Jacobs told me that you're going to die, Mummy – *die*, I said! So don't tell me everything's going to be all right. I'm not a child. I'm not Tom!'

Barbara waited a few seconds till the sobbing slowed, and Anna looked up at her with angry red eyes. Then she said, as if she were indeed addressing Anna at six and telling her that neither fairies nor Father Christmas dwelt at the bottom of the garden, 'But darling, don't you think . . . we've all got to die one day? I'm sixty-eight. I've enjoyed my life. It doesn't seem to me to be such a bad thing, to die after all that.'

'People live till they're ninety. You could – if you wanted to.'

Anna noticed that her mother's mouth set a little at the corners, as she made a stitch, and did not look up. 'Anna,' she said, 'I don't know what Dr Jacobs has been saying to you, but he hasn't been telling me lies. I know what I can expect, and I'm prepared for it.'

Her voice was not only resigned, it was almost pleased, and it irritated Anna. 'All he's been saying to me is that you don't have to be in here. Did he tell you that he thinks your attitude is negative?'

'Whatever do you mean, Anna? I don't know what you mean.'

'I mean – oh, nothing. Mummy, why did you give up your flat? You didn't have to – not yet. Dr Jacobs told me that you could manage at home as long as you had someone to keep an eye on you. Couldn't Molly and Harry have helped a little – and all your other friends?'

'But they're all old, like me, darling. I couldn't possibly expect them to keep trotting round to see me.'

'But they do anyway. They visit you here.'

'That's different.'

Anna remembered that note of stubbornness in her mother's voice, and it exasperated her as it had done when, a teenager taking her father's part, she had flounced from the room thinking that her mother was impossible. Her voice was weary, 'I know it's different, Mother. I'm just suggesting an alternative to you sitting here day after day.'

'But I enjoy sitting here day after day, it's so peaceful.'

'And so expensive, no doubt.'

Barbara's hands folded themselves into a tight ball. Her voice became guarded and the lines at the corners of her mouth deepened. 'Well, Anna, I know you mean well but . . . it is my own money. Daddy would have wanted . . .'

It was as if two ancient gates strained against their hinges and broke within Anna's head; she heard her own voice, almost a scream, in that quiet room. 'Oh for God's sake don't start telling me that my father would have wanted you to sit here, rotting away!'

As soon as the words were out she felt cheap. Barbara stared at her, her mouth working, and then raised the tapestry to her face. Her small breaths were hesitant, as if she did not have the right to cry. Anna leaned forward and tried to pull the piece of needlework away, but it was held in place firmly, as much anger in the resistance as in Anna's shout.

'Why do you come here . . . to say things like that?'

'I didn't mean it, you know I didn't.'

Barbara sniffed, letting the fabric fall and wiping her eyes upon her sleeve. She asked for the tissues and Anna, fetching them from the bedside, saw her father's face again in the photograph, and felt miserable, sick.

'Please . . . I am sorry, Mummy,' she said again, 'please try to see that I'm just stunned, that's all. It's been a shock. I didn't mean what I said. You must do what you like – and we won't talk about it.' To her surprise her mother nodded slowly, looking at her hands with swollen eyes.

'I think that's best,' she whispered. 'Best not to . . . talk about things like that.'

'But I do want to understand. I want to try.'

Barbara shook her head.

'She's dismissing me,' thought Anna, with a return of that futile rage. 'She's putting me into exile once and for all, damn it.' Aloud, talking quickly about anything, she told Barbara about Tom, how he loved spending time with George and how he had found a new friend in his 'windsurf boy'.

'What's that?'

Anna forced a laugh. 'Oh, it's the name he's given to a teenage boy who is staying in the village. You remember the road down to the church, Church Lane, with all the little cottages in it?' Barbara nodded. 'Well, this boy's parents bought a plot between two cottages – I think it must once have been the Masons' long vegetable garden but I can't remember – and built a hideous mock-Spanish house. You should see it! Anyway, we went there for a drink – the Treadles introduced me – and met the son, who was the boy Tom had watched windsurfing. Don't you know what that is? It's sort of standing on a water-ski which has a sail, so you're almost part of the boat yourself. Oh, never mind. Still it's lovely to watch . . . lovely.'

'God, how I'm rattling on,' she thought, faltering and staring up out of the window at the sky. Barbara was saying something, but she did not hear, consumed suddenly with a need to flee from that room and see people, anybody, people who would talk about trivia, or Matthew with his talk of tacks and gybes.

'How old is he, this boy?'

'What? Sorry, oh he's about fifteen.'

'Too old to play with Tom, then?' Barbara was regretful.

'No, he's very good with him. Really patient, considering.

Tom loves him. It really helps having him around, at least, I think it will.'

Barbara had relaxed, and smiled her old indulgent smile. 'Yes, dear, I'm sure it will be very nice for you all. Nice to have young people around. Why don't you . . . oh no, you wouldn't want . . . Yes, why don't you bring him in one day, this boy, with you and Tom, and introduce me? It would make such a change to see, you know, young people.'

'We've only been here five days and already she wants a change,' thought Anna, imagining how the prospect of a visit to 'The Park' would cloud the face of that teenage boy she hardly knew. It was an absurd suggestion.

'Well, maybe. Perhaps later,' she said dubiously.

'I'm sorry dear, I know it's a bore,' Barbara replied.

'No, of course it's not. You know it's not. It's just that . . . I don't know him very well.'

'Dear God, why the hell are we talking about that silly boy? Why does my mother always make me shift ground and make excuses, and . . . what's the point?' she thought, closing her eyes briefly so that the world turned red.

'Tom is already deep in hero-worship,' she said, adding, 'it's not surprising, really. We all need someone to hero-worship.'

'Like your father.'

Anna looked up, surprised. 'Yes.'

'You know, Anna, I've never said this to you, but you were his favourite child. His favourite.'

Warm blood rushed to Anna's cheeks. 'No,' she said, 'that can't be true. He loved all of us. He wouldn't have favourites.'

'Why not? People can't help it. Anyway, he loved you so much, darling. You were his little girl.'

Anna winced, something in her chest folding shut.

'Don't talk about him, Mummy. Not now. I can't bear it.'

'I suppose not,' Barbara said, and smoothed the tapestry upon her lap, from which the crimson wool trailed, un-threaded.

Eleven

Something had been arranged, Anna felt, between her mother and herself, a secret that she could barely sense, let alone explain. For the first time she who had always harboured the suspicion that her parents, at least her mother, held no key to the mysteries of her own life, began to suspect that the mystery lay elsewhere: within that building, within that room, even within the piece of tapestry with its muted colours and tiny stitches, that might have hung upon a castle wall for generations, and survived invasion, fire, neglect, flood and death, all the air-changes of history, to find salvation in an ordered museum. It was like one of those old nursery riddle-rhymes: the branch on the tree, and the twig on the branch, and the nest on the twig and the egg in the nest ... and somewhere is the key to the kingdom.

Preoccupied, she did not notice Tom run into the car park. Matthew, hands in his anorak pockets, followed slowly behind with his slightly rolling walk. Clouds had covered the sky, quite suddenly, and the breeze from the river was colder than it had been since they arrived. Anna looked up and shivered.

'Mum! Mum!' He ran up to her and held out his arms for a hug, panting, his cheeks red. Anne knelt to receive him, and pulled him close, too quickly, so that he pulled back with a squeal and squirmed away.

'Why are you pulling away from me?'

Imperceptibly, he glanced over his shoulder, and whispered, 'It's not that I don't love you.'

'I know. It's because you don't want Matthew to think you're a baby. Is that right?' He nodded. 'But it's not babyish to hug people, you mustn't think that.' Anna saw that Matthew was only a couple of yards away and added, raising her voice and looking over Tom's shoulder, 'I bet Matthew's mother still cuddles him.'

The boy grinned. 'Not any more, she doesn't. No fear! We're not like that in our family, anyway.'

Anna smiled. 'Well, I suppose you are a bit big.'

'He's bigger than you are, Mummy.'

Anna stood up, as if to prove Tom's point. 'Yes, well most people are taller than me.'

'I like girls who are small,' Matthew said, after a pause.

Tom shrieked with laughter. 'But Mummy isn't a girl, she's a lady!'

Irritated, Anna snapped, 'For goodness' sake, Tom, he wasn't talking about me, silly!'

They walked along the lane to the top of 'Ahoy's' orchard, and Matthew slouched beside her without being invited and without talking. Anna felt uncomfortable, drained by the visit to her mother, wanting him to go. After a few desultory questions, and his monosyllabic answers, she looked at the sky with exaggerated interest and said, 'There's quite a wind. Aren't we keeping you away from your hobby?'

'Yeah, well I've had him all morning haven't I?'

'That's what I mean. Well, don't let us keep you now.'

'That's OK. But I might go out. Why don't you come and watch me rigging and launching?'

Tom caught her hand, 'Oh, can we, Mum? Let's go with him!'

Anna felt leaden. 'I don't think so, not now, Tom.' She looked at Matthew and noticed, distantly, the perfection of his face. 'I've been visiting my mother, you see. Tom's grandmother. She's very ill.'

'I know. Mum said.'

'Will you tell your mother that I'm very grateful to her for helping me out, with Tom?'

He looked impatient. 'Oh, she doesn't mind. Nothing bothers her.'

'Do things bother you, Matthew?'

'Some things.'

'Like falling off your windsurfer?'

He grinned again, 'No, not that. I hardly ever do. I'm too

good. Come and see. Bring him down to watch.' And he ruffled Tom's hair with his hand, the shift from sullenness to charm miraculously complete, so that Anna felt bewildered suddenly, and taken over. She hesitated for a second, looking at him. 'Well, I'll have to go and change into my jeans. We'll meet you on the pontoon in about ten minutes.'

There were few people on the river and the pontoon was quiet and almost deserted. There was nobody waiting by the ferry bell, and through a cottage window Anna glimpsed the flickering colours of a television programme. It was one of those August days that carry, on the wind, an intimation of autumn. The sound of the pinging from the boats was tinny, fast and insistent; small white waves reflected the grey sky; seagulls threw themselves in enormous arcs upon the wind.

In those days there had been no television in 'Ahoy'. In rainy summer weather William would cut through their cries of boredom by organising games of Monopoly, in which he and Richard invariably dotted the board with their profitable hotels, whilst Anna lost all the money she had fanned into a pretty shape. They would turn to snakes and ladders, hilariously inventing crimes for which each rapid, reptilian descent was a suitable punishment, and adding forfeits to make the retribution even worse.

Then, the games exhausted, William would rise and give the quiet instruction, 'Come on, team,' not listening to their groans. Raincoats and boots would be pulled on, and their father would lead them along the beach, up and across two fields and around the village, saying that the way to cope with rain is to go out into it. Sometimes, if the rain was light, they would collect twigs and leaves to take back to Barbara. Once, when the downpour increased so that it beat upon their faces, half-blinding them and running into their mouths, William had led them to shelter in the village church, and Anna remembered how they had fallen silent in the musty stillness, listening to the rain drumming on the roof and the timid drip from their oilskins on the ancient stone floor.

'How I loved that time, those walks,' she thought now,

knowing that even then she had wanted to keep things poised for ever – the three smaller figures following the burly man along a wet beach that hissed and gurgled with its own private sounds, whilst a million pebbles, alike in the monotonous greyness, each glinted uniquely, transfigured by a streak of light that shone through parting clouds.

On the way home she would stop and watch the rainwater gushing downhill each side of the lane, carrying with it tiny broken twigs and the heads of wild flowers, and stained red by the russet soil. Her father would stop too, and turn, and call, 'Come on, dilly daydream,' or else he would point out a beetle, shining in the undergrowth. He had loved days just like this one, when the unseasonable weather kept all the holidaymakers indoors, and the place was left to the Syne and its own people. And when they returned from their rainy walks Barbara would have a tray ready, and they would drink cups of strong, sugary tea and eat chocolate biscuits in front of the electric fire, whilst the rain poured down the windows; but they knew it would be fine the next day.

Tom hopped along the pontoon, slapping his hands upon the wooden rails.

In this place, Anna thought, her life revolved around her father as it always had, and yet there was an emptiness at the centre, where he had been but was no longer; so that Anna felt herself drawn helplessly into the vacuum. There was nothing else, except Tom, of course, but sometimes his presence pricked her, reminding her that John had gone, and family life as she remembered it had finished for ever. 'Gone in search of his lost youth too,' she thought wryly, thinking, without the usual surge of rage, about the girls in their twenties who were still in nappies when John was listening to Elvis Presley. 'I should have told him it's a waste of time,' she said to herself, 'but it's too late now.' He had gone; and William was dead, and Richard and Hilda were like those familiar close planets we can see and study but never reach.

And now Barbara was submitting to her curious, but common death, beyond the reach of any of her children, as

97

if the tea-trays by the electric fire, and the Christmas stockings she had filled, and (back, back . . .) the tenderness of her breasts, had never been. 'It is a common death,' Anna said aloud, as Tom ran backwards and forwards, waiting for Matthew. William's death had been common too; and it suddenly seemed to her monstrously insufficient that the lives which gave her life, and all the love that she remembered, should still be subject to the ordinariness of pain, weariness and decay. Diminished, she stared out over the grey bay, the hollows inside her resounding with echoes; waiting, and thinking, 'Dear God, there must be something.'

In the distance Matthew appeared, plodding down the hill towards the pontoon, dressed in a black wet suit that removed all the grace from his body and turned him into a comic fish-like figure. He waved one hand absurdly; the other carried a mass of equipment.

'You look as though you've got long johns on,' she giggled as he drew near.

'What are they?'

'Never mind. Come on, get on with it.'

Matthew was bending over the long white board, shaped like a flattened dinghy, or a fattened ski, which he had left on the pontoon. Tom crouched next to him, saying, 'Yes . . . yes . . .' as the older boy explained the rigging in a stream of incomprehensible jargon.

'You see, this is called the hull, and all this is the rig – that's the mast, the booms, the sail and all these ropes – it's all called the rig. You attach the rig to the hull by this thing here. It's called a Universal Joint because it's pretty useful. See?'

Tom nodded energetically, and picked up a piece of rope, only to be told sternly to put it down again.

'That's the inhaul line, Tom!'

'Oh,' said Tom, with deep conviction.

The craft was taking shape. A gust of wind rippled along the nylon sail – pale blue flashed with white and inset with a clear 'window' – that lay spread out along the pontoon. Anna thought it beautiful and delicate, like a patch of sky.

Matthew's litany continued, '. . . you see, you have to put

the wishbone booms parallel to the mast, and get the front of the booms as close to the inhaul line as possible, see? There. That's a half-hitch knot; you always use one of them. I'll teach you, Tom, another time.'

'It's very kind of you, Matthew.'

He looked up at her, and stared for a few seconds, saying nothing. Anna felt embarrassed. There was a confidence in his gaze that was wrong, because it made her put a hand up to her hair automatically, to stop it blowing so wildly. She looked away.

'I'll teach you too, if you like,' he said, 'to tie knots, and windsurf, everything. I think everybody should learn.'

'Why?'

'Because it feels exciting.'

'Yes, but why does it feel exciting?'

'You're as bad as your son. He never stops asking questions.'

'Don't you ask questions, Matthew?'

'Not much.' He was tying a knot, deftly.

'I don't suppose there's much he needs to know, self-confident little creep,' she thought, with some hostility.

He squatted on his haunches. 'I'll tell you what. You watch me windsurfing in this weather – there's a good wind up now. Just watch it. Then when I get back you can tell me why it's exciting. Because it's obvious. Even you could see it.' He grinned cheekily as he said the last words, so that she was forced to do the same.

He bent and lifted up the board, his left hand holding the rig that bent and flapped like a broken wing. Anna automatically bent forward to help, but he shook his head.

'I do this by myself every day. Don't need anyone to help ... Look Tom, this is the daggerboard ... it goes in that slot when it's in the water – there, like that.'

He lowered the whole thing into the water, and Tom jumped up and down on the spot with excitement, as the wind caught the blue and white sail, which flapped freely.

'Now we're ready for the launch,' Matthew said. 'All I do is step on the hull, pull on the inhaul line until the mast is upright and the boom clew swings free. I keep the hull square to the wind, get hold of the rig, and go.' He looked elated.

'I envy you,' said Anna.

'Why?' He looked at her curiously, his head on one side.

'I'm afraid to do things,' she said quickly, surprised as she said it. 'I'm . . . scared of the water.'

He laughed. 'You don't go in it, stupid, you're on it, sailing, and the spray doesn't do you any harm.'

Anna felt a gust buffet her back and looked anxiously at the water. 'Will you be all right? Are you sure it's safe?'

He laughed. 'Course I will! This is brilliant. You can get a terrific speed up – really go.'

'Oh Mum, stop making a fuss,' said Tom.

'We might not stay here till you get back. Why don't you come to the cottage for a cup of tea?'

'OK. Sure. See ya!'

They watched as he stepped out upon the unsteady craft, balancing perfectly and manoeuvring with his feet until the wind caught the sail. His arms were straight, holding the boom firmly, hands about three feet apart. As the windsurfer drew away from the pontoon with gathering speed Matthew leaned back against the increasing pull of the sail, turning the rig so that the wind filled the sail completely, bellying it out tautly. Soon he was a miniature black figure in the distance, his sail a toy sail, or (thought Anna) the wing of a tiny, unusual butterfly, struggling against an alien climate yet preserving its extraordinary grace.

'Look at that!' Anna turned round. Some people were standing outside the pub, bored with television, or waiting for opening time. Two young women in the group were pointing at the figure of the windsurfer out in the bay. 'Whew, it's fantastic, isn't it?'

Anna looked down at Tom, saw his face, and suddenly realised that the expression it wore exactly mirrored her own; it was pride, a sense of reflected glory, because they had been with the windsurf boy. She did not want other people to look at Matthew, but felt he was theirs to watch – and that his presence in this village gave to their holiday its single potential for happiness.

'Mum – do you like Matthew?'

'Yes, darling, I do.'

'Then why were you so bad-tempered with him before?'

Sometimes Tom's accuracy astounded Anna; it was as if his blue eyes could see into her soul.

'Are you frightened of him, Mum?'

'Of course not, silly. I'm ... well ... I feel sad about Granny.'

'Is she very sick?'

'Yes.'

'Will she die?'

Anna hesitated. 'Yes, Tom, in time.'

'I don't think she will,' he said, confidently.

After a few minutes Anna guided Tom away and back along the pontoon; she no longer needed to watch Matthew. They had seen him; she felt calm. To her surprise Tom did not protest at the end of the vigil, but as they walked up the hill he asked again why his grandmother was so ill. Anna took his hand and he did not pull away. 'You see, my pet, we all have to die some time or other, and Granny is ... well . . . quite old.' How pat and feeble it sounds, she thought, like a school scripture book, and a nice time in heaven with the angels is just over the page. 'So you see, we can't help the fact that Granny got ill, because that happens to people sometimes and we can't do anything about it. But she won't die for a long time yet, because you and I are going to try to make her a bit better, aren't we?'

He nodded. Then he looked up brightly and asked, 'Do you think Matthew will come and have tea with us? Will he really come to our house?'

'He said he would. I think he will.'

She felt half-relieved but half-hurt that he had left the subject of Barbara so quickly; as if her mother and the windsurf boy had been weighed in a scale, and Matthew found to be much heavier in interest.

Twelve

'There are four walls here, enclosing this space which is mine. The flat was mine too, but before that everything was shared, with William and the children, with my cousin in that tiny flat in Courland Road, and before that at home, and all of us tiptoeing around in terror of disturbing Father. I can barely remember that house, now, and yet its geography ought to be engraved on my mind like braille. It's faded away, like an old photograph exposed to the sun, leaving a blurred picture of little girls in frilly white dresses and floppy hats, under a copper beech, with that little dog ... what was his name? We loved him. He was run over by the coal wagon ... but his name has gone now. Probably Spot or Fido or something unmemorable, like the names we give our children. Ordinary names, the names everyone else chooses, Richard, Anna, Hilda, Sarah, Barbara, Susan ... that sort of name, which will not stand out. How your children would hate you if you made them seem different, by giving them a fanciful name, one that could be mocked at school. So we all take refuge in complete ordinariness, because I suppose we know in our hearts that all of us are the same, and can expect the same fate. Richard, Anna, Hilda ... oh, her name has dated now, William's choice, I never liked it.'

Barbara lay, oozing sleep, although it was early and the room still light. 'Like a child, resisting the idea of bed, but glad when somebody comes to insist; mother, or a nurse. They help me undress and for a second I think that I'm back there again, in that house I can hardly remember, and somebody, mother or a nurse, forgetting the joints of my shoulders as they cram me into a nightdress. You resent the fact that things are always being done for you and to you when you are a child. Then you rush through the rest of your life serving other people, doing things endlessly for your husband and children and looking on the once-yearly tray in bed as a luxury. Then you get old, and things are done for you and to you all that time, until it seems that your life has been taken over by a regiment of mothers or nurses or daughters, what does it matter who they are? At first you dread the fact that you'll end up a senile invalid, totally dependent and not knowing it. Then, sometimes, when they are coming at me with all the needles and putting that machine over me, and walking in here all the time to check my functions, then I hate this feeble, collapsing body and want not to know any more, to drift into a second infancy like going to sleep.'

Though her eyes were closed she could see the soft purplish light in the room, as if her eyelids had grown transparent, no longer guaranteeing darkness. She wondered, for a second, what it would be like to die, what that light would be like, filtered through eyelids closed for ever. 'Dark blue, perhaps, or a sort of heavy red, that's what death must be like. Not black. Nothing is black . . . Though perhaps when I close my eyes and escape, and see that whiteness all around my head, light and insubstantial like fluffy clouds from a plane, perhaps death is like that. Perhaps that is a form of death, it seems too real to me, and when I open my eyes again the colours in this room, or in the nurses' faces, seem so drab, so lacking in life . . .

'Goodness how assured they all are!' she thought, her mind giving a buck of irritation. 'Why is it that a doctor, a nurse and a daughter for that matter can see me lying in this room, in these four walls which are mine whilst I'm paying for them, and assume that because I am a decaying scarecrow I can't think for myself? So they know what's best for me, or so they think. Ha! What they don't know is how much I know what I do want. I always have . . .

'Oh, Will, you know what I'm like. I've never changed, not since I made you marry me, and you so ridiculously shy for a professional man of thirty! I can remember all that without any trouble, and our poverty-stricken honeymoon in Cornwall, when things were so short, but the war was ending, and we were so happy. The guest-house next to a farm outside Bude so there were eggs, and the cows lowed us to sleep in that lumpy feather bed. You read *The Woodlanders* to me, and when we came to the end I sobbed and sobbed because the pain of it all was so unbearable, that Marty should lose him and yet stay faithful even after he was dead. And you put your arm around me and said that life was like that, full of sadness, and so we have to seize on all the scraps of happiness while we can. Oh, you were a good man too, and you did good things, Will, my darling, always good things. I wonder what you'd think if you saw me here? My breast is misshapen now and it hurts, Will, and my leg looks funny where it didn't set properly, and what an old stick I must look when they help me have my bath. I don't need them to help me, but since they want to I might as well let them. Give them something to do . . . What was I thinking? That's another of the sickening things about being old, that at least you missed, Will, because it would have been much worse for you than for me. You lose a thought even when you're in the middle of it, one minute it's there and if it's a nice thought you roll it around your mouth like a delicious taste, enjoying it, then – it goes. Anna came to see me today and now she knows everything, just as you do . . . It makes it easier. I don't want to talk about it all or explain what I want, Will, do you understand? Yes, I know you do. Every morning I wake up with you, and every evening I remember you, and I can't help it any more than she could, that girl in the book who loved him so much . . .'

Nurse Massey knocked on the door, then gently opened it, poking her head around. She listened. Barbara was breathing evenly, not harshly as she sometimes did.

'Are you asleep, Mrs Lewis?'

There was no reply, Sandra walked with soft feet across to the bed, and straightened the sheet. Barbara's head was on one side, her eyes were closed, and her expression was serene. Very gently Sandra straightened the pillow, and pulled the bedclothes up slightly, to cover Barbara's shoulders, just as she had done each night, when her children were small and she tiptoed into their room to make sure they were all right.

'You're babying me again, Sandra,' murmured Barbara, without opening her eyes. 'I'm all right.'

'Did you take your sleeping pills? The new sort?'

'Yes, yes. They seem to be fine. I expect I'll have nice dreams tonight, Sandra.'

The nurse looked at her with a tenderness Barbara did not see but sensed, in the calm of the woman's presence as she paused by the bed, without speaking, before saying good night.

Thirteen

Tom was asleep. Anna sat with her novel open upon the arm of the chair, and jumped when the telephone rang. Years ago Richard had organised a pay-phone for 'Ahoy' because, tired of controversial bills, he had pointed out that it was unfair for them to subsidise each other's calls. Anna had protested that the ugly grey box on the sitting-room wall reminded her of a pub or a railway station, to no avail. 'It is a railway station,' he had quipped, 'because we're all just passing through.'

She picked up the receiver, expecting to hear John's voice, although his previous call had been in the early evening when he could speak to Tom, which was his only purpose in phoning at all. Stiff and polite to Anna, he had conveyed information about the weather in London and told her his holiday plans, then asked for his son. That call was over quickly.

There was a faint 'peep' and she heard a newly-acquired mid-Atlantic accent say, 'Hi, Anna – it's me.'

'Hello Richard.'

'Hey, your voice sounds awful. What's going on?'

She looked around the sitting-room, covered now in toys

and odd sweaters they had both pulled off without bothering to put them away, and the remains of their sandwiches on a tray, and said, 'Nothing's going on. I'm on my own, and Tom's in bed so life goes on as usual.'

'You sound down. How's my mother?'

'Our mother isn't very well at all,' said Anna, trying to make her voice gentle, succeeding in making it sound brittle. She took a deep breath, 'Richard, she's got cancer. Cancer of the breast and . . .'

There was a silence, yet she heard him gasp, clearly, as if he were in the next room.

'Oh Jesus, Anna, I'll get the next flight home.'

'There's no point in doing that. She isn't going to die tomorrow. Come back when you were going to come back, in September. You can't actually do anything.'

'Why didn't she tell us?'

'I don't really know.'

'Anna, stop answering in that tone of voice. For God's sake, tell me what's going on. Where is she – still in that nursing home?'

'Yes, she is – unfortunately. Her doctor told me that if we can get her home she has a reasonable chance of living for at least six months, maybe more. But if she stays there she'll go down and down. He said she'll probably be dead by Christmas.'

'Christmas! I don't understand it . . . Well, for God's sake get her home right away.'

'Richard, she hasn't got a home any more.'

'Well, if she stopped paying through the nose at that place she could still afford to buy a new flat in Synemouth. A smaller one. Make a new start.'

Anna sighed. A new start. Just like that. Make up your mind and there you are: mortality at bay. New starts for old. It was so absurd she wanted to howl and said so to her brother, hearing him tut with irritation, suddenly sounding much more British. 'Surely you can persuade her, Anna. And listen, since John has left, why don't you take her to London to live with you? You've got the room. We could all see her then, because Lisa and I will be back for good.'

Her mouth went sour. 'Oh yes, of course,' she said, 'you'll zip back to your smart Holland Park flat and Hilda will pop over but of course she has her family to think of, but no doubt you'll all give me support as I sit by myself and watch our mother die. Thank you very much.'

'There's no need to be like that about it. What's got into you?'

'Our mother has got into me.'

'I'm sorry. Must have been a shock.'

'Just don't try to plan my life, or hers, without thinking first, Richard. As it happens I've already tried to persuade her to leave that place but it's not easy. I think I will get somewhere, I think she'll leave, but it'll take time. The first stage is to convince her that she wants to live. We can think about where she lives later.'

He had begun to reply before she had finished, so that his voice was lost for a second, with the transatlantic overlap. When it came back she heard his helplessness, '. . . if she thinks that. Anyway, she has to want to live. Nobody wants to die, except suicides. She's not like that.' When she said nothing he asked if Hilda had been informed.

'They're still in Brittany. Camping. I can't get in touch.'

'Couldn't you put out one of those emergency messages? Even Alan must listen to the radio sometimes.'

'You're just being dramatic again. What's the point of spoiling their holiday, bring them rushing back?'

'I suppose so. What's happened to all mother's furniture and stuff?'

'In store. For us to divide up, or sell.'

There was a silence. Anna felt that her brother was waiting for her to speak, to tell him something else, but there was nothing she could say. Better silence than more of this inconsequential talk of furniture, she thought. She could hear him breathing heavily across the miles and imagined him sweating slightly in the New York heat. Too fleshy – the stocky little boy who saved his pocket money instead of spending it upon sweets transformed into a man with thinning hair and a bulge of business lunches under his thin American suit. Children of the same mother, they each pressed the receiver to an ear, wondering that the faint, regular 'peep' upon the line should be the heartbeat of their silence.

'I guess I'd better go. This phone call is costing. Are you sure you can cope?'

'Yes, Richard, I'm sure.'

'I want to come.'

'There's no point; you'd have to cancel things.'

'So what?'

'You never usually cancel things.'

'My mother isn't usually dying, for fuck's sake!'

'I know. I'm sorry – really. Do as you please.'

His voice was quiet. 'I don't know, I'll talk to Lisa about it. We've got to come back in September because she'll be six months. Tired of waiting around too; it's so bloody hot here.'

'Always is in New York, isn't it?'

'I'll phone Mum, and talk to her. I'm glad to know ... thought something was up. And Anna ...'

'Yes?'

'Keep yourself together, OK?'

'Thanks Richard, I will,' she said.

As soon as she put the phone down, feeling the silence wash around her, Anna thought about Matthew Paul. They had watched the tiny figure windsurfing in the bay, losing sight of him occasionally, as he sailed beyond the viewpoint of the sitting-room window. Tom had said, 'He'll be coming soon, Mum,' and so she had put the kettle on, and arranged chocolate biscuits on a plate. For the next twenty minutes Tom drove her mad. 'Why isn't he here? ... He must be putting all his stuff away first ... Why hasn't he come yet?' and so on. Then, seeing how the child's mouth drooped at the non-appearance of his hero, Anna put her arm around his shoulders and whispered, 'He didn't promise to come, Tom. I only said if he felt like it.'

'Well why didn't he feel like it?'

'Darling, he's a very big boy. You have to understand that he won't always want to be with you. He's fifteen, and you're only seven.'

'Fifteen – is that nearly like a man?'

'Well, yes, nearly,' she had replied.

Now, walking round the room and picking up the familiar objects as if to know them again, Anna admitted to herself that she had been just as disappointed as Tom. His grief was soon assuaged by a plateful of chocolate biscuits that did not have to be shared. She felt, in an indefinable way, let down – as though an intimacy had been betrayed, or she had made herself look foolish by assuming that the boy would want to come. Yet foolish to whom? To herself, certainly, but what if Matthew too found it funny? That thought was intolerable.

She sat down again and picked up the book, but as she stared at the page an image of the windsurf boy floated across her mind once more. 'You're pathetic,' she said aloud, slapping the arm of the chair so that the volume fell to the floor. Leaning her head back against the chair she laughed, looking at the ceiling. A 'single' mother, dumped by her husband, who has just discovered that her mother is dying, and that a boy with the face of a Renaissance youth can bestow favour by his presence and emptiness by his absence ... 'It's ridiculous,' she said to the room.

Restlessly, she walked over to the fireplace. By the still clock was an old snapshot in a wooden frame, the image slightly faded and out of focus. William and Barbara stood on the strip of beach outside 'Ahoy', dressed in baggy slacks and sailing jumpers. His arm was loosely round her shoulders. Beside them, sitting in a rowing boat that had been pulled up from the water's edge, were Richard, Anna and Hilda, staring at the camera with broad toothy grins.

'I remember,' Anna said. It was their second summer, so (she calculated) she must have been eleven, Hilda nine, and Richard thirteen. William had bought the new rowing boat as a surprise for all of them on Richard's thirteenth birthday – though the surprise was soured on subsequent days by Richard's assumption that it was his boat, so that William sighed that it was impossible to please children, they always spoilt things.

Yet on that day, the day of the photograph, Richard had

been willing to pose with his sisters like three men in a tub, climbing aboard after the mock 'launch', to grin whilst George, who happened to be passing, snapped them with William's box camera.

Anna stared at the photograph. There was something odd about their smiles, beyond normal self-consciousness. Then she remembered. They had been singing; mouths stretched wide. 'One ... two ... three ...' their father had called, and they had struck up,

> Row, row, row the boat
> Gently down the stream
> Merrily merrily merrily merrily
> Life is but a dream.

They had sung in unison then in separate parts, until the whole song became a cacophony and they collapsed in giggles; then William helped them from the boat one by one, murmuring, 'Come on team, quieten down.' Afterwards the five of them had sauntered to the Treadles' shop to buy ice-cream.

'Gently ... down ... the stream ...' sang Anna, her voice quivering, thin; then she stopped. How extraordinary that the simple little song should carry with it such associations of summer, warmth and utter peace and acceptance, under a blue sky. 'I'm always missing something,' she thought, and tried to imagine how it might have been if her father's heart had not given up, and if he and Barbara had retired to this house as they had planned. Would their rugs and china and velvet chairs have absorbed, like blotting-paper, the memories that hung about the atmosphere, and would 'Orchard Cottage' have silenced the echoes of 'Ahoy'? 'Probably not,' Anna shrugged, 'because I would have come to visit them, crammed into the small back guest-room, and I would have been annoyed at every change they made, missing it as it was; just as now I search for its past, though it still looks the same as it was. Like Chinese boxes, disappearing off inside each other, back and back, until you reach the end, the last mystery.'

She walked softly into Tom's room, as she always did, to

110

check that his covers had not fallen to the floor. By the light from the hall, kept burning all night for him (as it had been for them) to keep the dark at bay, she saw his hair sticking up in points, his mouth open, and one hand thrown across the pillow, the other around the old teddy bear.

His frowsty little body reassured Anna, and she bent to kiss him on the cheek, noting the new, faintly sour smell which proved that he was already losing the purer fragrance of childhood. She saw that his nails were dirty and that there was chocolate around his mouth. 'You didn't even clean your teeth, you grubby little beast,' she whispered, tucking him in. 'Gosh, and we'd have been yanked out of bed for less.'

With that rueful memory came an accompanying wistfulness, that death meant a barrier between people you love, who would never know each other. Prematurely William had planned his days as a grandfather: the picnics, visits to local places of historic interest, the model-making, if these phantom grandchildren were boys. It was clear to him how it would be: the retirement, the sense of *pater familias* increased, the long hours for reading. 'And how he'd have loved you,' she said aloud, to the almost-snoring child.

'Too much – it's all too much, and I'm wallowing in it, as if there wasn't enough to be fed up about,' she thought, angrily, banishing the thought of her father with a mental leap, like the action of someone swatting a persistently buzzing fly. 'It's no good; it blights everything; suffocating me, damn it.'

She undressed quickly, thought about cleaning her teeth, then decided not to bother. In the darkness she tried to ignore the noises from outside the cottage, the river noises, but drifted off to sleep thinking, quite deliberately, about Matthew Paul.

Fourteen

The days arranged themselves into a pattern. Every other afternoon Anna drove Tom into Synemouth to visit his grandmother; each day between she spoke to Barbara on the telephone, gently talking of the weather and what Tom had said and done, avoiding all reference to the future, or the past. The visits were always free of tension now, and only the slight breathiness and the hollows in Barbara's face were a reminder of the truth. Tom was like a cushion between the two women – something soft and comfortable which enabled them both to rest, and yet a safety barrier too.

Daily, Matthew Paul attached himself more and more to them, as if he were bored at home, as if (thought Anna in wry moments) there were nothing else to do. The day after he had failed to arrive for tea, he had turned up at the back door, and apologised. 'Dad came and got me,' he had explained. 'He came running to the end of the pontoon and I told him he'd better be careful or he'd have a heart attack or something. God, he's unfit! Anyway, Mum had been making a fuss because she had some more people coming for drinks, and I was supposed to get changed and hand the peanuts round, like a flunkey. Yuk, I can't stand all that rubbish! They all hang round getting pissed and Mum starts pawing me, and when Dad gets drunk he gets stroppy and shows me up.'

'What do you mean?' asked Anna innocently, pleased at the unusual length of the boy's speech, and enjoying this glimpse into the Paul household.

'Oh, he starts to go on about school and how it's a waste of his money because all I think about is sport. He said all that when you were there, I think.'

'Yes, but is it true?' she asked.

He grinned, pleased with himself. 'Yeah, it is really. I'm in the gym display group, and all the house teams, and I'm middle-school diving champion. At the end of term swimming gala I won the best overall cup.'

Impressed, Anna murmured that he should work hard too, and he groaned. 'Don't you start! I didn't think you were like that, I mean like them, Mrs Lewis.'

'I'm not Mrs Lewis, I'm Mrs something else, at least, I was. We'll shake on it – I won't mention school again if you remember to call me Anna.'

'Done!' He paused, then added, 'I suppose they are right. Dad's said that if I don't do well in my O's next year he'll sell the windsurfer. I couldn't stand that. I'd rather freesail than do anything else.'

'Why, Matthew?'

'There you go again! Why do you think? Because it takes you away from everything, you're on your own, no one can get at you, you haven't got to think about anybody because there isn't time, and you feel great – in control. All that. It's obvious really.'

Anna had agreed that it was indeed obvious, that all questions were superfluous.

It was as if she and Tom entered into a conspiracy. If, one day, Matthew failed to call at their cottage, to chat for a few minutes and leave them satisfied, Tom would say, 'Shall we go to the pontoon, Mum?' and she would agree, knowing that he intended to search for Matthew. Or she herself might say, 'Shall we go to look for your windsurf boy?' and they would walk along the beach and wait until the tiny figure, grasping the booms like a mountaineer clinging to his rope, would catch sight of them, and release one hand to wave a greeting. If ever Matthew was missing altogether, and could not even be found in the shop chatting to George, Anna would have to stifle h   urge to ring the bell at 'Hacienda' and ask for him.

Tom talked about the older boy incessantly, and Anna did not discourage him. One day he asked, 'Mum, do you like Matthew's face?'

Taken aback she replied, 'What an odd thing to ask ...
But yes, I do. Yes.'

He looked deep in thought. 'It's a nice face,' he said
slowly, 'and he's quite kind, you know. I wish I was strong
like him. I want to be like him when I'm grown up. I'm glad
you like him so much, Mum.'

Since that first drinks party Anna had avoided 'Hacienda'.
She felt she knew too much about the Pauls to be able to
keep a straight face in any gathering, especially if Matthew
were to smile at her from across the room. Treating her as
a friend he told her things that would have appalled his
parents: how long, for instance, his mother took getting
dressed in the morning, how she infuriated his father by her
expenditure on clothes, and how there was a very good-
looking male friend, the owner of a chain of shoe shops, who
dropped in to see her at times when Adrian was not there.
'He must fancy her, wouldn't you say?' he asked, looking
at Anna out of the corner of his eye, so that she could not
decide what he understood.

She had learnt that Valerie was exactly the same age as
herself. Matthew was sprawling in the grass at her feet,
tickling Tom's neck with a long leaf as he tried to put the
wheels back on his toy car.

'How old are you, Anna?' he asked.

'Why do you want to know?' She felt annoyed, both at
the question and at the trace of archness she could not keep
from her voice.

'No reason. I like knowing people's ages. Funny, but kids
like Tom say I'm seven and a half, and that half really
matters to them. Then people like my grandad say I'm
ninety-nine, or whatever,' he mimicked a quavering elderly
voice, 'and you're supposed to say well done. I mean – me,
I'm always pleased when people tell me I look seventeen,
but I don't mind them knowing I'm not.'

'So?'

'Don't you see what I'm getting at? Somewhere in the
middle people don't want to mention age. Mum says it's
rude to ask someone how old she is, almost as bad as asking
how much a man earns. I don't see why it matters.'

He looked serious, looking up at Anna and leaving Tom alone. She noticed that the hairs under his arms were golden and beaded with sweat. The sun was very hot, and Tom was lying down on Matthew's shirt. Anna said, 'Your face is smooth, that's why. You aren't worried about grey hair, or wrinkles, or aches and pains. It'll be years and years before you have to think of getting old. But all people are afraid of it. It's as if, by not mentioning the number of years, you can stop them. I must say, I wouldn't mind.'

'But you're not old,' he protested.

'I think that was where we came in,' she laughed.

Matthew appeared to have forgotten his original question. 'And I'm damned if I'm going to volunteer the information,' she thought.

'The trouble with people,' he said, 'is they have too many secrets. Things that don't matter. One day I told somebody, a friend of Dad's, that Mum always said she'd had me when she was twenty and that was it. She didn't want to spoil her figure, so no more kids. D'you know, she didn't speak to me for two days!'

Anna threw back her head and laughed, but waved a finger at him in mock-gravity. 'You shouldn't have said that!'

'But it's true.'

'One thing you'll learn is that people don't like the truth.'

Tom was interested now. 'Would you have liked a brother or a sister, Matt?'

'A brother, I think. I don't like girls – not little ones, that is.'

He glanced up at Anna flirtatiously, and she raised her eyebrows, looking away. But Tom was staring at her, as if a thought had only just crossed his mind. 'Mum,' he said, 'I'd have liked a brother too. Let's have another boy. Why don't you find somebody to have a baby with?'

She felt her cheeks flush as Matthew started to laugh, looked at her, then turned his face away towards the river. There was an uncomfortable pause; then quickly he leapt up and asked Tom if he would like to go rowing.

'Can I? With you?'

'Sure, if you promise to sit still.'

Gratefully Anna went into the hall to find the smallest lifejacket; then she watched them as they walked away along the beach, the small boy running to keep up with Matthew's strides.

One morning Anna was washing up after breakfast when she saw the heavy form of Adrian Paul descending the orchard path. The sun was already warm. Tom had taken out his toy boats, and they had set up the leaky old paddling pool on the grass. 'Hello, young man, having a good play?' boomed Adrian, in the tone of someone who has no interest in any possible reply, but likes to think he knows about children.

He knocked at the kitchen door, and walked in, looking round with open curiosity. 'Hello and good morning! So ... this is your little place?'

'Um,' Anna mumbled, already feeling her hackles rise.

'Jeez, somebody certainly had an eye for bright colours, didn't they!'

'It wasn't us.'

'Are you going to do it up one day?'

Annoyed, she muttered that it was hardly worth it.

He looked interested. 'Why, are you going to sell it? Done up it would be worth a lot, especially with the river frontage. Ask old Jasper Herbert, he'll give you some advice.'

'No, I mean that it isn't worth doing it up because we've all got used to it the way it is, and we like it.'

'Have you? – Oh.' In the face of life's mysteries Adrian Paul always resorted to what was familiar, and so he fiddled with his teeth, extracting a morsel of food from behind his left canine.

Repenting, Anna offered him coffee but he refused. 'Thanks, no ... look, I came to ask you if you'd like to come on a trip. Val asked me to ask you – not that I don't want you myself!'

Groaning inwardly Anna asked, 'Do you mean today?'

'Yes, we thought we'd go for a spin to one of the beaches. To tell the truth, we've bought a new boat!' He could hardly contain his pride, and Anna smiled inwardly, feeling a sudden affection for this man who was Matthew's father.

'How exciting for you – yes, we'd love it. Oh, it was our day for visiting my mother . . .'

Her face clouded, and there was an awkward pause.

'Couldn't you cancel it? Go tomorrow?'

She decided. 'Oh yes, it won't matter. I'll give her a ring. It's only fair – for Tom, I mean.'

'Yes, that's the spirit. 'Cos Matthew will be coming, needless to say. Matter of fact it was him who . . . No, sorry, forget it.'

Curious, Anna pressed him.

'No, Val says I'm always putting my big feet in it. It's good that Matt's got you two here, because he gets a bit fed up with us, you know what kids are like. Someone else is a novelty. To be frank, Val wouldn't let him bring a friend this time – she's a bit difficult like that. So before you arrived he was spending damn near all day on that bloody windsurfer and not talking to a soul, or mooching at home and moaning. I can tell you, he's been a lot better company since you've been here. Must be your good influence.'

Anna carefully wiped each side plate, a task she normally left. It was important to hide her smile. 'Oh well, better go and get the stuff ready. We'll pick you up at the end of the pontoon at 12.30, OK? How d'you fancy a picnic on the river?' He chuckled and nudged her. 'My problem is, I fancy anything!'

She watched him climb the orchard path, very slowly, as if he were an old man, until he disappeared into the waving greenery, the sunlight on his back. Then she flung down the cloth, ran outside and squatted beside Tom, throwing an arm around his shoulders and kissing him repeatedly.

He ducked. 'What's the matter? What's wrong with you?'

'Typical!' she said, with a peal of laughter. 'Just because I'm feeling happy you think there's something the matter with me. Shall I tell you something nice? We're going on a boat with Matthew's Mum and Dad today.'

'Yes, but will Matt be there?'

'Of course he will! I think it was him who asked them to ask us.'

Tom smiled, 'Do you think he likes us a lot, then?

'Oh yes,' she said. 'Matthew likes you all right!'

A bird sang in the tree above their heads; it was as if Anna's ears, finely tuned, could hear even the tiniest sounds, even to the rustle of each individual leaf in the light breeze or the imperceptible wash of ripples beyond the garden wall. She noticed the golden down on Tom's neck, as he bent to his boats once more; noticed too how the morning light intensified the vivid green of the long grass which had once been a cropped lawn. About a yard away a bee was droning heavily around the mouth of a brilliant pink foxglove. It jagged hither and thither until it located the entrance, then tucked itself inside to suck nourishment from the flower – dark against its veined translucence. After a few moments the bee disentangled itself; it flew off on wings that could hardly bear its sated weight through the shimmering air. Anna, rapt, saw the almost invisible dusting of pollen upon its body.

'Mum – why are you so excited?'

Momentarily embarrassed she said, 'I'm not.'

'Yes you are. I can read your mind, Mum. You're excited about going in the boat.'

'Well, yes. I think it will be nice for you.'

Tom looked up gravely, with that awareness in his eyes that disconcerted her, since it was so new – the seeing through this placid surface of adult pleasantries into whatever swirling, murky waters lay beneath. Anna met his gaze, and smiled at him nervously, dreading his knowledge.

'No,' he said with an air of calm finality as he dropped a plastic boat from a height, and watched it sink, swamped by its own waves. 'No, Mum, you're excited because Matthew's going. Shall I tell you a secret? I think you're in love with Matthew!' And he pursed his lips in the soundless whistle he had learnt from boys at school.

'Oh Tom,' Anna said, flatly, 'I wish you wouldn't have to be so childish all the time.'

Fifteen

'Of course, darling, don't worry about it at all, see you when I see you . . . 'Bye.'

Barbara replaced the receiver and shrugged, fighting down her swelling disappointment. Her towel and toilet bag were on the bed; Nurse Anderson stood expectantly at its foot.

'I don't think I'll bother with a bath this morning.'

The nurse clicked her tongue, 'Now then, we can't let standards slip, can we? You always have a bath, Mrs Lewis. It's nice to freshen up.'

'They aren't coming today – my daughter and grandson. Going out on a boat trip up the river with some friends.'

Nurse Anderson picked up the towel and hung it over her arm, moving her body towards the door as if to encourage this patient who really got on her nerves, though she did not know why. 'Oh well, you can't blame them really, can you? Not very nice for a little boy, visiting here, let's face it. Not nice always being with old folks, let's . . .'

'Oh, I know.'

'Now let's get this bath over, Mrs Lewis, I do have a lot to do.'

Feeling drained of all resistance, Barbara sighed and followed her to the door.

The trouble began when Anna went to the bedroom to pull on her old denim shorts, then stared at her reflection in the full-length mirror on the wardrobe door. White legs, covered with stubble; fleshy thighs, mottled, with a streak of pink down the front where she had caught some sun. 'God, I'm ugly,' she thought, 'Matthew will take one look at me and throw up.' For a second she wanted to cry; then walked with some determination into the bathroom.

The razor (probably left by her brother-in-law Alan, since Richard always used his travelling electric) was old and blunt, but Anna set to work on her legs. Five minutes later three rivulets of red traced a delicate path over the contours of her flesh, gathering in a pool in the hollow of her thin ankle. She swore, but finished the other leg in much the same fashion, blotting the blood with Tom's brown face flannel. Then, after rinsing the sprinkling of scum and stubble from the bath, she took from the cabinet a bottle she had bought two days earlier. The label announced that 'Instabronze' would turn her into a golden goddess in just ten minutes – an experiment that Anna, who cherished the devout sceptic's secret longing for miracles, decided she must try.

She supported one leg upon the bath, unscrewed the lid and poured the yellowish-white cream into the palm of her hand. 'Spread quickly over the surface of the skin making sure that the "Instabronze" is spread evenly.' Anna smeared the stuff all over her calves and thighs, finding it hard to reach the backs of her legs, and allowed herself a cursory glance by way of a check. Now for the arms. She repeated the process, slopping more and more of the cream into her palm and slapping it on her skin. There was a problem at the shoulder: did you stop at the high point of a sleeveless tee-shirt or continue to the neck, stopping at the face – which would then peer wanly from its stem like a snowdrop stuck on a brown twig? The trouble with the 'Instabronze' was that it became absorbed so quickly into the skin that whilst Anna was wondering where to go with it, she forgot where she had been. It was rather like trying to complete a 'Paint by Numbers' with invisible ink.

Anna stared at herself in the mirror, remembering suddenly something she had forgotten: the extraordinary concoctions she and Hilda had made in the kitchen of 'Ahoy', because Barbara used to say that it was wasteful to spend their money on suntan preparations. 'Of course, Dad was on our side,' she thought. He had laughed one day to find them stirring and mixing, whilst their mother had gone shopping in Synemouth. Anna had played safe with vinegar and olive oil, suspecting none the less that Barbara would be less than pleased to find the expensive oil cooking her daughter in the sun. Hilda, who had read in a magazine that something called cocoa butter was an ingredient in expensive American lotions, decided to combine melted butter with drinking chocolate, thinning the sticky mixture with some of Barbara's cologne. They had smeared their inventions over their limbs (young and firm then, Anna thought), taken the two pale-blue bath towels and stretched themselves hopefully on the lawn. William had chuckled, saying they were like a fish and chip supper followed by hot chocolate, and offending their teenage dignity by slapping both of them on the bottom as he passed. After an hour he called softly from his deckchair, 'Excuse me, you two beauty queens, I think you ought to know the Queen Mother is coming down the path!'

Anna started to laugh quietly as she remembered her mother's face. The kitchen was covered with debris; half a pound of butter wasted; the open bottle of cologne; and the sight of two daughters standing by towels stained with long greasy marks. Two days later she had produced a bottle of Boots' suntan cream for each of them, and William had whispered that vanity always vanquished prudence.

Smiling to herself Anna suddenly remembered that the instructions on the 'Instabronze' had emphasised the importance of washing the hands immediately – and she had been daydreaming with it still coating her palms. She looked down. Already a tracery of fine brown lines showed against the orange of her skin. Horrified she attempted to scrub the stain away, but her skin remained orange. Reaching for the abrasive cleaning powder she sprinkled it over her hands and rasped them together, then took the scrubbing brush and ground the powder into her skin, wincing at the punishment. She looked down and saw the long, uneven streaks spreading over her thighs like a sunset, matching her striped arms. Her elbows and knees closely resembled the wrinkled skin of an ancient orange, left too long in the fruit bowl.

As she was filling the bath, with tears of panic gathering in her eyes, Tom came in. 'What are you doing Mum? You've gone a funny colour.'

'Well, that's pretty clever of you,' she muttered.

'Yes, honestly,' he explained, innocently helpful. 'You've gone sort of yellowy, on your shoulders there, and your legs. Were you trying to make yourself as brown as Matt?'

At 12.30 promptly, they sat on the end of the pontoon and Anna felt sourly as if she had been scrubbed all over with a wire brush. She wore a long-sleeved tee-shirt and jeans, even though the sun was at its hottest, and wished – as the kind of boat her father used to call a 'floating gin palace' swung slowly round towards them, with Matthew in his swimming trunks upon the cabin roof – that she had never set eyes on the Pauls.

George Treadle lumbered along the pontoon behind them and called Matthew to throw him the rope. 'I saw them bring her up from the Marina last night, Anna. She a fast one, that's for sure,' he said. George reached out, caught hold of a rail of gleaming chrome, and held the boat steady as Adrian Paul lifted Tom aboard, holding out a hand for Anna as she clumsily scrambled across, nervous as always of the streak of cold water beneath her.

As it had approached them *Invader* had reminded Anna of a tiered wedding cake, decorated by strange flying protuberances. It seemed curiously top heavy, as if at any moment the laws of science must insist that it sink slowly beneath the little lapping waves of the river, a sacrifice of modernity to its age. Now, on deck, Anna felt like a fly in an empty swimming pool, tiny and exposed.

'Well, what do you think?' Adrian's face was flushed. 'I'll show her around,' said Matthew, leaping down on to the deck. 'No, you won't, that's my job,' called Valerie, waving him aside. The three of them wore the same expression, like children, Anna thought, with a new toy. She felt touched. Already Tom was running around the deck screaming, 'Look at this, look at this!'

Invader swung out, making the people fishing from their dinghies bob wildly from side to side.

'Well, do you like her?' Adrian repeated.

'Yes, it's . . . lovely,' Anna replied.

'You look hot in all those clothes,' said Valerie, looking dubiously at the jeans and tee-shirt and resting a hand on the brief white shorts which revealed her own long brown legs.

'Yes, well, I forgot to bring shorts. It doesn't matter.'

Anna screwed up her eyes against the dazzle of sun on white fibreglass and shining chrome. Matthew had climbed aloft again, and was lolling on the cabin roof, dark against its whiteness. His swimming trunks were brief; Anna averted her gaze, shaking her head when he called to her to come up and join him.

Instead she wandered in to Adrian, who sat at the wheel. 'Not bad, eh?' he said over his shoulder, and without waiting for an answer went on to list *Invader*'s assets. 'She's got twin diesels, goes about twenty-five knots maximum, not that that's much good to us along here. The limit's five knots – too slow. That's radar up there, and we've got VHF and autopilot, so Val and I can have a cuddle and still keep on course!'

He winked at her. 'Want to take the wheel?'

'No thanks. It's safer in your hands.'

Adrian reached out and put an arm around her waist. 'You know all boats are female? Well, no female's safe in my hands!'

Valerie stood in the doorway. 'There he goes again,' she said, with no emotion in her voice. 'Come below and I'll show you the galley and cabins. How would you like a glass of cold white wine?'

'Bring me a beer, love. Terrific to have a fridge on board,' Adrian added to Anna, so that once again she felt oddly touched at the childish quality of his pride.

Matthew joined them. 'Give her a burst, Dad.'

'Use your head, Sonny Jim. What's the point of getting into trouble when we've just got her?'

Matthew looked sulky. 'What's the point of being able to go really fast if they won't let you? It's stupid to have a speed limit. A river's not like a road.'

'But you once complained to me', Anna said, 'about motor cruisers not knowing the river rules enough to get out of your way in good time when you're windsurfing. And whizzing past making unnecessary wash. You've changed your tune a bit, haven't you?'

'We didn't have one then. It's different when it's your own.'

'Whose?' Adrian laughed. 'While we're on the subject, this is mine. You've got that magnified water-ski of yours.' Matthew peered at the instruments panel with its battery of dials. 'I'd rather have this thing,' he said.

Anna felt disappointed, and turned to look for Tom. He was sitting perfectly still in one of the folding chairs, staring at the frothy wake which churned from the stern, his face full of ecstasy. 'Mum, isn't this great?' he whispered. 'I've always wanted to go on a boat like this. A really fast boat. Do you think it's the fastest boat in the world?'

'Oh, I wouldn't be surprised,' she said, turning away.

The cabins had teak edges to the berths; frilled curtains, patterned in turquoise, navy blue and white, hung at the rows of portholes; the shower had a sliding door of reeded plastic. Valerie displayed the boat's virtues, including what she called 'two decent toilets that work properly'. So Anna found herself peering down a lavatory bowl and making admiring noises. The interior of *Invader* shone; the manufacturers had allowed no meanness with metal or Melamine or teak or tweed to detract from the impression of lavish uniformity.

Valerie switched on a radio, so that quiet pop music filled the galley, and opened a fridge stacked with wine and beer and soft drinks, commenting, 'Look – Ade's got his priorities right!' She started to unpack the large hamper that lay upon the table, pulling out chicken legs, hunks of salami and garlic sausage, soft cheeses and bags of tomatoes. Two French loaves were wrapped in a red-checked tablecloth.

'You didn't get all this from the village shop,' said Anna.

'No, I only get basics like tins from there. I get most of our food in Synemouth, and use the freezer. Actually, I saw you in Synemouth – the day before yesterday. Were you visiting your mother?'

'Yes.'

'Is she getting on all right?'

The question was merely polite. 'Yes,' replied Anna – then thought how dishonest, how foolish to try to protect this woman, standing amidst her picnic in all her health and prettiness, from truth.

'Well, no, that's not strictly true. Sometimes when I see her she seems better, but it's an illusion. She's got cancer, Valerie – breast cancer. I still find it hard to say. I don't really know how long she's got to live.'

Valerie Paul folded her arms across her chest, each hand rubbing the smooth skin it touched, and she shuddered. 'Ooooh, it's awful. I can't bear to think about it.'

'Don't you think', Anna asked quietly, 'that we have to – at some stage? Have you ever had a relative who died? Someone close to you?'

'No, thank goodness. Ade's mother died when he was little, and he hardly remembers her. His father lives in Manchester, and he's all right. He married again and his wife's much younger than him. My parents live in Dover, but to be honest, I never see them.'

'Why?'

'We never really got on. I was an only child and they didn't really want me to get married so young – all that sort of thing. Mind you, they'd like all this. They like Ade, now he's done so well for himself. Actually, I've always found them a bit . . . well, a bit of a pain. There's no rule that says you have to like your parents, is there?'

Anna shook her head. 'So you never see them?'

'About once or twice a year. We used to have them at Christmas, but Adrian and Matthew like coming down here for every school holiday, so it's a bit of a problem.'

'Yes.'

'Anyway,' Valerie added, taking turquoise plates from a cupboard and piling them on the table, 'they get on all right. I think old people like to be left alone to get on with their own lives. You shouldn't interfere all the time, don't you agree?'

The day before yesterday Barbara had laughed, telling Tom stories about when his Grandad was a little boy and there was no television and few cars. Tom had been incredulous, full of pity for the terrible life they must have led, but Barbara had smiled her secret smile, and said that it was not terrible. In those days, she said, people talked to each other, and when the bombs fell on London they all scurried underground into the shelters and everybody was friendly, everybody helped. Anna had sat, listening to the tales she had heard before, remembering how the same stories had drawn each one of them, as children, into a vivid world of sirens and blackouts, rations and camaraderie, and how that history had seemed heroic, enviable to her – themselves a generation deprived. Sometimes she used to detect a note of wistfulness in her father's repetitive anecdotes about the army, as if it was the last time he had felt free. Yesterday, beneath the mirth, Barbara had sounded wistful too.

Did she want to be left alone? In a sense she did, Anna thought – despite her repugnance for Valerie's complacency, her easy explanation of her own neglect. Barbara wanted no interference, in that she had set her course for death and needed only the emotional sustenance of quayside parting with her family. 'And yet she's wrong – so we have to do something about it,' Anna thought, remembering how she had interfered after William's death, meeting with Hilda and Richard, arranging the cremation, arguing about 'Ahoy' ... and since then, nothing. When her mother had written that slightly coy, slightly questioning letter about her friend the Brigadier (whom none of them had met, deliberately), Anna's reply had given information about John's new job and the house they were going to buy, and finally (in a postscript) answered her mother's delicate hints about the possibility of future companionship with the blunt and breezy observation that it was nice for her mother to have new friends, but of course no one could take the place of Daddy. That, Anna had decided at the time, was not interference; simply an expression of the obvious. Yes, she thought, I too told people that my mother loved being left alone to live her own life. Richard and Hilda agreed, during those odd quarrelsome Sunday lunches, when the gravy congealed upon our plates as we sat, drowsy with wine, and wondered why the accident of blood should draw us into unsatisfactory rites with these familiar strangers. So we left our mother alone, as Valerie leaves hers alone, and yet now I want to change her mind, to alter the course she has chosen.

Valerie was looking at her, asking for approbation, yet dreading (Anna could tell) that her guest would continue this uncomfortable conversation. 'Perhaps they do want to be left alone,' Anna said, 'because they've had enough of us. But what if they grow desperate without their children, and wonder what was the point of having them, just as we will one day?'

'Oh, I doubt that,' said Valerie, with a tense smile and a toss of her head. 'All I can say is, sometimes I can't wait to have Matthew off my hands. Life'll be much easier. Let's face it, kids can be a terrible nuisance at times, can't they?'

Again she looked hopeful, and suddenly Anna felt pity for this woman's inability to shift outside the limits of her own language. Such clichés, she admitted to herself, formed the syntax of her communication with her own mother – so she above all must allow some charity towards the fear they hide. So she shrugged and said, 'Oh sure they can,' and saw the smile spread across Valerie's face.

They ate their picnic when Adrian dropped anchor, about fifty feet away from the leafy bank, at a quiet bend in the river. Valerie peeled off her shorts and tee-shirt, and sprawled on a brightly-patterned 'lounger' in a lime-green bikini. Adrian removed his shirt, and Anna averted her eyes from the hairy stomach which swelled over the belt of his khaki shorts. 'Thank God Matthew takes after his mother,' she thought, watching as the boy leaned against the rail and smoothed his mother's suntan oil over his arms and chest, rubbing it in slowly until his flesh shone in the sunlight. She felt hot and hemmed in by these bodies which offered themselves to the heat like chunks of meat under a grill. Shamed, almost.

'Aren't you hot, Anna?' Valerie pointed at Anna's arms, covered by the long-sleeved tee-shirt. 'I've got a spare bikini in the cabin, if you want.'

Anna thought of her orange piebald body and shook her head. 'No, I don't feel the heat. I'll stay modest today.'

Adrian opened his fourth beer. 'Spoilsport! Eh, Matt?'

'She can do what she likes,' said the boy sullenly.

'Can't you take a joke?' Adrian's face reddened.

'Don't think much of your jokes. They're embarrassing.'

'Oh, for God's sake, you two, don't start squabbling! See what a hard time I have, Anna, keeping them apart?' Valerie lit a cigarette and glared at her husband and son.

Embarrassed, Anna fussed over Tom, who had spilt lemonade on his bare legs. He had, with unusual lack of shyness, permitted her to strip him to his underpants, and now pinkened in the afternoon sun. When she looked up, Matthew was staring at her, but switched his gaze immediately to the river bank, where birds called harshly in the stillness. His nose was straight, the face in profile harsher, older-looking. Anna gazed at his face, noticing how his hair, damp with heat and oil, curled in tendrils over his ears, then dropped her eyes, seeing the oil gleam on the planes of his flat stomach, and observing how it flattened the hairs on his brown thighs. For a second there flashed across her mind an image of him naked, but the thought curled at the pit of her stomach, so that she looked away, feeling ashamed. Sweat trickled coldly from her armpit down her side.

'Have some more food, Matt,' said Valerie, holding out a plate to him. 'You've hardly eaten a thing.'

'Don't want much,' he muttered, but took a fat portion of chicken and squatted down at his mother's feet, pulling and gnawing at the meat. His tongue slid out to lick his fingers. Soon there was a ring of grease around his mouth, and he wiped his hands carefully on his own skin, adding to its lustre.

'Oh, why the hell can't you use a serviette?' snarled Adrian.

''Cos I don't want to.'

'Why don't you go for a swim and clean yourself up a bit?'

'I was going to anyway, Dad. Thought I'd give you all the honour of seeing me perform.'

Matthew hauled himself up the ladder to the top deck, and stood looking down at them, screwing up his eyes against the sun.

'Don't be so daft as to think you can dive from up there,' Adrian called, 'come down and go off the back.'

Valerie stared sleepily up at her son. 'I must say, even though he's mine, that he's turning out a handsome kid. Don't you think he's beautiful, Anna?'

'Course she does!' said Adrian, with a wink at his wife, 'Anna can't take her eyes off him, can you Anna? All you women are the same!' He threw back his head and laughed, so that his stomach shook. Valerie joined in. 'Well,' she screamed, 'if you put any more weight on Ade, I tell you I'll be inviting that new young milkman in for morning coffee.'

Tom looked puzzled, his head turning from one adult to another, trying to understand the incomprehensible laughter. Though loud, it was not infectious; it shut him out, and made his mother look pink and irritated, even though she forced a laugh as well.

'Can I swim too, Mummy?' he asked, sensing dimly that she needed him to help her. But she looked through him for a second and he saw a dreadful vacancy in her face, the faraway sad look that seemed to afflict her more and more. Though Tom did not understand he was afraid she might be going to cry, and so he jumped up and repeated his request.

'It'll have to be in your underpants,' she said, shortly.

Matthew stood on the stern and plunged cleanly into the water, showing pink soles as he disappeared, a long shadow beneath the surface, before bobbing up some distance away, to shake the hair from his eyes with a wild toss. He struck out for the boat, his arms cleaving from the water, and glittering drops of spray cast upwards from his churning feet.

'Matthew won't want you to spoil his swim.'

'Yes he will. I won't spoil it anyway.'

Dubiously she helped Tom down the ladder into Matthew's arms, and watched anxiously as the child doggy-paddled in a small circle.

'Stay near to him, Matthew,' she called.

'Don't worry, I'll look after him. Hey Tommy, you're quite a good swimmer.'

Adrian and Valerie lay flat, their eyes shaded by dark glasses, whilst the debris of their lunch grew shiny on the folding table, and half-finished wine warmed within the glasses. Few boats passed them; there was not wind enough to sail and only a single daytrip boat made *Invader* rock upon the chain, as rows of curious and envious faces peered at them from its decks.

Matthew tickled Tom and lifted him in the water, never leaving his side. He pretended to race the child, and Anna smiled to see him pace himself, absurdly containing his own strength, so that Tom pulled out ahead. Suddenly, it was as if something within her softened like the butter left on the side of their plates, and she rested her head upon her arms, tenderly. The hot sun burned her back, and, with eyelids half closed, Anna felt suspended, listening to the two voices from the water, remembering nothing but the sight and sound of the minute just gone, whose echoes still reverberated in her head. She smelt her own skin and liked the fragrance, one that she associated with Tom folded into his towel after an evening bath, with that totally unthreatening love. Matthew's voice called, 'Anna! Anna! Look at us. Tom's beating me!' and Anna opened her eyes a fraction, still with her head resting, to see Matthew smiling up at her, his teeth white and his face shiny with water, the smell of the salt river mingled with the fragrance of suntan oil and filling her nostrils and, it seemed, the air all around.

Under her breath, her stomach folding as it does when an old lift starts its descent, Anna said, 'I love you.' She leaned forward to help Tom up the ladder, and said aloud, 'Love you,' thinking it did not matter, after all, if she was as unspecific as the sun, especially as the wine was making her drowsier and drowsier and the movement of the boat upon its anchor was gentle, soporific. Matthew was good; he had been patient with Tom, when he must have longed

130

to swim alone, and now he was reaching up to her from the water, holding out his hand to her and smiling, pleading in mock helplessness to be pulled up the ladder. Happily Anna held out her hand, which he grasped tightly, pulling himself over the top and scattering drops of water in her face, so that she shivered slightly at the sudden coolness.

She wrapped Tom in the towel, and whispered, 'Isn't this perfect, my love? It's completely perfect.' Then they both watched silently as Matthew stepped over his sleeping father and climbed quickly up the ladder to the top deck. He stepped carefully over the chromium rail, balanced for a moment on the edge of the wheelhouse roof so that he was silhouetted against the brilliant blue sky, and then made his exquisite, forbidden dive into the river.

Sixteen

Anna was dreaming. There was a lane, warm and fragrant with wild flowers, and the tall hedges each side were like walls, so tangled that they allowed no chink of blue sky through the leaves. Birds sang; there were minute rustlings within the hedgerows, and every now and then a cabbage white flitted heavily from one side of the narrow lane to the other.

She was walking along, slowly and at peace, just as she used to do when she was a child, but now she was no child but an adult. Bending to gather red campion, Anna saw the shiny beetles scuttling through the waving grasses, and felt such a deep sense of happiness, and love for the lane and its inhabitants, that she grew dizzy, intoxicated by the smell of wild honeysuckle and dog rose. As she straightened her back and walked on she felt that, slowly and imperceptibly, she was shrinking, like Alice in Wonderland, into one who could walk through the tiny door, into an enamelled rose garden where her parents would suddenly loom large, stooping to pick her up as she bent to gather the flowers.

Down and down the lane wound, so that she could not see around the bend, where the trees behind the hedge each side mingled their branches overhead, making a shadowy tunnel. Anna walked on, down the lane, into the tunnel, and suddenly it was as if she had not shrunk, but the lane itself had, so that gradually it was enclosing her with its reddish darkness. Fearing nothing, but trusting that somewhere at the end of this journey William would be waiting, holding out his hand to encourage his child, Anna felt no need to hurry.

She heard her own footsteps. With no reason, the birds had stopped their singing, and in that second she noticed that the rustlings and buzzing too had ceased, as if all nature was poised, waiting. Anna listened too. In the distance she heard the drone of an engine, a noise that gathered speed and intensity, as she stopped and glanced back along the lane, seeing nothing but how silent, dark and claustrophobic it had become. She walked on. The noise grew louder, and louder. Looking back again, up along a straight stretch, she saw a car turn the corner in the distance, gathering speed. She waved, thinking it might slow down, but instead it went faster, filling the lane, bearing down on her.

In that dull light she could not see the driver's face, but waved again, begging the car to slow down. Dark red and streaked with dirt it picked up still more speed, brushing back the hedge each side of the tunnel, and bowling down the hill towards her.

Anna screamed, and ran in terror like a fox, on and on, down and down, hoping that there would be a gateway on one side or the other, somewhere she could press herself into and let the thing go by, but no such passing place occurred, no doorway small or large. On and on she fled, not daring to glance back, but feeling from the sound, the urgency, the car drawing closer and closer with every second, with no possible escape.

Then it was as if, dreaming, she transcended her own dream self, so that she was simultaneously inside that terrified body, its heart and blood pounding, and outside it,

132

above and looking down. *Run, run,* that Anna called to the fleeing animal, who still looked over her shoulder, panting, yet still believing that the car would stop. She turned a bend in the lane, and saw in front o." her the River Syne, silvery and placid in the sunlight. But back in the darkness and heat of the lane the car still gathered speed; and now, looking back at it, Anna saw, for the first time, the face behind the wheel. It was John, her husband, and his face was full of malicious happiness.

Look out, look out, the other Anna sang above her, but it was not for a few seconds more that her first self saw the reason for that cry. Numb with horror and panic she ran on, seeing the river ahead, and assuming that there would be some way of escape – a sliver of beach which no car could pass. And then she saw that this lane ended as no lane in real life ends, by leading into the river itself – the tunnelled trees ceasing suddenly, and the dusty lane toppling over a tiny ledge into the cold and flowing stream.

One part of her rejoiced that this blunt red car in pursuit would meet its own destruction, unless it stopped; and soon, with the momentum of all things, it would be too late to stop. And yet the self that ran, still ran towards that ending, could see no way of escape ahead, no promise of safety, only the horrible arrogance of the water's relentless movement over whatever stones and broken shells and slithery creatures lay upon its bed.

Jump, jump, jump now, she called to herself, and she paused fatally upon the edge of that lane, staring at the water, more afraid of what was in front than of the thing that came from behind . . .

Anna woke, calling, 'I can't, I can't,' and her nightdress was soaked with her sweat. She was panting, and lay for a second in the darkness, limp. Then she got out of bed, pulled the nightdress off, and noticed with distaste that the sheet was wet too, and must be changed. She was shivering, with cold and remembered horror, so she pulled on her dressing gown and wrapped herself in the duvet as if it were a sleeping bag, huddling upon the bed.

It was hard to get warm, and she did not want to go to

sleep in case she should be betrayed again. Yet she could not prevent herself from thinking of that dream. As she relaxed, feeling her own warmth spread, Anna began, with deliberate defiance, to construct an ending. It would have been all right, she thought, had Matthew been coming along, not on his windsurf board, but in the dinghy, so that she could have leapt aboard at that second and been carried to safety. Then they might have put ashore somewhere, in a field studded with buttercups, and slowly the boy would have stroked her, calming her, and telling her that she was beautiful. Anna closed her eyes, feeling herself loosening, as she fantasised the moment when, naked to naked, Matthew Paul would enter her flesh, but gently, and in innocence.

Barbara was not in her room. The door was ajar as Anna approached and she hesitated before entering, afraid of the bed and of Barbara herself. She had not been to 'The Park' for four days, the pattern of her visits broken. On the telephone she explained to her mother that she simply had to concentrate on 'giving Tom more of a holiday'. Barbara had agreed and asked what they would do, satisfied by Anna's vague talk of picnics and days out. She did not know that Matthew Paul would invariably accompany them on these odd, unsatisfying journeys through traffic jams, to fishing villages they did not particularly want to see, or to crowded beaches. But had Barbara known she would have approved of the idea of 'company for Tom', as Anna justified the boy's inclusion to herself and to the Pauls, when she telephoned yet again and asked if they could 'borrow Matthew for the day'.

Halfway through their holiday she had felt stifled by the continued visits to the nursing home, and grew to hate the carpeted corridors, and even the way Barbara would smile as they came through the door, apologetically, as if her life were a nuisance. For his part, Tom tolerated the visits to his grandmother, but such was his obsession with Matthew, and the possibility that they might see him, that now his face would screw itself into a grimace when Anna announced that it was time to leave for Synemouth. She had taken to

134

bribing him: the trip to the town came to mean an ice-cream, or a small cheap toy, or a round trip on the car ferry, and only incidentally the tense three-quarters-of-an-hour in Barbara's room.

But how cruel we are, Anna thought one night, as she leaned on the wall in the gathering darkness and looked at the river, to resent even such a fraction of time from our own lives – one boy of seven united with a woman of thirty-five in an unconscious but universal rejection of the old. Or is it that we are subtly infected by the arrogance of someone else: Matthew with his easy beauty and muscled health, and way of accepting all gifts calmly – and by his acceptance giving enough?

'Enough. Yet is it enough?' With sudden discontent she stretched her body like a cat, and brooded, half-ashamed. Her waking dreams centred upon Matthew; he banished even the thought of William from her mind, and for that, for depriving her of memory, Anna was not always grateful. In the cottage he made the furniture look pale and shabby, and when he picked up an object like an ashtray or a book, glancing at it idly before putting it down in a different place, those clean fingers tanned by the wind as they clung to the wishbone booms disturbed a cherished thing that suddenly lost all life. One day he flung himself down upon the window seat to gaze at the river, and Anna, pinched by his apparent boredom, heard the old wood creak and crack under his weight.

Tom was oblivious of such moments of boredom. Sometimes Anna ached at the openness of his admiration, his love, and at the way he expected Matthew to play with Lego and cars, as if he too was a child and could be trusted. She dreaded the moment when her child would see, would realise that the older boy would come until the time he ceased to want to come – and in that instant Tom would gain a bitter foretaste of all the loss and longing that would fill his life, until the day that he, like his grandmother, lay somewhere upon an iron bed, waiting.

Molly Black had telephoned the night before, timidly, to ask if Anna would please take in a book, and some magazines, that is if she ... 'Yes, I'll be going tomorrow,' Anna said hastily, angry to be exposed.

Anna deposited *The End of the Affair* and two thick, glossy women's magazines upon the bed, and looked around the room. Some more roses had been given dimension in her mother's tapestry, but that was the only change. Without its occupant the room seemed drained, colourless; Anna felt surprise that Barbara, though frail, still possessed the capacity to transform her surroundings, just as she would when, years ago, she would visit Anna in her student rooms, and leave fireside light behind when she had gone.

The wardrobe door was open, and Anna looked in. There was one dress and one jersey suit on hangers, another dressing gown, and a pile of folded nightdresses on the shelf. That was all. Wire hangers hung empty, rattling slightly as Anna moved the door. 'And when I was a child I used to hide in her wardrobe, and lose myself amongst the rows and rows of coats and dresses, until Richard, who always knew, found me there and gave me a fright.' She had always dreamt of approaching the big mahogany wardrobe in her parents' bedroom and passing through it into a world of talking beasts, but in her dreams there was no witch and no lion, no threat of evil or promise of redemption, simply a painted fairytale scene framed by her mother's pretty clothes. The emptiness of this veneered cupboard shocked Anna. There was nothing to hide amongst, nothing to pass through, and the back of the wardrobe showed clearly for what it was – cheap wood, but solid for all that.

'Hallo, dear. What are you looking for?' Barbara stood in the door, supporting herself against its frame. Her face was grey; she was panting and holding one thin hand across her chest. Anna could not suppress a small cry of shock at her appearance, and stood with one hand stretched out, but not moving.

'Where's Tom?'

'Oh, he's with that boy Matthew.'

Barbara shuffled forward, touching the wall at intervals, and waving aside (though gently) Anna's sudden movement towards her. Lowering herself into the armchair Barbara threw back her head, trying to regain her breath, so that Anna saw the white skin of her neck, its slackness stretched taut and the adam's apple fluttering as Barbara swallowed again and again. 'What is it, Mummy? You don't look well.' As soon as the words were out Anna saw the absurdity, and bit her lips.

'What were you looking for in there?' Barbara repeated. 'Did you want a tissue, or something?'

'No, just closing the door. It was open. But, Mummy, where are your clothes? All your clothes, I mean?'

'Oh, those. Well, one or two things are folded up in cases and with the furniture in store. You and Hilda can go through them later. Shouldn't think you'd want much of it, only there's that rather nice beaded cape, and the musquash stole, and Hilda always liked the green velvet . . .'

'Don't, Mummy, please,' interrupted Anna.

'I sent all the rest away to Oxfam and the church jumble sales. No point in keeping any of it – old jumpers and things like that. You wouldn't want any of them, would you?'

'But you might want them, that's the point.'

Barbara looked straight at Anna, and shook her head. 'Don't think so, somehow, darling.'

'But how do you *know*? Dr Jacobs told me . . .'

'Anna, I don't care what he told you, I know. I am the person to know.' Barbara's voice was firm, but Anna refused to give up. She sat down, took a breath, and consciously made her voice cajoling. 'I know you are. I understand the way you feel, but I don't think you really mean it, Mummy. We must talk about the future. It worries me that you've made up your mind to stay here until – well, stay here indefinitely. You don't want me to interfere, but can't you see that I can't help it? You know as well as I do what your doctor thinks. He says that if you leave here and go home you can still enjoy, well, a good chunk of ''e.'

'Home?'

Anna felt uncomfortable. 'We can work something out. I promised Richard I'd try.'

'When is he back? When is Hilda back?' Barbara's voice

was plaintive suddenly, like a very old lady who resents the least delay in attention to her wishes.

'They're both back next week, I think. They'll both come and see you when I've gone back to London.'

Barbara looked away. 'I don't want them to trouble over me.'

Angry, Anna gritted her teeth. Martyrs choose their dying, after all, so should not seek pity in the lion's teeth, not try to deny the importunate self which led them to their fate. 'Of course they'll trouble over you, Mother! How can they do anything else? You talk as if none of us care about you. All right, I know we've all been very busy in the last few years. You probably felt left out. But it happens that way. It'll happen to all of us when our kids have grown up. But it doesn't stop the children caring, does it? And it doesn't stop you needing to know that we do bloody well care!'

Barbara said nothing. Anna made an effort, and started again. 'Look, I've been thinking. If I could find you a small furnished flat to rent, near Molly and Harry, would you consider that? We could take it in turns to come down at weekends, and Molly would keep an eye on you.'

'I couldn't live with someone else's furniture,' Barbara said stiffly.

Determined to be patient, Anna made her voice more soothing still. 'I can see that. Well, never mind, why don't I look for an unfurnished place in the middle of Synemouth, and we'll take your own favourite things out of store. There's no reason why we shouldn't make you a nice new home, but without all the effort of buying. What do you think? Please say yes.'

Barbara's mouth was set in a line, but her lips folded inwards, as if to preserve that countenance. In a small voice she said, 'I don't want to live somewhere new. I don't want to be there alone when I die. I'd rather be here. Why don't you all understand that? I know what the nurses think, and I know what Dr Jacobs told you. They think that I'm difficult, and that if only I would put my mind to it I could live a reasonable life for another year or two. That's what

138

they think, don't they? What nobody tells me is why I should want to. Why should I? What for? I'm tired of it, Anna.'

Anna sat back in the chair, helpless. 'But why?' she asked.

Tears gathered in her mother's eyes, and for a few seconds she said nothing. Anna looked away, her confusion increasing, and sensing that if she were to kneel and bury her head in her mother's lap, asking for the comfort she herself could not give, Barbara's hands would not fold about her head.

'Tell me, darling, do you remember your father?'

'Of course I do, of course.'

'I mean really remember him. You can't remember him in the way I do – children never can. You were all too busy growing up and getting married, all those things.'

'Whatever do you mean? I loved Daddy. I was devastated when he died.' How ridiculous it was, thought Anna, that she should justify herself in this way, when Barbara had no inkling of how the thought of William had followed her through each room in 'Ahoy'; and how sometimes when Tom was asleep Anna wanted to run back through the emptiness, calling out like a child lost in a wood, and to feel the roughness of his tweed jacket against her cheek as he picked her up, loving her as John could never have loved her – certainly not in the damp passion of their bed.

She felt jealous of this old woman who was trying to claim him.

'Of course you were, Anna dear. I didn't mean that you weren't.' Now it was Barbara's turn to soothe. 'But you know, he and I used to sit and talk, when you had all left home, about our future, and that was when he made all his plans about the boat.' Her voice trembled slightly, then grew firm again, like that of a storyteller who is suddenly moved, despite himself, by his own tale. 'We used to torment ourselves by talking of the day when one of us had to die, and wonder which of us it would be. You do that, when you really love somebody. You spoil all the happiness of the present by thinking about the sadness of the future. Do you remember doing that, with John?'

Anna flinched. 'Oh yes, we did. When we were first

married we used to say that it was impossible to imagine not being together. He used to say that he hoped that he would die first, because he couldn't bear the idea of being without me. John was such a romantic,' she added bitterly.

'Yes, it is romantic, I suppose,' Barbara went on in a dreamy voice. 'The trouble is, when we talk about things like that we don't have any idea of what it will actually be like. It's a game; or a play you write for yourself, with a happy ending because deep down you don't believe in the sad one. Even when he died I couldn't believe it. I kept thinking that it was a mistake and that I'd see him again. Then I got so angry . . .'

Abruptly Anna muttered, 'Yes, I know,' as if to silence her mother, who still would not stop.

'. . . when I realised that I wouldn't; I felt left behind and I didn't want to be. It was like being stuck on a moving staircase, endlessly going on up, like one of those in the very deep Tubes – Holborn or Highgate – except that you never reach the daylight. On and on, Anna . . . can you imagine what that is like? With nobody.'

'But what about us?' The question was automatic. Then Anna thought of herself and her brother and sister, and the family Christmases that had tapered out, and felt ashamed that she should now ask her mother to consider them, as if a debt were owed.

'Yes, Anna, I know you all care about me. But I've always dreaded being old and asking someone in the family to look after me. And be waited on – a nuisance. When I was in that geriatric ward I saw what it was like. The families had put the old dears there, because nobody could find room for them, or for whatever reason. All good reasons, I know. The woman in the next bed to me had been looked after by her daughter, but the daughter couldn't stand it any more – she told me one day while her mother was in the loo. She cried, Anna, because she felt so guilty. I dreaded doing that to all of you. When they told me I had cancer I decided I wouldn't tell you at all. I just wanted to die as quickly as possible. It's dignity, you see. Dignity is what all those old ladies wanted as they dribbled and wet the bed and cried in the night and bumped into each other in the corridors, and looked towards the door at visiting time, when nobody came! They knew they'd lost their dignity, and they cried for the shame of it, every night. I used to cry too, only one night I realised that I wasn't crying for myself, but because of them. For them, I mean – and because I realised that their dignity hadn't been lost, it had been stolen from them; taken away by their families and by that flock of clockwork dolls called nurses.'

Barbara was pink now, her cheeks flushed and her eyes bright. Anna had never heard her speak so passionately, not even after William's death.

'I know, Mummy, I know.'

'But you don't know, Anna! How can you possibly know?'

'Please don't be irritable. I'm trying to understand.'

'I'm sorry.' Barbara's face softened, as she reached across and took Anna's hand. 'You have to make allowances for a foolish old woman, getting worked up about nothing she can alter. Sometimes it's so hard to explain what you mean to other people, because how can they understand? All I'm trying to say is that I thought then that it could be infinitely more dignified to die than to live like that. I would watch the doctors and nurses doing their rounds, and keeping everybody alive as it's their duty to do, but I wondered then what was the point, and I still wonder it now.'

Her voice was wistful. Anna looked away, catching a glimpse of her father's photograph and wanting to run from the room. It was as if she had heard all this before, somewhere at the back of her mind, like a warning ignored.

'Daddy died too soon,' she whispered.

Barbara's breathing had quietened. 'Yes,' she said, 'but why do we say that? I used to say it all the time, as if there were an amount of time we could pay for, like putting money into a parking meter. But – too soon for what? Will it be too soon when I die, or will you be able to console yourself by saying that I had ten years longer than he did?'

'No,' Anna said, 'it always comes too soon. I hate death – I think it's obscene. Every death is an outrage, to me, and I don't think we're ever ready for it.'

Barbara gave a wry smile and shook her head. 'Oh, but that's all very well, dear. It's too fanciful for me, and not always true. Shall I tell you something I've never told anyone else? When I buried my own parents – within six months of each other – I felt such relief! All that worrying was over. I didn't have to explain myself to them any more, and put up with their sense of disappointment that the three of you didn't always want to be worshipping at the throne of their old age.'

Shocked, Anna asked, 'Did they really feel that – Grandpa and Grandma? I didn't think . . . I'd never have guessed.'

'Of course, that's the whole point.'

'Do you feel disappointed, like that?'

Barbara put her head on one side and looked quizzically at her daughter. 'Ah, and will you feel relieved, like I did?'

It seemed to Anna that her mother was looking through her skin and bone to the back of her mind, and smiling at what she saw there. Angry tears filled her eyes. 'Of course not,' she said through clenched teeth, 'or would you prefer it if I said yes? You'd feel satisfied then that you'd got a secret from me, and then could let yourself feel knowing and sacrificial if I didn't come to visit. It's like a trap. A trap for me.'

Barbara's face had closed like an oyster shell. 'Are you in a trap, Anna? You can walk out of here now. I would have thought it was me in the trap. I have to lie here looking at those tree-tops, knowing what I know.'

Spreading her hands in her lap, Anna allowed her right forefinger to trace the indentation on the third finger of the other hand, where the wedding ring she had taken off still left its mark – a pale circle, ghostly relic of the life that John had seen as a trap. She sighed, realising the futility of all their anger with each other.

'Oh, everybody thinks they're in a trap, and we're all imagining that other people are somehow free, or at any rate freer than we are. So we look on those people who are closest to us as gaolers, whether it's children, wives or parents. It's all trying to shift the blame, Mummy. Look at me – I'm thirty-five and getting older every day, my cells are falling apart, my skin changing, and that's the trap I'm in, like any wild animal. Or like you. It's nobody's fault. It's just being born that does it.'

'You sound so sad, Anna. Tell me this, do you ever wish you hadn't been born? Or that you'd never had Tom?'

She thought hard, then shook her head. 'No, never. Not even at the worst times. I often think about when we were children, and I like remembering all that. I feel nostalgic, but not sad. That was the happiest time. So I'm glad there was that time.'

Barbara was smiling again. 'When you're at the cottage, do you think of all our holidays?'

'All the time.'

'We had some marvellous times, didn't we?'

'Yes, we did.'

'I suppose we shouldn't always be looking back. It uses up your life – if you're young, like you. It's all right when you're old. The past reassures you, though sometimes there's something you can't remember, just round a corner in your mind, and it drives you mad, trying to remember it. Sometimes I do a kind of exercise, Anna, and I set myself a task of listing the names of people at our wedding, or the names of Daddy's important clients, things like that.'

Anna was thinking, only half-listening to this. She had a sudden vision of her father within the oxygen tent, his face grey, his mouth gaping foolishly behind the paraphernalia. Not prepared – not him, nor Barbara, nor any of them; the boat at the boatyard waiting prepared, the firm prepared for the retirement party, the future in 'Ahoy' all waiting, and all the little human preparations hollow at the centre, waiting, in innocence and ignorance, for the end. And since William's fight and failure within the oxygen tent, all those years ago, Anna realised (with that kind of sudden insight that is like a blow) she too had been waiting. She had been preparing for her mother to die too, and dreading it, not because that death would mean that this frail body in the chair beside her would be gone for ever, but because it would sever the last real link with William.

Leaning forward she took her mother's hand and stared

at it, not hearing what she was saying. 'She loved him. These hands in front of me held him closely when they were young and offered her children to him. They cooked for him, smoothed his bed and ironed his stiff, collarless shirts, and they wrapped his birthday presents, year after year. And older, blue veins sticking out, these hands covered his as they turned the pages of his sailing magazines, and brought him tea on a tray, loving him, indulging him, until the day they closed his eyes for ever, and the hands beat frantically against the wall because it was all gone.'

Anna looked down at the dry palm within her own, and wondered what she would hold when it was gone, as if to hold it were to reach, in a childish ring o' roses, right back to her father. She panicked and spoke quickly. 'Mummy, why don't you come to London with me? You could live with us.'

'No, dear, I couldn't. Though it is kind and sweet of you.'

'Why not? Tom would like it, and there's the room. John isn't there. It would be good for all of us – and right.'

Barbara looked closely at her. 'Do you get lonely?'

Anna shook her head vehemently, then stopped as suddenly, and shrugged. 'Yes,' she said.

'How could it have all gone wrong?' asked her mother with a sigh. 'I remember how your father used to hate doing divorce, and the way that people fight over the children . . .'

'Well, at least that hasn't happened with us,' Anna said shortly. 'A child around would cramp John's style.'

'Darling, that's an awful thing to say!'

'But it's quite true.'

'Do you think we ought to say what is true, all the time? Your father used to tell me that since he could never be sure whether his clients were telling the truth it was better to leave the idea of truth out of it altogether. Do you remember Percy Wright, that barrister Daddy was so friendly with?' Anna nodded. 'He died last year, by the way . . . anyway, there was one evening, not long before your father died, when they both got quite tipsy and gloomy together. They finished off the whiskey! I remember Percy saying that he'd spent his life persuading juries that guilty people were innocent, and Daddy said that his professional life had convinced him that nobody tells the truth and that innocent people all carry a great burden of guilt. All of us – guilty.'

'I can't imagine Daddy talking like that.'

'Can't you? No, I suppose not.'

'Mother, you haven't answered my question, about coming to London.'

'I think I should have a little rest now,' Barbara said, pulling her hand back.

'Are you really tired, or are you avoiding making a decision?' Anna asked gently. 'Promise me you'll think about it when I've gone.'

'I promise. It's a nice idea, darling, and you're . . . kind to me. We'll talk next time. You're not going back to London yet, are you?' Her voice was anxious.

'No, not for another two weeks. I insisted on having the full month because I thought Tom needed it. He'd been very upset over John, but since we arrived he's hardly mentioned him. John phoned once, but I think he's taken some girl on holiday now.'

'I'm so sorry, dear.'

'Oh Mummy, forget it. It's not your fault, after all. Not anybody's fault, really. Do you remember what Dad used to say when Hilda and I had boyfriend trouble? It's all part of growing up!'

Seventeen

After she had gone Barbara pressed the bell. Five minutes passed before the door opened. Neither Sandra Massey nor neat Nurse Anderson stood there, but a young nurse Barbara had not seen before.

'Did you want something?'

'Oh, I . . . we haven't met before.'

She felt panicky at the sight of the stranger, no friend and no familiar adversary, but someone who must needs take her at face value. In a voice that trembled she asked for Nurse Massey.

'Oh she's busy with another patient at the moment. What is it that you want?'

Barbara tried to rise, but her leg buckled beneath her and she fell back in the chair, gasping. The new nurse marched across the room, an expression of exasperated concern upon her face. 'Now, come along, Mrs Lewis, where are you trying to go?'

'I want . . . I need to go to the loo,' Barbara whispered.

The nurse looked at her dubiously. 'I'm not sure that's a good idea at this moment. It looks to me as if your visitor has worn you out. You stay there, and I'll go and get you a bedpan. Much more sensible.'

She turned on her heel and left the room. 'No, I won't. I won't,' Barbara said to herself, closing her eyes for a moment at the stab of pain in her chest, and biting her lip. 'They won't make me. Nobody is going to make me do anything, Will. You wouldn't let them, and I won't either. I won't. I won't.'

She could not understand where her bones had gone: it was as if her spine and her legs had turned to soft plasticine. Making an enormous effort she pulled herself up by resting all her weight upon the arm of the chair, which tipped perilously. The sudden pressure on her bladder made her desperate, and she forced herself to stand upright, swaying on weak legs, small waves of pain rippling up her back. Tears filled her eyes. 'Oh God, please help me, please help me,' she whispered, letting her head loll forward, 'I must . . .'

When the nurse returned a minute later, carrying a bedpan under one arm, she paused in the centre of the room and made a tutting noise with her tongue. Barbara still stood there, her body half bent. There were tears on her cheeks; she was staring down at the pool of water which was spreading on the floor between her feet.

Anna walked into Elaine's Boutique in Synemouth's main shopping street, and riffled through the clothes that hung,

146

shapeless, on red and green plastic hangers. Over the thudding bass of the monotonous disco music she heard two brightly made-up girls behind the counter laugh about the exploits of the previous evening.

'... so by the time he's come out I'm in the car and I leans out the window and shouts, "See you somewhen!"'

'You are awful, Jean!'

'Well, what about you with that Dave? Flirting with a married man ...'

'No, they ain't together no more. Don't reckon so. Anyway, who cares? I don't wanna be involved ...'

'Hey, it were a good night, weren't it?'

The blouses were cheap, synthetic, decorated with stiff frills or scraps of nylon lace. Summer dresses had threads of gold in the fabric, or floating ribbons in pastel colours, low-slung waists, and full skirts. It all seemed like fancy dress to Anna, or theatrical costumes destined to take their place upon a stage, before the curtains swish back to reveal, beyond the footlights, darkness and emptiness. She glanced at the mask-like faces of the two girls, who shivered rhythmically to the music and chatted about their lives: 'He said ... she didn't ... and so I thought ... why should I ... always try ... he said ... I said ... no point in it all ... no way ...' One of the girls tapped long nails varnished the colour of blackberries upon the counter; the other gazed for a moment at the street outside, blankly, as if she were staring through the crowd of people in their new holiday clothes and away beyond them, into a vision of perpetual boredom.

Skirts – some with frills around the hem, some tight with side splits and wide belt loops. Strange trousers, gathered and cropped at the knee, like the garments of the dwarf-fools who hover disconsolately at the corners of Spanish paintings. Skin-tight jeans, tee-shirts frosted with glitter ... miserably Anna pulled at them all, loathing the limp garments empty of promise, and the fact that she was searching there for something to graft upon her person like a new skin. And she had gone first into a chemist's to look at the face creams. '2nd Debut' she had chosen, salmon pink

147

in its tall, expensive bottle; muttering blackly to herself as she left the shop, 'I'm promising myself a second debut when I haven't even made my first.'

'You can try anything on, anything you fancy.' The tall girl, with nails like clots of blood, stood by her. Anna looked up, afraid.

'No, er . . . there's nothing I really like.'

'Oh.'

With a shrug the girl turned on her spindly heels and walked back to her friend. Anna called out, 'I'm sorry,' and her voice was easily heard, now that the tape had changed, and the voice of a girl rasped out her sad complaint that 'Love hurts' – reminding Anna of all the nights she had spent, years ago, longing for this boy or that, enjoying her own melancholy in the conviction that it was all a prelude, that perfection lay ahead.

Both girls looked surprised at the apology. The tall one smiled, and it was as if a tight veneer suddenly cracked and peeled away, exposing the soft wood underneath. She was very young, just seventeen perhaps. 'Don't worry,' she called cheerfully. 'You just look. It don't worry us. T'aint our shop or our money!'

'I'll have this.' Anna handed over a pale blue sweatshirt, decorated on the front with a little yacht appliquéd in white satin, and the words 'I am sailing' embroidered underneath.

'That's nice. That'll suit you, that will,' said the smaller girl, in a tone that was almost comforting, as she folded the garment and pushed it gently into a bag.

Anna watched, wondering why she had bought it, why she was in the shop at all. All the clothes, the cheap changing fashions, had nothing to do with her, and yet she desired them, like those women in their forties and fifties who cram themselves into pink dungarees or girlish dresses, craving youth. 'Anyway, it's no good trying to deceive myself,' she thought, wryly handing over her mon . She allowed her mind to loll into its daydreams about Matthew Paul, to escape from the memory of Barbara, and of William too. It made her happy, as it always did. Suddenly, passionately,

Anna wanted to be new once more, like all these fresh and pretty clothes upon their hangers, waiting to be chosen.

Still feeling this odd euphoria Anna decided, on impulse, to call on Molly and Harry Black before returning to 'Ahoy'. Their welcome reminded her of a childhood and visiting a grandmother, who offered sugary biscuits and asked all the details of her life. And yet, she reflected, her mother had cast doubt upon that fantasy too. Anna frowned, and Molly saw, thinking it was because of something she had just said.

'You must have a really lovely holiday, and I know you mother won't mind if you don't pop in and see her quite so often. She told me that. And . . . I hope you don't mind me saying this, but she told me all about . . . your difficult times with your husband, with John. You need a rest now, dear. You need to enjoy yourself.'

There was a pause; Anna nodded and smiled and said it was all right. Once it would have annoyed her to think she had been discussed. Now it gave her a different kind of pain – to think of the two old women sitting in that room together and giving her their compassion for John's betrayal, not knowing that it did not matter any more.

Eighteen

George Treadle leant on the polished counter and did what he rarely dared to do; he disagreed with his wife. She was rearranging the deep-freeze cabinet and her hands were red and cold, making her irritable.

'It just don't seem right,' she muttered, throwing down some lamb chops, which hit the sausages with a dull clunk.

'None of our business, Mary.'

'With all the years I've known Mrs Lewis I should think it is my business,' she snapped.

'Be fair, Mary, they'm on holiday.'

'No reason to go on neglecting your poor sick mother, is it? An' her with not long to go.'

'Now, now, we don't know that.'

'Anyway, George, all I'm saying is that I'm disappointed with Anna, I am. You'd have thought she'd have been at that hospital every day, and be making up for lost time – but every time I do see her she's walking round the village with that Matthew and giggling like a schoolgirl!'

'No harm done, Mary,' he said mildly, relieved that a man had walked into the shop to buy some cigarettes.

'Mum?'

'Yes?'

'I like hearing you talk about all those things.'

'What things?'

'You know – what we've been talking about.'

Anna was sitting with Tom in the attic bedroom, explaining how the three of them used to sleep up there if their parents had adult friends staying in the small back bedroom downstairs. Otherwise Anna and Hilda would always sleep downstairs, leaving Richard to lord it over the attic, unafraid – he said – of the ghosts.

There were two sets of bunks, and two folding beds stored against the wall, so that (she explained) they could have friends to stay as well.

'It must have been fun,' Tom said.

'Oh, it was.' She ran her hand over the old ticking mattress. In one corner stood a small cupboard, its paintwork chipped, and when Tom opened it a pile of broken toys spilled out upon the linoleum. There were Dinky toys with no wheels, a naked blonde doll with one arm missing, and countless odd bricks and jigsaw pieces, jumbled together with skipping ropes and dead batteries.

Tom looked at the pile of rubbish, and sighed.

'Fun with lots of people. More fun.'

'Than what?'

'Nothing ... well, there's only you and me really, isn't there, Mum.'

Anna tried to joke, looking around the room and saying,

150

'Well, apart from a few broken dolls, yes,' in her lightest voice.

'No, I don't mean that. You know what I mean. Sometimes I wish I had a brother or sister, like you did. Sometimes, when it's only you and me, I think about Dad, and then I think about you getting old and dying, and I don't want that because I don't want to be on my own.'

'Oh, Tom ... don't think about things like that. Don't, you funny little boy.' Anna held out her arms to him, feeling a sharp pain in her chest.

'I do – sometimes.' He came to her.

'We all do.'

'Even you?'

'Especially me ... By the way, darling, Matthew hasn't got any brothers or sisters either, and look at the fun he has. He doesn't seem to mind, does he?'

'No. But I'm a bit fed up with him, Mum. He doesn't play with me so much.'

Her voice grew sharp. 'What do you expect, when you're so much younger?'

'Oh, let's go downstairs now, Mum. Let's take some toys down.'

She did not want to leave the room. How nervous she had been, even at thirteen; awed by the thick silence and dreading that something might lurk behind the little door into the eaves, where the cistern gurgled. At night they would keep each other awake, listening to the sighing wind, until gradually the replies grew fainter as Hilda drifted into sleep, leaving Anna alone. But below, if she listened carefully, she could hear the little sounds that reminded her that their parents were still awake – a kettle being filled, music on the radio, footsteps across the hall, the lavatory chain being pulled, Barbara's laugh – fragments of sound, meaningless in isolation, that united to tell a well-loved tale, of which Anna was sure that she knew the beginning, the middle and the end.

Tom looked disconcerted. He picked up a plastic lorry and ran it to and fro on the bench between them.

'Mum, when are we going home?'

'Oh not yet, Tom, don't worry.'

'I wasn't worrying.'

'Do you want to go home? Is that it?'

He nodded, then looked up anxiously. 'I don't mean that I'm not having a nice time, but . . .'

'But what?'

'Well . . . I'd like to see Dad. He told me on the phone he'd be back near the end of August. Is it that yet?'

'Not yet – no.'

'Oh.' He looked sad. Anna's stomach pitched.

'Never mind. All this'll be over soon enough, and you'll be back. I expect he'll have bought you a present, as usual.'

It was easily done. Tom's face lightened; he turned with new animation to gaze out of the dusty window.

'Look, there's Matthew, on the river! Can we open the window and shout to him?'

'He wouldn't hear. He's too far off.'

Anna stared at the now-familiar figure on the windsurf board. Each time she saw Matthew out on the river her throat contracted with the beauty of that movement, the simple communion between wind, water and flesh. 'My windsurf boy,' said the voice inside her mind.

'He looks so free,' she said aloud.

'Of course he's free, Mummy. He doesn't have to pay. It's his own windsurf board.'

She laughed. 'I didn't mean that sort of free. I mean . . . well, free means that you can do as you like. You're not in prison. Or – there's no rules for you.'

'But he had to learn all the rules of how to put that thing together, like he showed us. It's very hard.'

She could not drag her eyes from the boy on the river. 'I know,' she said, half to herself, 'but once he's out there he can do anything he likes. Nobody can reach him.'

Tom understood. 'His mum can't tell him to have a wash,' he said enviously.

'Yes,' she went on, dreamily now, as if the child was no longer with her, 'and you feel when you watch him that he'll be like that for ever and ever, beautiful, and never change, never go to hospital, never get old, like the rest of us. And he doesn't need to know . . . anything . . .'

'Oh, I expect he'll get married, Mum.' Tom's voice was practical, and, with a curious infusion of spite, he added, 'I bet he'll get fat too.'

'Oh no,' Anna said, still staring out at the river.

The sun had gone, leaving the evening sky flushed pink and purple; a bright silver light still shone on the water. It was high tide; the river brimming almost to the wall of 'Ahoy'. Tom was in bed, and already asleep, bored and tired by the warmth of the day and by their aimless wandering around the village. They had seen nothing of Matthew, after that glimpse from the window, and Anna allowed herself to brood about him – ashamed, all the while, when she looked down and saw that Tom was waiting for her to notice him, to speak.

She poured herself a glass of white wine and walked through the front door to sit on the low wall around the terrace. It was still warm; the air had dissolved into a mothy indistinctness Anna associated with . . . what? . . . romantic love stories, she supposed. In the distance, from the direction of the pub, she could hear laughter and a faint sound of music. She knew that the bar would be crowded and smoky, as people told jokes and swapped sailing and fishing stories and the holidaymakers said that home could never be like this. They would eat pasties hot from the microwave oven and order another round.

Out on the river, little pinpoints of yellow light showed where people stayed on the boats, perhaps warming tomato soup in the narrow galleys, or savouring the smell of frying bacon in the evening air. Later they would wriggle down into their sleeping bags, softly whisper good-night to each other, and drift off to sleep to the sound of lapping water and the rigging beating out its gentle tattoo above their heads. Now and then a laugh would float across the water, or a fragment of conversation, as people sitting on the deck forgot how easily voices carried in that river-stillness. Sitting alone Anna thought of them all, and of the myriad shapes of pleasure, as you might think of the happiness of children

153

at a circus – tenderly, although now there seems nothing funny in the cruelty of the clowns.

As she looked to where the pale shape of a crescent moon showed ghostly against the sky Anna realised that now – at this moment when all the people around her were conforming to a paradigm of holiday enjoyment, and elsewhere millions of other souls existed in their daily patterns – now she had far more in common with her mother than at any other time in their lives. It was as if a vast invisible cord stretched the six miles down river to where Barbara lay in her bed in the nursing home, uniting them, as they had only been united before the moment of Anna's birth. 'And even when I was actually a part of her I was moving towards a separation, like Tom from me, like all of us,' Anna thought. 'But we block up the chinks in our lives to keep that knowledge at bay, cramming the time, clinging to each other, stuffing our lives with sex in search of a second's unity once more. But sometimes a glimpse of a solitary figure, walking across a yellow field in autumn, will remind us of the truth, the sadness that surrounds everything we do. Alone. It's so hard to accept though ...' She wrinkled up her face as she thought. 'Can I accept it? What is it? That I am alone as she is alone, but that in that aloneness she and I are closer together, and closer to the truth. Each of us is, in a different way, abandoned.'

She heard a click, and saw, with a little tremor of fear, the latch of the tall gates move. One gate swung inwards, and Matthew Paul walked into the garden. He closed the gate carefully behind him then turned, grinning at her expression. 'Hello! Thought I'd surprise you. Mum and Dad have got some people in for a meal so I said I was going to bed and slipped out by the window. Nobody'll notice. They're all well pissed as usual so I thought I'd come and make a nuisance of myself with you here. I came down through Parsons' field so I wouldn't have to pass the shop.'

It did not occur to her to ask why he had taken such care; she knew her delight shone in her face, and felt foolish, dipping her head to sip her wine.

Silent in his gymshoes Matthew took the three steps at

154

one bound and sat beside her on the wall, looking sideways cheekily. 'Are you on your own?'

'Yes – I always am. Look, your feet are wet.'

'Tide's high. I only just made it – there's only about nine inches of beach outside your gates.'

'Take them off.'

'Oh, I can't be bothered. You unlace them for me.'

He held each foot lazily towards her, and Anna unlaced the dirty plimsolls, letting them drop in turn to the ground.

'Aren't you going to give me a drink, then?'

'You don't drink wine at your age. Anyway . . .'

'Aw, come on, Anna! It was you that bought me a beer the other day. Even Dad lets me have the odd glass of plonk nowadays. I'm nearly sixteen, not a kid.'

Saying nothing, she rose, went indoors, and returned with a second glass and the bottle. He had stretched himself full length on the little wall, arms folded across his chest, staring up at the sky and leaving no room for her. She stood for a second looking down at him, then smiled. 'Help yourself. Since you've taken up all the wall I'll have to get a chair.'

Settled in the folding chair, about two feet from Matthew's head, Anna started to chatter. She commented that he had not poured himself any wine, asked what his last servant died of, splashed the drink into his glass, talked about the nightmare of dinner parties, reminded him that he had promised to teach her to sail, but had not – and praised, in quick succession, the warmth of the night, the colour of the sky and the atmosphere in the village pub.

Matthew said little. Every so often he raised himself on one elbow to sip his wine, grunting agreement with her words. When her own voice died away Anna was aware of the silence between them – which had never before been allowed to grow, since Tom was usually there, and the bright daylight was filled with noise. In this mauve light, lying still, Matthew reminded her of a youthful knight on an old tomb, hands crossed on his breast, retaining his chiselled beauty for ever in stone. She wanted to put out a hand and touch him, but did not.

'You know why Mum and Dad didn't ask you tonight?'

he asked suddenly. 'They talked about it, but they think you're too clever for them. They like you, but you make them nervous.'

Anna was incredulous. 'Me? That's rubbish, Matthew, I don't believe it. Anyway, you shouldn't be listening to them talking, and you shouldn't be telling me.'

'Why not, if it's true? Mum knows you work in a publisher's – that right? – and she's never read a book in her life! She can just about manage a cookery book but that's a strain. You're different – to her.' When she said nothing he swung his legs around so that he was squatting on the low wall, looking directly at her. 'Don't you want to know why I say you're different?'

She laughed. 'Well, I think you're going to tell me whether I want to know or not!'

He was grinning broadly, showing his even white teeth. 'Right! You're not like them, or most of their awful friends, because you like me. You talk to me – I mean proper talking, not just larking about or treating me like a kid, or a dumb waiter. Nobody else talks to me like you do.'

Anna felt embarrassed. 'But surely,' she protested, with no conviction, 'surely Adrian and Valerie talk to you.'

'Oh yeah,' he said making a gesture of disgust, 'they go on and on about my marks and nag me to do better and bore on about my prospects, whatever they are. I can't talk to them about what I really like doing. They don't wanna know.'

'You mean your windsurfing?'

'All that. I've told you, and you understand a bit, don't you? As for school – yuk!'

He sounded like a very young boy again, like Tom discussing school meals. Anna felt tender towards this overgrown child in front of her. 'What do you want to be, Matthew, later, when you've left school?'

He sighed. 'Oh, I don't know. I'd like to be a windsurfer. Go out to Hawaii, where they have the races and you can do wave jumps. I've got a book about it, and you should see the pictures! You can get custom-built boards, and really fly! I'd like to do some distance freesailing too – you wear a harness for long trips. It would be hot all the time and I'd be fantastically brown and sexy, can you imagine that?' She looked at him quickly, but he was continuing like an excited child. 'You could come and see me out there. Better than cold old England.'

He paused and sipped his wine, and the light suddenly died from his face. 'I don't like thinking about the future, really. Growing up, and all that. I hate the thought of changing, getting old and not wanting things. Know what I mean?' She nodded. 'You see, I have all these dreams of being a champion windsurfer, or swimming for England in the Olympics, but I'll probably end up as a dentist or an estate agent or something equally boring.'

'Oh, don't say that.'

'Mind you,' he said gulping back his drink so that he held out an empty glass to be refilled, 'as long as I can make some good money it won't be so bad. Dad makes a lot of dough. All those people who spend a fortune having their teeth crowned and done up. Because they're so worried about their beauty, we can have *Invader* and I can have my windsurfer. Can't be bad. But I don't fancy staring into people's mouths all day.'

He hesitated then looked at her with open flirtatiousness. 'Mind you, it'd be all right looking into your mouth.'

Surprised, she turned her face away, and there was a silence again. To break it she said lightly, 'I must say, I'd like my teeth capped.'

He looked at her with that directness she had noticed the first night at 'Hacienda', a look that bore no trace of the archness she had just heard. 'You don't need to. You've got nice teeth. In fact ... I'm going to tell you something. I think you're much prettier than Mum. I mean, she's very glam and all that, but you look – nice. I'd rather have girls who look like you than the ones who plaster themselves in make-up.'

If it were light, she thought, he would see that her face was crimson. She felt extraordinarily, but simply, happy. But she ducked her head so that her hair covered her expression. 'Compliments, compliments,' she muttered.

He laughed, and patted her head, as if she were the child. 'There, there. Don't get all shy on me.'

The sky was much darker now. One or two stars already studded the luminous blue, like sparks of light aboard boats moored in the universe. The river glowed purple, streaked with ultramarine and black, and the masts glistened like the trunks of silver birches. There was a smell of salt mingled with the scent of night flowers, earth and water mingling in the air, so that Anna, breathing in the fragrance that had permeated their cottage as she slept, each night, through all the summers, felt that time had lost its boundaries.

She stood and walked down the steps and across the grass to the big wall, and stood leaning on it, gazing at the river in a trance. Matthew followed, leaning his elbows on the wall close beside her, and talked desultorily about the boats they could see, which he liked, who owned which one, which was expensive, which fast. 'But you can't see *Invader* from here,' he complained.

'Will you always come here?' she asked.

'Oh yeah – we love it, even Mum. Next year though, I think I'll bring a friend. Only trouble is, windsurfing is something only one can do. Except – some people take girls, and do sort of acrobatics on the water. Don't fancy that.'

'Why – because you don't like girls?'

'Don't be stupid, Anna! As it happens most girls my age are too ... well young, for me. Giggly; get crushes on you. All that. But what I meant was, I like to keep my windsurfing to myself.'

Anna nodded, as if she knew. After a short silence he looked sideways at her, and asked, 'Will you two be here next year?'

The question was irrelevant, but Anna shrugged and said that she supposed so, yes. A sudden picture of summer after summer, and Matthew getting older, flashed into her mind, so that she turned to him with a brilliant happy smile and repeated, 'Yes, I think we'll come. It's nice – for Tom.'

'But ... what about your mother?'

It was like a douche of water. Irritated, she snapped, 'What about her?'

'Sorry, I put my foot in it. But . . . will you come here if she's dead? Will she be dead?'

'Yes, I think she will. But', she said, injecting a heartiness into her voice, 'we'll go on using this place. Things don't come to an end.'

He was gazing at her, his nose wrinkled up in a mixture of embarrassment and sympathy. 'I can't imagine anybody I know dying. Not being there any more, ever again. Sometimes when I have rows with Dad I go into my room and wish I could kill him, or that he'd have a crash in the car, and be dead. Do you think that's awful?'

She shook her head. 'No, it's not awful. Everybody thinks things like that at some time in their lives, only most people don't admit it. Sometimes when you love somebody very much you want them dead, and you feel guilty about that, because it alters the way you love them.'

He looked puzzled. 'Do you feel like that, about your mother?'

'I don't know. I really don't know what I feel about anything or anybody.' She could not keep the despair out of her voice.

Matthew had turned, so that his back was to the view, and he stood leaning nonchalantly, his elbows on the wall, bearing his weight. In his denim shirt and jeans he was hardly visible in the darkness; only his eyes, teeth and skin gleamed, full of health. Anna could smell his sweat, not stale, but a clean, sharp natural smell.

'Don't be sad,' he said in a gruff voice, 'I'm sorry I asked about your mother.' She said that it was all right.

'Anna?'

'Yes.'

'Do you like me?'

She forced a laugh. 'Oh, typical, you'd rather switch the conversation to you!'

'I didn't mean that.' He sounded disappointed, 'I just meant . . . er . . . well I like coming round here because I like being with you, see. But I don't know whether you think I'm a stupid kid, or not. That's all. And I wanted to know.'

For a second Anna was tempted to escape, to insult him

gaily, to let him down. But she took a breath and said, 'Yes, Matthew, I like you very much,' feeling her own words flit into the darkness, like tangible things.

He shuffled his feet. She looked down at her own arms, that rested upon the wall. They shone pale blue in the gloom; she was wearing the sweatshirt she had bought in Synemouth, and her fingers kneaded the fabric of each opposite sleeve, as if she were cold.

At that moment Matthew noticed it. 'Hey,' he said, as if relieved, 'You're wearing something new. Let's see it.' He reached out, took her by the shoulders and turned her towards him. Anna felt limp, like a doll pulled into position by its owner. Still holding her shoulders he stared down at the sweatshirt, his head on one side, and it seemed a long time before he muttered, 'Yes, that's nice. I like it.'

Anna saw him smiling at her, his face indistinct so that she could not quite trace the origin of that smile. For a second she thought he might be mocking her; then she heard his breathing and knew that he was not. Still staring at her Matthew released one shoulder, and lightly placed his hand upon her breast, covering the little appliquéd satin yacht. 'That looks like me, windsurfing,' he said.

She stepped back quickly and turned her head away, feeling tears prick her eyes and wanting to cry aloud at her need and the hopelessness. Her impulse was to reach out, to stretch her arms so that he would have to hold her, just as he had in all those dreams and fantasies she had dismissed, stroking her, tenderly fusing with her flesh, and in that act of generosity transferring to her all his freedom, his beauty. And yet, what if it were not so? In novels and French films such moments are full of aching sensuality. In real life, Anna knew, the gulf is much harder to cross, and the awkward bones unite with custom to resist, to conquer fantasy.

So she turned away, still feeling his hand on her chest, and strode across the grass, calling over her shoulder that it was time for him to go. He followed, protesting that he wanted another drink, that nobody would notice he was not at home. Anna ran up the steps and stood framed in the doorway, snapping on the hall light behind so that the night outside seemed blacker, and less beautiful. Matthew's face was impossible to see. Then he stepped forward into the pool of light from the door, and a moth flitted into his hair. 'What's the matter with you?' he asked, beating at it with one hand, puzzled and offended by the rejection he sensed but did not understand.

'Matthew, you must go. Your parents might well go and look for you, and they'll be worried. Can't you understand that? Soon it'll be too dark for you to see anything. You must be sensible. Go now, but come to see us tomorrow. Come and see Tom and me tomorrow – will you?'

He stood for a second, looking up at her. Then he spread his arms in a clownish shrug. 'Good-night Anna!' he called, as he turned and ran off silently round the house and up the hill through the orchard, where small hard apples studded the trees, promising a good crop.

Nineteen

Susan Anderson closed the door behind her, none too gently, and paused for a second outside the door looking at her watch. It did not worry her that she had been even brisker than usual with her patient; in five minutes' time, she knew, Dr Elkins took a break for coffee in the case-study room, and there would be time to slip into the staff lavatory and mend her make-up before she happened to return some notes at just the moment he sat down. Nurse Anderson folded her arms across her bib in satisfaction, and walked stiffly along the corridor.

Anna, reaching the top of the elegant staircase, noticed that the nurse had emerged from her mother's room, so stopped her. 'Excuse me, I'm Mrs Lewis's daughter. Can you tell me how my mother is today?' There was a slight tutting sound, just controlled, and the nurse's hand flew to the watch that was pinned to her chest, playing with it as she spoke.

'Ah yes. Mrs Lewis is doing very well, considering. She went to the hospital for her treatment this morning, and she didn't want her lunch when she got back. But she's had a sleep and she looks fine now. I told her – I keep telling her – that she's not doing herself any good, you know!'

Nurse Anderson shook her head and waved a finger, as if admonishing Anna, then tucked both hands comfortably within the pouch behind her bib, under her breasts. She was about twenty-five, Anna guessed, and had the look of someone who has few doubts about her own ability to cope with life, and death. 'Pretty, though,' thought Anna sourly, 'so pretty that she hardly needs to have imagination.'

'What do you mean?'

'We always tell our patients that the best treatment they can have is the one they can give themselves. Mrs Lewis should be at home. She's quite capable of looking after herself, if she really tried. I said to her today, we've got to try. We can go to the hospital for treatment, but at least we'll keep our independence.'

Infuriated by the nanny-like assurance, Anna asked, 'Oh, are you ill too?'

'I'm sorry?'

'You said "we" can go for treatment, so I assumed you must know what you're talking about because you're ill too.'

The hands were withdrawn from the cosy pocket; Nurse Anderson gave Anna a look of dislike, and lifted the watch face so she could see it. 'I think you understood what I meant, Mrs . . . er . . . It isn't easy for us, you know. Now if you'll excuse me, I have a patient to see to.'

Barbara was in the chair, as usual, resplendent in a scarlet velour dressing gown, with a hood. Richard and Lisa had sent it from New York, she explained, pointing to the Bloomingdale's box that lay under the window. 'Looks a bit hot,' Anna said, then felt ashamed and praised the robe, fulsomely. She thought that it made her mother, thin with pale hair and parchment skin, look more faded than ever.

'How are you?' Anna asked.

162

Barbara's breast rose and fell, as if she were trying to contain an enormous emotion, which, released, would crack the fragile shell in which it was cased. 'The same as ever. I hate going to the hospital. I wish I didn't have to go.'

'But you do have to go, Mummy. You need your treatment, to make you better.'

Anna heard her own voice lose conviction on the last words, and Barbara heard it too. She looked up with the faintest of smiles. 'That's the trouble, dear. It seems pointless to me.'

'Don't start talking like that again,' Anna begged, 'you mustn't. It gets us nowhere – and today I've made up my mind that we're going to come to some decisions.'

Her mother sighed. 'That's what Hilda and Richard said. They both rang last night. They said they'll be coming down after you've gone back to London. Hilda got back from Brittany yesterday. She said she's bought me a shawl.'

'What else did she say?'

'Oh, she gave me a little lecture. She said that Richard had told her that you were going to sort it all out, and that I've got to leave here as soon as possible. She was very concerned, Anna. But ... well, I understand how you all feel; it's just hard for me to believe it's all as important as you all seem to think.'

'What's important?' Anna was frowning.

With a wry smile Barbara said, 'Living, I suppose. Oh I know that when I say that it's hurtful to people around me. It diminishes them, and their concern. On the other hand, I've never said what I feel so perhaps it's time I did. You know, I've been thinking – when people say they don't want someone they love to die, perhaps it's because they don't want to lose another bit of their own world, rather than that they want to keep that actual person alive. Of course, I'm not talking about you ...'

'Perhaps you are,' Anna said.

'Anyway,' Barbara went on, unsure of her daughter's tone, 'it's not meant to be a criticism. I just think that people are like that. Do you remember that quotation, that famous

163

one, which says something like, any man's death diminishes me?'

'John Donne.'

'That's right. Well, it's quite a selfish thing to say, isn't it?'

Anna laughed. 'Actually I think it's meant to be the opposite of selfish. That whole passage is about being one with other people.'

'Is it?' Barbara looked doubtful. 'I always took it to mean that you should care about other people, not for their sakes, but for your own. Like a sort of insurance.'

Anna decided to make a new effort. 'Never mind all that, Mummy. Will you decide to come to London with me? There's room, and we would love to have you. You can go to St Thomas's for treatment, and we'll all be near you. You must say yes. You must be brave about it.'

She half-expected her mother to turn away, that gauze across her eyes. Instead Barbara leaned forward, as if she had just heard something startling.

'Why brave? Why do you say brave?' she asked.

The question confused Anna, and she was silent for a few seconds, thinking. 'Well, to be really truthful, I can't help feeling, after all I've heard from the staff, that your attitude is ... well ... just a bit cowardly, Mummy. It's as if you've just packed up. I think that if you were to say yes, I want to live as long as I can and so I'm going to try as hard as I can – that would be brave.'

Barbara reached for the tapestry that lay on the table in front of her, and made five or six tiny stitches before saying quietly, 'I wonder why I have a different view to the rest of the world? People always think it's brave to soldier on, see things through, grit your teeth and survive. All that. But I don't understand why it should necessarily be brave to want to live, to struggle on pouring drugs inside yourself, having bits of yourself cut off ...' Anna shuddered and made a small noise of protest, but her mother took no notice, '... and doing everything possible to squeeze a few more miles out of the old machine. Sometimes I think that the medical world has gone mad. Doctors assume they're doing their duty if they hitch people up to all sorts of machinery to keep them alive. It's all got out of proportion. You see, everybody's afraid of death, even the doctors and nurses. Nobody talks about it; they all shy away and pretend it's not coming to them. If you want to talk about your own death, or the death of someone you love, people cross the street to avoid you. After your father died I realised that. After all, you didn't talk about it, did you?'

Anna shook her head. She remembered the day of her father's cremation. They had insisted upon a cremation, Richard, Hilda and herself, despite Barbara's faint noises about 'a proper funeral'. Too shocked to take part in the arrangements, she had given way. The bleak, modern crematorium; flowers arranged in rows upon the pavement; the coffin sliding through the little door – no sense of ending, merely of anti-climax. Anna had thought then that the fire was pure and clean.

And yet, through the ritual of dust returning to dust, and moss growing in the churchyard, they might have retained an intimation of their father's presence, instead of consigning him to nothingness so cleanly and swiftly, then changing the subject whenever their mother mentioned his name.

'No, you're right,' she said. 'We always talked of something else. It's easy to explain it, but it doesn't stop it being inept. I'm sorry.'

Barbara was changing the colour of her wool. 'Oh, Anna. It's such a long time ago. It's all over. It doesn't matter now. All I'm saying is that I don't think it's particularly brave to want to live. We've all got to face dying, just like I had to face up to Daddy's death. What can we do to stop it? In the end – nothing.'

'But what about when a child dies?' asked Anna, with aggression in her voice. 'Can you accept that easily? Or even if I got run over tomorrow, at thirty-five?'

'It's hard then,' said Barbara, 'but you still have no choice. The Victorians faced that all the time, didn't they? They put themselves in black and made a proper thing of it – much healthier in a way.'

'We're not talking about Victorians.'

'All right, dear. Well – you can rage away about it being too soon, but that's pointless. If you accept the fact that you're alive you have to take death as well. It helps if you happen to believe that all this', she waved a hand at the view from the window, 'isn't everything. Quite apart from the fact that I'm sixty-eight, and I've had a good run, I actually feel . . . oh, you'll laugh at me.'

'Go on.'

'I feel that I will see your father again, one day soon. I believe it Anna. I couldn't have gone on without him if I hadn't thought that one day we'd see each other again. I don't know for sure. I wish I did. But I think so.'

Anna was looking closely at her own fingernails; for a moment Barbara rejoiced to see her daughter so disconcerted. From her height she watched, smiling. Then Anna asked, in a tight voice, as if she were angry, 'But why do you think that? You and he weren't great church-goers. I didn't realise . . .'

'It seems to irritate you, dear. But why should you have realised? As it happens, I have started to go to church in the last few years, though never if any of you came down for a weekend. There's always so much to do, cooking Sunday lunch, but when you're alone there's nothing to do and so it's easy to go to church. But don't you remember that Daddy used to go, sometimes, when we were on holiday? He loved that village church. Just before he died he'd started to read a great deal about God. He loved the *Lives of the Saints*, and that sort of thing. And he prayed.'

'What? Did he really?'

'Why does it surprise you so much?'

There was nothing to say. Again Anna felt as if she were, in an undefinable way, being made a fool of. She felt angry with her mother who, like all bearers of good news or breakers of secrets, looked faintly complacent. In the silence, a strange and disturbing thought filled Anna's mind, of William and Barbara safe within their great mahogany bed, reading of Saint Teresa perhaps, or praying. She found it intolerable.

Barbara was saying something, and with an effort she

166

yanked her imagination back to the present. 'Don't you . . .
I mean, isn't there something you believe in, Anna dear?
Surely you must feel . . .'

'Oh yes, I feel things,' said Anna, dryly.

'No, I mean something special. We never discussed things
like this as a family. Families never do. It's as if all there is
to life is passing the time as comfortably as possible, with
no disturbing questions.'

'What's wrong with that, Mother?'

'Nothing, I suppose. But . . . don't *you* wish that there is
more than that?'

'No,' said Anna.

Barbara insisted, 'Wouldn't you like it to be true?'

Anna stood up. It was as if all her sadness had drained
away, taking with it her horror at the thought of those
prayers sent into the vacancy, and with the oxygen tent
around the corner. 'No!' she cried, 'I wouldn't. Not for a
moment! Most people would, I know, but I don't want to
believe in anything that makes dying any easier. All I believe
in is being alive. This is all we've got, and no matter how
much we suffer, no matter how disappointed and lonely and
rejected we might feel, it's still worth it. There's always the
chance that things might be better, and there's kids like
Tom, growing up. The kid, Matthew, I told you about, full
of life and health and with so much to do . . . and when he's
out on the river I can look at him and the water and the sky
and it all seems beautiful. There's always the possibility that
you could save . . . well, that you might be able to protect
kids like him and Tom from all the – shit. I'll cling to that,
thank you very much. I don't want your acceptance. When
I'm dying I hope I'll fight till the last second, because I don't
want it to be over, I don't want to go into the darkness. Not
even to see Dad – if I thought there was a possibility. It's
too big a gamble, and nobody is worth that sacrifice, not
even him.' She hesitated, shaking, then shouted, 'I don't
want you to die!'

Barbara's hand was trembling, but she still tried to make
her stitch. 'What you or I want doesn't matter. I've been
ready to die ever since I lost Will, so why should I fight it?

I tell you I believe I'll see him again, face to face, but I know I could even be saying that simply as a way of coming to terms with it all. It's reality, Anna. You, Tom, me, Richard, Hilda, even that baby inside Lisa – we are all dying. If I say it's the will of God you'd make a face; if I say it's human fate that comes to the same thing. Listen, I've been cursing God for years, since Will died. Then one day I realised that I'd grown dependent on having him to shout at. I used to cry, "Why me?" each night at first, because he'd taken away my husband so soon, and left me alone. Then one night I thought, "Why not me?" and I felt more peaceful after that. Ordinary, like everybody else. And now I feel that I want to, I don't know, get back.'

'Back where?'

'It's odd, I don't know why I said that. But you know how when you're an adult, and you tuck a baby up in its pram or cot, when it's freezing cold outside, and you think how nice it would be to be that baby, even to being snug and warm and innocent inside your mother? Well, it's a bit like that, this feeling, as if I'm going to step into a warm darkness, a nothingness that isn't empty. Going back, to God, and to Will.'

Anna shook her head and her voice was harsh. 'I'm sorry, but you talk about reality in one breath, and you describe fantasy in the next. Oh, it's pointless to talk. We're a million miles from each other.'

Serene, Barbara looked at her and smiled. 'Not necessarily,' she said, as if she knew something of which her daughter was ignorant. 'Shall I tell you something, dear? I've always worried that you couldn't cope with things, face up to things. It's as if everything that happens to you surprises you, somehow. You were always in a dream, always needing help. That's why your father had his special soft spot for you, because he thought you needed him. Richard and Hilda were always so practical – rather like me. You and Daddy, with your walks in the rain, and your daydream games, and always wanting things to stay the same ... You're still the same. Some days you look like someone who's just fallen in love, all distant, but sad. Is that it? Is there someone, now that John has gone?'

Quickly Anna looked at her mother's face, fearing that she had guessed and wanting at the same time to bury her head in her breasts and cry that it was true. But Barbara was stitching rhythmically, just casting gentle looks from time to time that had no undercurrent of knowledge. 'No, there's nothing like that. I don't love anybody, except Tom – and you. I'm all right. I'm just getting used to things.'

They sat in silence for four or five minutes, both exhausted, until Barbara stopped her work and flexed her fingers with a grimace of discomfort. Then she stretched her arms, arching her back with a grunt. 'Darling, could you do something for me? I'm tired, and my hands are so stiff. Could you just sit with me for a while and do some of this for me? There's so much of the background to do. My fingers can't keep it up, and I do so want to get it finished. It takes so long – and sometimes, I'm afraid that there won't be enough time.'

For the first time Anna heard a note of dread in her mother's voice. She wanted to cry, but held out her hand instead for the piece of cloth. 'I'm not as good as you are, but I'll try,' she said; then slowly and clumsily began to make the small half-cross stitches in regular rows, while Barbara leaned back in her chair and watched.

Twenty

George and Tom were nowhere in sight. 'Anna! Anna!' called a voice, and she knew it. The smile was already on her face before she turned. At the side of the pontoon, holding the rowing boat off with both hands, was Matthew. Two girls sat with him in the boat, their hands gripping the gunwale with white knuckles. Anna guessed they must be sisters from their identical straight black hair. One of them wore it tied back with a red ribbon – she looked about fourteen and boyish in her scarlet dungarees. The other girl was older, sixteen probably, with hair hanging straight to her shoulders. Matthew grinned up at her.

'Anna, this is Jane and that one with freckles is Nicola. I've had them forced on me!'

'What a cheek!' said the older girl, whilst Nicola put her hand across her mouth and laughed.

'Are you here on holiday?' asked Anna.

'Yes,' said Jane, 'in that little house along the front at the end of the row.'

' "Rose Cottage",' Anna said.

'They've never been here before,' Matthew explained, as if somehow he felt he owed the explanation, 'so Mum said I was to show them round the place. Mrs Treadle's idea, really. They don't even know how to row.' The swaggering note irritated Anna, and she said nothing.

'You said you'd teach us, Matthew, you did!' squealed the younger girl, then looking shyly up at Anna she added, 'He's good at it, isn't he? Have you seen him on his windsurfer? I think it's lovely.' Jane shuddered, self-consciously. 'I wouldn't have the nerve to do that. It's not for girls, is it?'

'Not really,' said the boy complacently, pushing off from the side. He called to Anna, 'Tom's up at the shop. Haven't seen much of him today because of being lumbered with these two. Shall I call round later?'

She nodded, and watched them for a few minutes as Matthew pulled strongly on the oars. Both girls were staring at him with open admiration, but he looked across at Anna. 'Going to show them *Invader*,' he called, and she waved her hand, as if to give him permission.

George Treadle was standing behind the counter and smiled when Anna walked in. The low door that led into their sitting-room was ajar and she heard the sound of the television. The old man nodded towards it. 'He's in there with Mary. She's bin givin' him crisps and chocolate biscuits and all kinds.'

'He'll love that! It's really kind of you both, George.'

170

Anna hesitated, then went on, 'You know my mother is very ill?' He nodded. 'I do have to see her on my own sometimes, George, to talk things over, so I don't know what I'd have done without you and Mary – and the Pauls.'

He shook his head. 'We'm not being kind, Anna. Kind got nothing to do with it. He's a lovely little lad, and he do bring life back to the old house. By rights we'd've 'ad big grandchildren of our own by now. But that weren't to be.'

'I'm sorry, George.' She stopped, then took a breath. 'Does it make you very sad, to think of that?' He looked up, surprised, then dropped his eyes to the counter, rubbing one index finger to and fro on one spot. 'Bound to, ain't it? You'm don't get over such a thing, not ever, I reckon. I looks out and I sees the river, and I thinks as how she'm always there and so my boys is always there. They're in the churchyard yonder, that's as maybe, but every day when I takes my ferry out on that water I thinks of them as there, in the river, for ever like.'

He looked up at her, and Anna saw with pity that his eyes were watery. 'And each year I do think what age they'd have been now, and Mary, she'll always cry on November the twenty sixth, 'cos that were the day they was born.'

'Were they twins, George?' she asked softly. 'I didn't know that.'

He nodded. The hysterical chatter of a cartoon film drifted through the sitting-room door. Anna heard Tom laugh, and Mary say something in a soft low tone – a note rarely heard in the shop, but one which Anna recalled from her childhood when the three of them would go to the shop for errands and be spoilt by the stout woman. Her parents talked in whispers about the tragedy that had happened the year before they bought the cottage, warning the children in louder tones always to be careful on the river.

'Just seventeen they was,' he was sighing, 'and fine big lads. And you should have seen the way the girls ran after them! They was a dev'lish pair, our Thomas an' Edward.'

Anna smiled at him, amazed all the while at her own courage. 'I bet they were good-looking, George, just like their father!'

'Oh aye, that's for sure,' he said, and after a second the far-away look disappeared from his face, he winked at Anna and turned to call his wife. At the sight of Anna, Mary Treadle's smile faded a fraction, but Anna did not notice. Tom ran after her. 'Oh, it's you, Mum. Can I stay a bit longer? There's a good programme just starting.'

'No Tom, you must come home now.'

'But it's boring down there and the telly's no good.'

'Yes it is. It's perfectly all right, Tom.'

'But it's not in colour. And you never let me watch . . .'

His voice had become a whine; Mary Treadle seemed self-satisfied, looking from mother to child, her arms folded. George frowned. 'Now you listen to me, young man,' he boomed. 'When your mother do say "Go 'ome", she do mean go 'ome. You be good to your mother, now, because she's the only one you'll ever get. Now you think about that.'

Tom looked at him, his mouth open, suprised at this unfamiliar tone from his friend. Then he followed Anna from the shop quite meekly, muttering 'Thank you for having me', in response to her jab, and quite forgetting to ask about the television once they were home.

That night Hilda telephoned and Anna's heart sank as she recognised the mood of decision in her sister's first words. 'Hello, I'm back. How's mother?'

'Just the same. How was Brittany?'

'Oh, the usual chaos. Our equipment worked perfectly, of course, and the new tent is marvellous. Two rooms. But the camp site was terrible, and so we had to move on. The next one was just as bad. The loos were absolutely frightful. Disgusting. I made Alan go and complain but it didn't do any good. How's your holiday?'

'Oh fine, considering.'

'That's what I was coming to. Tell me about Mummy. Richard's filled me in with all the details so I'm not going to waste time saying how awful. What I want to know is, has she decided?'

'Decided what?' asked Anna, determined not to help.

Hilda clicked her tongue. 'Honestly, you are vague! Richard told me you were going to persuade her to leave that place and come back with you to London. I bet they're not treating her properly anyway. She'd be much better going to a London teaching hospital where we could all keep an eye on things. Alan knows a radiotherapist at Bart's, it always helps. It's quite ridiculous for her to use up all her savings down there, when she'd be so much better with you – and us.'

'She doesn't seem to think so.'

'Oh Anna, it's nonsense. Have you talked to her – I mean, really talked to her?'

Annoyed, Anna spoke sharply. 'Look Hilda, I've talked more to our mother in the last two weeks than ever before in my life. She's quite determined to stay put, and you know what she's like when she's made up her mind.'

'But she's just being silly.'

'Maybe she is,' said Anna, 'but frankly, if she wants to be silly I think she has the right to be silly, and we should leave her alone.'

Hilda sounded shocked. 'Anna! How can we leave her alone if we know she's doing the wrong thing?'

Picking at the peeling wallpaper with her nails, Anna asked, 'How do we know it is the wrong thing?'

The conversation bounced backwards and forwards for several minutes, with Hilda's irritation growing, and Anna's answers becoming shorter and shorter. She tore a long strip of paper down, revealing the plaster underneath, with its mottling of damp. At last Anna interrupted her sister's flow. 'Hilda, I've done all I'm going to do. I'm not suggesting any more that she comes to live with me, because to be honest I don't want her to. I didn't really want her to when I made the offer, and maybe she sensed that. Now I've got my own life to live, and to be honest with you, I think she's got her own death to die, and we should all respect the situation. Is that clear?'

The voice on the other end of the line was cold. 'Well, if that's the way you feel, Anna. I'll see what we can do when Richard and I see her. When are you coming back?' Anna told her. 'Oh good. That means, let's see, there's a week before the boys start school. We'll drive down on the Monday. It's a pity we'll miss you.'

'Yes,' said Anna, thinking wryly that they still had to go through all the motions of affection.

There was a short exchange about leaving the cottage clean and tidy (from Hilda) and not trying to browbeat Barbara (from Anna) before the sisters said goodbye. Anna reflected gloomily, as she prepared for bed, that surely her sister could never have believed in anything that was nameless – and certainly never have left a teddy bear to cope with it.

Twenty-One

It was four mornings from the end of the holiday, and the sky was cloudy. Anna lay still for a moment, then stretched, thinking of how much better Barbara seemed, now that she and Tom went every day, and the future was no longer mentioned.

Tom ran into the room in his pyjamas; when she stretched out an arm he climbed gladly into her bed, cuddling up against her as he used to do. Anna smelt his hair and noticed how dark it was at the roots, so that the child who had been pale blond would end up a man with ordinary brown hair. Brown eyelashes shadowed his cheek, long, like Matthew's.

He asked what they would do that day, but Anna shivered and snuggled farther down into the bed. 'It sounds really stormy out there. It'll probably pour with rain later, so we'll just go to town and say hello to Granny as usual, then come back and play games.'

'I don't want to stay inside. Is it autumn yet?'

'No, not quite. But sometimes at the end of August the weather's really bad, and the river's rough. That's why you have to bring lots of woollies, because you never know.'

'I don't mind it when it's stormy,' he said.

174

'It can be fun to go out in it, like we did when I was a little girl. Long walks in the rain.'

He made a face. 'No fear.'

There was still no day when they did not see Matthew Paul, though more often now it was they who sought him, as they had at the beginning, always in the vicinity of the river. He rowed, or fished from the end of the pier, or waved to them from the deck of *Invader*, and if there was a wind he would spend a part of each day on his windsurfer – sometimes waving to them, sometimes oblivious to everything but his own motion.

He had become, Anna thought, an essential part of this landscape: something that had never been there before, in twenty-five years of seeing this same river and those distant trees, yet something so beautiful that now the river would seem incomplete were a day to dawn when Anna could no longer glimpse that blue and white sail.

Now and then she would see him far off, talking to the sisters from 'Rose Cottage'. Sometimes the three of them would be lounging at the end of the pier, forgetful of the river's reverberating stillness, so that scraps of their conversation would float across the water to where Anna stood, leaning on her garden wall. Things she had forgotten – school meals, the top twenty, straight-legged cords that could be tapered, mock exams, parents. Their laughter would reach her.

Those moments pinched her, although she made the effort to tell Tom that it was good for Matthew to have friends his own age, and so he must not mind. 'He must not mind . . . !' she thought, taking a certain pleasure in the irony. Then, an hour or two later, Matthew would loiter by to say hello, and she would tease him about his girlfriends, pleased when he denied them, scowling. Then the odd, contracted feeling disappeared and it seemed as if she and Tom and Matthew were suspended, and that she was in her teens again whilst Tom was older, all of them, mysteriously, one. Their imminent return to London seemed unreal, meaning as it did that she must pick up the threads of another design, with work, and the morning rush to get Tom to school, and weekend following week so quickly, and John making his awkward visits. The month in 'Ahoy' had blended Sunday with the rest of the week; Anna felt that someone had unloosened the screws at the corners of her life.

Barbara herself noticed the change. That day as they were leaving she called Anna back and whispered, 'I'm so glad, darling. You seem to have come to terms with ... everything. You look much happier.' It was not so much true of Barbara herself. Her cheerfulness was like a glaze, applied too quickly in an attempt to cover up the flaws in a piece of pottery. She was often in pain and breathed with difficulty; her eyes and hair had lost their life. Neither of them mentioned it; Anna avoided all encounters with the nursing-home staff. There were no words now, she felt, and no point in miming to those uttered by others.

It was very stormy now. As they drove back from Syne-mouth huge drops of rain dashed against the windscreen and the wind increased, so that the tall hedgerows each side of the lane were tossed about, and they might have been driving in the furrow of enormous waves. Wild flowers were whipped from side to side; dried leaves and flower heads whirled upwards on currents of air.

'Wow, what a storm,' said Tom, pressing his nose against the car window. Then he asked, abruptly, so that Anna felt the question like a physical shock, 'Mum – is Granny really going to die?' After a moment she replied, 'Yes, she is, Tom.'

'When will it be?'

'I don't know.'

'Will it be soon?'

'Yes – I think so.'

'Why does God let people die?'

She caught her breath and said helplessly, 'I don't know the answer; I can't tell you. What do you think?'

There was a short silence, broken by the swish of the tyres and the regular slice of the windscreen wipers. Then he said, 'Because they've got bored with being old.'

'And what do you think of that?'

After another pause he said, 'Nothing, really.'

She was shocked. 'Don't you care, Tom? I always thought you cared about people.'

'I do,' he said defensively, 'I meant that I can't do anything about it, and so there's nothing I can say, is there? Granny is old, isn't she?' Anna agreed. 'Well, there you are,' he said, as if solving an experiment and writing QED at the end. 'I'll die when I'm old.' His voice was matter of fact; it made Anna feel rebellious.

By the time they had finished their soup the wind and rain had increased, and Anna went to find a sweater, even though the atmosphere in the cottage was muggy rather than cold. They sat on the window seat, warily because it sagged in the middle, and looked out at the river, leaden under its veil of sky, with the rain forming a mist as it drove across. The water was very choppy. Anna pointed out to Tom that there were no regular white-capped waves, only a churning and a bubbling as wind and tide fought against each other.

'Anybody home?' They heard the kitchen door open, then slam in the wind, and the voice repeated the question. 'Yes! In here!' she shouted. It was Matthew's voice. He appeared at the door of the room in a yellow oilskin, shaking drops of water from his glowing face.

'What on earth are you doing out in the rain?' she asked, happily, feeling the dull little room infused with light.

'I was bored in our house. Mum and Dad were griping at each other so I thought I'd get out.'

'What's griping mean?' asked Tom, but Matthew winked at Anna. 'Questions, questions,' he jeered. 'And you're too young to know the answers. You're a baby!'

Unoffended, Tom asked if Matthew would play Lego and help him make something complicated. 'Aw God, no. Anything but that. All your things are boring.'

Tom grappled with the older boy, half in earnest, and Matthew pretended to be afraid, retreating across the room. They collapsed in a heap, playing at fighting and knocking over the light coffee table so that Anna's books went flying. She groaned and turned to stare out of the window again, listening to the faint, desperate drumming of the rigging,

177

barely audible above the wind. She felt restless. The wind which tossed the boats upon their mooring penetrated the tiny cracks in the ill-fitting window frames so that she felt it upon her face. 'It never used to be as draughty as this,' she thought. 'This cottage is falling apart.'

Tom had started to cry in earnest now. 'He hurt me,' he sobbed, rubbing his head, and burying his face in Anna's breast. Matthew was sulky. 'I didn't. He always tries to fight properly, and expects me to take all his punches, while I go on pretending.'

'But you're so much stronger than he is,' Anna said reproachfully, rubbing Tom's head. 'You see, it always ends in tears.' Matthew snorted contemptuously, 'My gran always says that, but God knows what it's supposed to mean.'

'Don't you know what it means, Matthew? It's obvious to me.'

He walked around the room, picking things up, looking at them and then putting them down, as he always did. He left a trail of water on the floor as he rocked upon his heels. His restlessness infected Anna. 'Why don't we all go out for a walk?' she suggested.

'Oh Mum, it's too cold and it's raining,' whined Tom.

'It's not cold, it's August,' she said.

'More like October,' grunted Matthew.

She protested that they must do something. They discussed the possibility of snakes and ladders, only to reject it. It seemed to Anna suddenly that the room was growing smaller and smaller, so that some vast energy inside her was compressed, crushed into a tiny space, and she wanted to cry out with passion and frustration. Instead she said, in a cajoling voice, 'Matthew dear, think of something to do.'

His face lit up. 'I know. Let's go out on the river. It'll be great out there – wild! I'll row.'

She shook her head and Tom made a face, but Matthew was already on his feet. 'Well, it's boring in here, and boring just going for a walk, but if you get togged up like me we can get Dad's rowing boat and get a taste of the storm. Come on!'

Tom looked worried. 'Will it be safe, Mum?'

'Of course!' Matthew cried. 'It's not even very choppy out there. I've been out in much worse – and you know what a brilliant oarsman I am.'

With a surge of recklessness, Anna decided. It was as if all the windows of the little house had opened and the wind swept through, scouring the dust from all the corners and carrying with it the dried-out wild flowers she had stuck into a jam jar on their first day and never bothered to remove. For a second she fancied that the place was pure and empty, the useless objects tumbled into a heap at the bottom of the river.

'All right, we'll come. Why not?' she said. 'It'll be an adventure, Tom.'

Not giving him time to protest she bundled Tom into a small oilskin, and wellington boots, pushing her own arms quickly into an old oilskin jacket of her mother's. She tied sou'westers on both their heads, and he caught her mood, giggling up at her from under the brim, repeating, 'It's a real adventure.'

They left the house, not bothering to lock the door, and climbed the orchard path, slipping occasionally on the wet ground. Anna heard the drops of rain patter through the trees; the storm had even dislodged a few young apples and pears, before their ripeness. Walking quickly down the lane they passed the village shop, all silent, and hurried downhill to the waterfront. The pontoon was completely deserted. Only the gulls, wheeling and crying savagely above, gave life to the scene – except that the river itself was alive, tossing the boats on their moorings and slapping against the pier and pontoon, as if to threaten whatever man had put there for his foolish moments of holiday fun. A child's bucket, left on one of the walkways, was caught by the wind and skeltered along, crashing against upturned dinghies before being whirled into the water, where it was hurled about like a miniature coracle before it sank.

Matthew led them along to the pier, where, tied to the steps at the end, the Pauls' dinghy lay with its oars still inside – a carelessness William Lewis would never have tolerated. The boy climbed into it first, then held out his

179

arms, balancing expertly as Anna helped Tom down. He moved as if he had lost all use of his joints, moaning, 'I'll fall, I'll fall.' But Matthew guided him to the bows, then turned to help Anna into the boat. His hand was warm, but damp because of the rain, and she let it go quickly.

Matthew pushed off, then fitted the oars into the rowlocks and started to pull. From 'Ahoy' the river had looked choppy but not as rough as in winter; now they sat so low upon it that they were tossed up and down in an increasingly violent motion, and it seemed as if not even Matthew's strength at the oars could control their motion. The wind blew in their faces, and Anna laughed aloud with the spray in her face and the rain drumming all around. Her sou'wester had slipped back but she did not care; already her hair was wet and whipped around her face in long strands. Smiling to see the water cascading from Matthew's plastered hair down his flushed, smooth cheeks, she leaned forwards and tenderly wiped at it with both her hands. 'Thanks,' he said.

By now they were about a hundred yards from the pier, allowing the current to dictate their course. Over Matthew's shoulder Anna could see Tom's face, pale under the vivid yellow hat, and his knuckles white where they gripped. Seeing her look at him, he forced a grin.

'Isn't this fun?' she shouted.

'Yes,' he yelled back, his voice caught by the wind, his mouth wide open, so that he resembled a puppet, tossed jerkily up and down, its white wooden face painted in a permanent expression of alarm.

Exultant, Anna looked at the shore. She saw 'Ahoy' standing squat and square behind its protective wall, its two windows like blank eyes each side of the front door and the mast in the garden like a finger pointing upwards. She waved like a child, as if there might be someone within that house, standing watching at the window – a parent perhaps, smiling indulgently at the childish escapade, with tea and toast by the fire later, and even a story in the drowsy afternoon.

But the wind slashed at her face and she shook her head. 'There's no one there!' she cried out, loudly, throwing back her head and laughing so that Matthew looked at her in astonishment, and asked her what she was saying, what she meant. 'There's no one there. There's no going back,' she shouted.

Tom was looking frightened. 'I want to go back now, Mum!' he was shouting at her. 'Let's go back.'

'No, not yet,' Matthew called over his shoulder, 'I'm just beginning to enjoy myself.'

'No, not yet,' echoed Anna, mesmerised by the movement of the oars, and Matthew's head as it dipped mechanically towards her, with each thrust into the water.

After another five or ten minutes Matthew looked up at her and muttered, 'Jesus, the current's strong,' heaving all the while on the oars, his face glowing with heat. 'The wind seems to be coming from all directions,' he yelled. Anna saw that they had made progress out into the bay at an angle of about forty-five degrees from 'Ahoy', and all around them the water was churning, as tide, cross current and wind fought for supremacy.

'We'd better turn back,' she said, but Matthew looked uncharacteristically worried. 'It's going to be a bit tricky,' he mumbled, looking at the water; and just hearing this Tom began to wail the stiff, strangled sob of a seven-year-old who knows he is too old to cry, especially on an adventure.

Then, droning beneath the sound of the wind, Anna heard the chug of an outboard. 'Look!' shouted Tom. The ferry boat plunged towards them, George Treadle, swathed in oilskins, at the tiller. 'Whatever is he doing?' Anna asked, but Matthew shrugged, shipping his oars for a moment before dipping one of them into the water, ready to turn the boat in a tight circle, to head back for the pier. George was shouting, and after a few seconds they made out his roar. 'Matthew! Matthew!' They turned to see him making furious gestures with his hands, even letting go of the tiller for a second as he waved both arms frantically in the air.

'What's he saying? He's telling me to stop,' Matthew said, looking like a child whose balloon has suddenly been snatched away by the wind. The ferry drew alongside them, making them rock even more, and George screamed angrily across the intervening gap of water. 'What you'm doing,

Matthew? If you do put about now, like you was goin' to, you'll be in that water. If you'm don't know this river you got no business be out on her in weather like this!'

Rain streamed down his face. He did not look at Anna. 'Now you just do as I say,' he yelled. 'I'm staying beside you all the way, so you just follow my course in a wide curve. Don't you try and cut no corners! You try and do anything sharp an' she'll have you over!'

Silently Matthew dipped both his oars in the foaming water and began to pull, but wearily now. George chugged beside them, guiding them round in a wide arc, still pulling out away from the shore, and only then round at a shallow angle heading for the pontoon. Looking back Anna realised that if Matthew had simply tried to turn the boat around on the spot as he was about to do, there was a very real danger that they would have been swamped.

She felt cold. Matthew was bent double and grunted at every stroke, all elation gone from his face. The new course doubled the journey back, but never once put them in a position where they might have been caught between the wind and those treacherous choppy waves.

At last they reached the pontoon. George pulled ahead and landed first, so that he was ready to pull them in. When he held out a hand to pull Anna ashore the old man was not gentle, and there was an expression on his face she had never seen before. 'What in God's name did you think you was doing?' he shouted, his lined face grim. 'You should be ashamed of yourself, you should! Ashamed!'

The three of them looked at him in astonishment, then Matthew looked down at his feet, mumbling, 'It was my idea to go out, George. But there's no need to make a fuss. We'd have been OK.' Anna made her voice wheedling, 'Yes, George. Matthew thought it would be a bit of fun, and honestly, there's no harm done.'

'Fun!' he shouted. 'Yes, and it's good fun when the little lad ain't even got a life jacket on 'im! Fun if he was to get drownded in there!' He pointed at the river with a shaking finger, and with the other hand drew Tom to him, so that the child's face was pressed against his streaming oilskin.

182

Anna said nothing. No life jacket . . . it had not occurred to her, in that moment of leaving the cottage, of doing what Matthew said, anything, to please him. And their father had always taught them never to go near that deceptive river without one. 'But we can swim,' they all used to protest, but William used to murmur that you cannot put faith in what you think you can do – not near the river, which thinks only of its run towards the sea.

George could not stop. 'However could you do such a thing, such a foolish, wicked thing? A growed woman actin' like a child, that's what it is! You should be ashamed, Anna.' Matthew shuffled again, and mumbled that it was all his fault, his idea, nothing to do with Anna, and anyway, perfectly safe – but George ignored him, staring at her with passionate dislike.

'Oh,' he sneered, in an unpleasant voice, 'so it were his idea . . . and him only a kid too. Very nice! It's you what's to blame, Anna, so don't give me all that. Fancy letting an overgrown schoolboy take you and the little 'un out on the water on a day like this! Mary sees you walk past and she tells me, but I don't listen to her at first. Then I gets one o' them feelings so I walks down and sees you out in all this. After all these years I'd a' thought you'd've known these currents.'

She looked down. 'No, I didn't know. I'm sorry,' she whispered, but her humility enraged him still further. He wanted her to cry with shame, to fall upon the ground in her humiliation, not to stand there accepting it, like the boy. 'Oh, so you didn't know! But why didn't you? Why didn't you put no life jacket on him? Was you just too busy thinking about your friend Matthew, here, and doing what he wanted? Making a fool of yourself, following him round, at your age! Was that why you didn't think about your own boy? You'm entitled to go and drown yourself with 'im, but not an innocent child who's never done no harm to nobody. And you his mother too!' Still he hugged Tom to him and waved a dismissive hand at Matthew. 'It's no good trying to put the blame on him. He's just a stupid lad who's too big for his boots. He's too young to be trusted; but you – you're old enough to be responsible.'

Matthew Paul turned sharply on his heel, his face sullen, and started to walk away up the pontoon, without saying a word. 'I'll tell your Mum and Dad, I will!' George shouted at his back.

Tom had started to cry quietly, aware that there was something to cry for, even if it was simply relief from being out of that pitching boat. He looked from George to his mother, seeing the one face angry and the other about to break into tears, and redoubled his sobs, because he did not understand.

'I'm sorry, George,' Anna said quietly, looking at the old man with brimming eyes. 'Now will you let us go home? And thank you for coming to help us. Thank you.'

Her face was so desolate that he dropped his gaze, bending down to tell Tom to be quiet, for it was all over. Then he looked up at Anna with a different expression in his eyes, of pity. 'You get along then,' he said in a voice which rasped in the attempt to be gentle, 'and give the lad a hot drink. See ... folk don't know this river like I do. She can be an old bitch, she can ... an old bitch.'

With his last words he raised his voice slightly and turned his eyes to the water, as if he were addressing, not Anna, but the river itself. And he stood there massively as Anna took Tom away, looking like a Lear with nothing left to do but hurl imprecations upon the sky.

Twenty-Two

'Your mother tells me that your brother and sister will be visiting very soon.' Dr Jacobs leant forward on a desk that was completely empty, except for one buff folder which had Barbara's name upon it.

'Yes.'

'I imagine you'll be staying to see them?'

Anna shook her head. 'No. I have to be back at work.'

The consultant raised his eyebrows a fraction, and there was a short silence. Then he frowned, as if he had expected something from Anna, an apology.

'A pity. We usually find that relatives like to have a discussion – a family council. It helps . . . in a case like this.'

'In a case like what?'

'Well, where there is some sort of deadlock.'

'But there is none. Not now. My mother and I have discussed everything, and . . .' Anna took a breath, 'I don't think any of us have the right to make her change her mind.'

He shrugged. 'I was hardly suggesting you should make her do anything, Miss Lewis. As a matter of fact I think she has changed her mind. It seems to me that she has shifted her course somewhat, since you have been here, and that she could easily be persuaded . . .'

Exasperated by his conviction, Anna broke in. 'No, I'm sorry, but that's not right. She couldn't.'

'Hmmm. Perhaps I should discuss it with your brother next week. He is the eldest?'

'It really won't be necessary,' said Anna drily, amused to think of Richard in the role of *pater familias*. 'Oh, talk to him all you like. He'll agree with you. All I'm saying is that my mother has made a decision, and will stick to it. I must say, I understand it now. What is the point in her struggling on for another six months or so?'

Dr Jacobs looked surprised, even a little hurt. 'As a doctor I have to disagree with you – in this case. I always do what I can to make my patients want to help themselves . . .'

'I know. I do – really. Four weeks ago I agreed with you, and I was angry with my mother for being so defeatist. To be honest – I thought she was turning herself into a martyr. But now . . .'

She bit her lip, and he looked at her, curiously. 'What do you think now, Miss Lewis?' Anna was not sure if there was a touch of mockery in his tone, and the suspicion was enough.

'I'll tell you what I think. We're arrogant – all of us who

185

are healthy. Why should we assume that the sick always want to be like us? Why should you think that because my mother isn't too bothered about living she must have lost all sense of purpose?'

'My experience would indicate . . .' he began, but Anna interrupted. 'Just for this moment I don't want to hear about your other patients, or turn my mother into a case history. As far as I'm concerned, she's unique. And the point is this – since my father died she has had a sense of purpose, which is that one day she would be reunited with him. Isn't that a purpose?'

Dr Jacobs leaned back in his chair and looked at the ceiling. 'I . . . I'm not a Christian, Miss Lewis. And may I ask . . . are you?'

'No,' she said. 'But she is, and I didn't realise that was true, which says a lot about me.'

'But do you sympathise?'

She looked at him helplessly, and spread her hands wide.

'If you're asking me if I believe it, the answer's no. I certainly don't think she's going to see my father again in some cosy celestial sitting-room. No, I don't. But sympathetic – yes, I do feel that. It seems to me that it's a pretty slender straw to cling to, but if you cling to it thinking it's a lifeboat, then so what? Who am I to say she's wrong? I don't know, and nor do you. It so happens that my mother feels that she has to die – to be happy, if you like. And I think that all of us have to suffer a bit, or be humiliated, or whatever, before we can reach where she is already.'

'You admire your mother, Miss Lewis?'

She paused, surprised by the question, then nodded.

'Yes, I do. Much more than when I came down. I feel . . . well, fonder of her too, fonder than I have for years. I can't stand the thought of her dying, but I'm learning to – and that's all to do with her. It's necessary to learn – that's what she says. It's odd you know . . .', a bright smile lit up her face, 'but I think my mother is making me grow up at last.'

Dr Jacobs smiled too, unexpectedly. 'This whole conversation brings home to me something I've always talked about

– how an illness like cancer can serve as a focus, not just for the patient, but for the patient's family too.'

Anna nodded. 'It's – brought me back to life,' she said, very quietly.

'I'm sorry?'

'Nothing really. It's just that I've had a bad year, and this is the worst thing that's happened, and yet I've come out of these weeks of seeing my mother feeling tougher, somehow. In a good way. She is tough, you know.'

'I realise that.'

'And do you see why I feel that we have no right to impose our view of her life upon her, as if she were a silly old lady?'

'I do see what you mean. But your brother and sister . . .'

She looked at him, then smiled. 'Then will you promise to stop badgering her about standing on her own two feet? . . . Oh, I didn't mean badgering, I'm sorry. All I mean is, it's better not even to raise it with her. The nurses too! The only thing that worries me is, finance.'

The consultant polished the fingernails of his left hand with the thumb of his right, very carefully. 'That is . . . no business of mine. But I assume you mother has . . . er . . . resources?'

She nodded. 'Yes, my father left her a small income and she's sold her flat overlooking the harbour.'

He raised his shoulders in a hint of a shrug. 'Then she will have little to worry about. Sometimes I get old men and women who come here to die, and they panic that their savings will not cover the cost. They lie awake and worry because they've worked it out to the last penny – enough for, say, eighteen months or so. Which is, I'm afraid, pretty expensive. What they do not realise is that they have only two or three months left to live. They're the ones it's a kindness to tell, although sometimes even then I don't. Sometimes that worry is itself an occupation, something they need. In your mother's case – well, you know that she knows it won't be too long.'

He stood up, inviting Anna to do the same. 'I'll remember what you've said, Miss Lewis, and I'll think about it carefully. But will your brother and sister understand? Will you tell them? I'm afraid that if they make vehement efforts to make her change her mind ...'

'She's beyond that kind of upsetting. But I'll do my best.'

He held out his hand. 'Will we see you here again?'

'Yes, of course you will. I'll come down at weekends as often as possible, every week probably, until I don't need to any more.'

Tom was waiting outside on a chair, reading a comic. Together they walked along the corridor to Barbara's room, and pausing outside her door they heard the sound of music. Anna knocked quietly, then pushed the door open. As they stood on the threshold, music and sunlight cascaded over them in deafening and blinding waves, making Anna dizzy. Barbara sat in front of the two open windows in full sunlight, her radio turned up unusually loud. Anna felt suddenly light-headed, and closed her eyes for a second, sensing the dizzy arpeggios like pinpricks upon the surface of her brain, as a blind man reads his braille. Barbara made a movement as if to turn the radio off, but Anna stopped her. 'Leave it,' she said, 'it's so beautiful.'

'Yes,' said Barbara, looking wistful. 'This sort of music makes me remember so many things, happy things. Your father loved Mozart, do you remember? It still makes me want to dance, even though it wouldn't be wise!'

They listened for a few minutes more, then Barbara turned down the sound until the music was like a whisper, but still a presence in the room with them. Anna could hear the riotous birdsong from the trees, like another section of the woodwind.

'I've never noticed those birds before,' she said, 'not like today.'

'They're always there, darling.'

Barbara beckoned to Tom and whispered that he should look in the cupboard by the bed, where he might find something to interest him. He rushed across the room, rummaged, and turned round with an expression of ecstasy – brandishing a box bearing a flashy picture of a yellow streamlined racing car. 'It's a radio-controlled car! Is it really for me, Granny? I've always wanted one!'

Christmas, Anna thought, it's like Christmas. As he threw his arms around the frail old woman, she had a vivid recollection of other presents, when she was a child, and the snow was soft and glistening in memory, and the tree huge and light. Their house was full of secrets; parcels hidden like Tom's car in cupboards, and the glint of silver paper in a drawer. On Christmas Eve William always organised his ritual, each child holding a taper to the fat white candle that stood in the centre of the sitting-room window, then taking it in turns (the youngest always first) to read the Christmas story from the huge family Bible. There was a happy solemnity about that moment (repeated year after year until they became self-conscious teenagers who sniggered, so that their father, hurt, abandoned his ritual for ever) that was quite in keeping with the orgy of paper and ribbons and presents the following day, and the turkey sizzling in its fat. Nothing, thought Anna, that had happened since then could match the unalloyed joy, or the knowledge that the love within the ritual, the gifts and the ceremonial lunch was, quite simply, due – beyond gratitude, and indivisible from life itself.

'I hope you don't mind, dear,' Barbara was saying, 'but Molly got it for me because I wanted him to have something nice to take back. I know you don't like him to be spoilt.' Anna kissed her mother gently, saying that it did not matter, that she was kind, whilst Tom fitted the batteries into the toy car, and fiddled with its black controller. He was silent from that point on, putting the car through its paces, pausing only to utter rhetorical cries of, 'Did you see that?'

For a while Barbara chatted about what the nurses had said, and what the meals had been like, casting pleased glances at her grandson. Then she took a visibly deep breath, and said, 'Anna, dear, there's something I want to tell you.' Seeing the look of surprise and anxiety she added hastily, 'Oh, it's nothing about my health, dear, nothing to worry about. But you may think it's bad news, just the same . . . It's something I've discussed on the phone with Richard, because after all he is the eldest, but I feel guilty that I haven't told you too. You know I sold my flat?' Anna

189

nodded, waiting with a curious tremble in her stomach, for the news. 'Well, to be mundane I'm living off that money at the moment, to pay for Nurse Anderson's tender mercies! I've got my little income of course, but it's nothing nowadays, and it is ... well very dear at "The Park". I suppose you have to pay a high price for peace.'

'I know,' Anna said.

'The fact is, dear, that Richard and I decided on the phone together, or rather I decided ... that I should think seriously about selling "Ahoy". You told me the other day that it's in a bad state of repair. I can't ask any of you to take the responsibility of having it done up, and Richard said it would be hard to divide because none of you would want to put in more money than you would get out, in use. Do you see what I mean?'

'He would say that,' said Anna sourly.

'Don't be like that, darling. He was being very helpful to me. I know you hate the idea of selling the old place but I think we should. I really do. You can't cling to things for ever, can you? And if it isn't renovated soon it will fall down and be worth nothing. If we sell now we'll still get a good price ...'

'Yes,' said Anna, her voice full of irony, remembering the conversation in 'Hacienda'. 'I hear the market is at its best right now.'

'Is it, dear? I didn't realise you knew about those things. Well, good. There's two reasons for doing it now, apart from that. Firstly, I need to know that I can stay here for as long as I need to, without worrying. Don't pull a face, dear. Despite all our gloomy talks I fully expect to be here next summer! And secondly, I prefer to think that after I've gone there will be a nice sum of money that I can leave the three of you. It could be evenly divided, instead of all the complication of a piece of property that you want to keep, Richard wants to sell, or whatever. Daddy always said that people should never share property – it makes for awful legal and family wrangles.'

Mumbling, 'Yes I suppose you're right, I suppose it does,' Anna rose and stood by the window, looking out on the lawn

190

dappled with sunlight. It was hot; almost impossible to imagine the storm three days ago. Patients walked among the shrubs, or were walked by nurses or pushed in wheelchairs, and all the time the birds kept up their noise in the branches above. Above it all, in the distance, gleamed the water where the widening Syne lost its identity in the sea. The scene, so strange on that first day, now seemed beautiful to Anna; and so familiar that it was easy to imagine that this was the only world – the other one, of babies and weddings and gardens and boats, an illusion.

'Anna?' whispered Barbara, plucking at her skirt. 'Are you terribly sad? Are you really sorry to lose it? I can't bear to think . . .' Still looking from the window, Anna said, 'No, don't worry. I was just thinking that I mind less than I would have thought. Perhaps it's just the surprise . . . and I'm numbed. But I can't go on wanting to keep things the same, because they can't be. It's not possible. It's not . . . mature.'

Her mother frowned. 'I don't see what maturity has to do with it, darling. You're too self-critical.' Anna shook her head. 'No, I know what I mean, though it's impossible to tell you. Since I've been down here I've done . . . I've been stupid in some ways. Like a child. But never mind about that, tell me how we're going to handle it. Will Richard do all the boring things like getting an agent?' She had made her voice so brisk that it sounded artificial, and Barbara looked at her strangely. 'Anna, you're not being honest with me. Are you quite sure you don't mind about it?'

Sitting down again Anna buried her face in her hands, just for a second or two, before looking up at Barbara. 'Oh, I mind,' she said, 'but at the same time I don't. I think it's the right thing to do, by instinct, though I never thought I'd agree with Richard about anything. I do now, but for different reasons. I love that scruffy little cottage more than I've ever loved any place, but . . . it's damaging me.' Puzzled, Barbara asked what she meant. 'I'm too old to play at Wendy Houses,' Anna said dully, 'I don't expect you to understand, Mummy. But it's to do with what I just said, about keeping things the same, all the magical things, the things you remember. It's been an escape for me, that house: trying to get back, chasing something out of reach all the time. Perhaps I'll understand it more, what's been happening, when I'm back in London, and maybe I'll be able to tell you then – but not now. All I know is I've been wandering from room to room in the cottage in a dream, just as you must have done ten years ago, and now I feel it's all over. It must be. John, Daddy, you ... everybody. So I've got to learn to be on my own now – and actually that's thanks to you.'

Barbara looked amazed, and put a hand on her own breast, as if she were about to swear an oath.

'How?' she asked. 'I don't understand at all. I feel I've done nothing for you this holiday, except be quarrelsome.'

Anna grinned, unexpectedly. 'Oh, you've helped me a lot. You're a tough old biddy, you know, and you've toughened me up too. Anyway, it's good that "Ahoy" is ... er ... over. Over for me. I've been under its spell for too long.'

'But you won't forget?'

'Don't be ridiculous. I shouldn't need bricks and mortar and a heap of junky furniture to help me remember, now should I?'

They fell silent. 'I called by at Molly's house on the way here,' Anna said. 'I took her a bunch of roses, and him a bottle of Tio Pepe, because they're so good. They seemed pleased.'

'I'm sure they were, darling,' said Barbara in a far-away voice. 'That was so kind of you, to think of saying goodbye to them.'

'Oh, but I'll be seeing them again,' Anna interrupted hastily, 'when I come down, you know, soon. At weekends.'

Tom demonstrated how his new car could right itself, by its own power and momentum, when it crashed into the skirting board. When the noise and their exclamations of dutiful admiration had died down, Barbara asked, yet again, when they were going home. It was as if, Anna thought, she was incapable of storing the information she received each time, because she did not want them to go – or perhaps because it was not important enough for her to remember.

'Tomorrow,' she said, 'but not until the evening. I'd rather leave when most of the traffic has gone. I'll spend the day cleaning the place up, and packing, and saying goodbye. To the Treadles, and the people we've met.'

'And is it work on Monday?'

'No, Mummy! Monday's the bank holiday, but I'll never drive then – it's too much of a nightmare. I'll do the washing; and John sent a card to say he'll come and take Tom out for the day. I haven't told him yet . . .' she lowered her voice, 'because I knew he'd be beside himself and go on about it all the time.'

'You forget bank holidays, when you're my age,' said Barbara.

'I'm not surprised.'

'I don't suppose you'd want to drive back then.'

'No, I just told you! Anyway . . .'

'Oh no, dear, I quite see. When is Tom back at school?'

'Another nine days to go. He goes to his friends, the O'Briens, when I'm at work, remember I told you? I give her m . . . o . . . n . . . e . . . y, and it works quite well. David O'Brien is in his class. It's odd, but I don't altogether mind the thought of the routine beginning again. You can't stay on holiday for ever – but I'll miss seeing you.'

'Don't worry about me, dear. I'll be fine. It'll be nice to see the others . . . oh, by the way, I've got a present for you.'

With some effort now, Anna noticed, Barbara hauled herself from the chair and walked slowly and unevenly across to the wardrobe. Her arm shook as she reached up and pulled something wrapped in tissue paper from the top shelf. 'Here you are, Anna. You gave Molly some roses so I'm giving you some. Only these will last.'

Anna pulled the folds of paper apart, to reveal her mother's tapestry, finished now and neatly pressed. The crimson roses glowed in their blue vase, surrounded by an intricate border in subtle but sombre hues; and Anna raised it to her face for a moment, as if the pictured blossoms might come alive and fill her nostrils with their scent. She smelt the clean, dry odour of the linen and the wool, and looked closely at the thousands of small stitches that made up her mother's gift, whispering in a voice she did not trust, that it was beautiful.

'I wanted you to have it, darling,' said Barbara cheerfully, 'to remind you of me. All this time I've been making it, and moaning at you, so you deserve to have it. It will outlast me, darling, and that's for sure.'

'Don't, please.'

'It's all right, Anna. We have to smile about it all, and in any case, it's true. You'll be able to hand that on – I think that's why I love doing tapestry work. You know that it will last for ever, like the work on those Victorian footstools that's survived feet for a hundred years and is still intact. Can't say the same for us, can you?'

Anna shook her head, feeling stifled, although the windows of the room were still wide open. She folded the tapestry into its tissue, and looked at her watch. 'We must go in a minute. There's so much . . .'

'I know, darling.'

'Listen, I won't waste energy worrying about you, now, at least. I'll phone you a lot, and Hilda and Richard will see you, and once Tom's back at school I'll arrange it so as I come down every weekend. I'll stay in that guest house at the end of the road, or do it in a day sometimes.' She was speaking rapidly, as if to fill each fraction of a second.

'Oh, but don't let it get in the way of your . . .' Barbara started to murmur, but Anna interrupted. 'It won't get in the way of anything, Mummy. Because there is nothing for it to get in the way of. Do you understand that? I shall come because I want to come. I want to see some more of you yet.'

She was moved by the enormous smile that spread across her mother's face, like that of Tom when he saw the car. In that second Barbara did not look like an old woman, but like the girl who smiled from the wedding photograph, her hair dressed in a fashionable roll; or like the young mother Anna remembered quite clearly, holding hands with her husband in the garden's evening calm. She did not sound sad, only mischievous, as she put her head on one side and asked, 'So this goodbye isn't going to be the last one, dear?'

'Not on your life!'

'Good. I'm glad. Tom – come here and put that car in its box. Come and kiss Granny, because Mummy's going to take you back now.'

He did so, pushing against her with such exuberant roughness that Anna saw her mother wince, and hissed, 'Be careful, Tom, for goodness' sake.'

'It's all right, really,' Barbara protested, holding out her hand to Anna, and suddenly she sounded so weary that tears filled Anna's eyes. Impulsively she knelt upon the floor, putting her arms around her mother's waist and burying her face in her dressing gown, smelling from her lap the fresh scent of lemon talcum powder, and beyond it, the warm woman's fragrance she recalled from childhood, cuddling upon her mother's knee, or sulking in tears because of a childish quarrel. Barbara's hands folded about her head, stroking, and she murmured, 'There, there,' in a drowsy voice, as if in a dream, or as if she had become part of the memory, Anna could not tell.

They stayed like that for a long time, whilst Tom stared silently, excluded and disturbed by an emotion he did not understand. As the gentle fingers wound the strands of her hair around and around, Anna felt as if she were melting deep inside, and rushing backwards, buried within her mother, for ever, whilst all the time that fragrance made her happy, the scent of lemons. Outside the birds still sang, and in the corner of the room the radio continued to mumble, its music finished now – a familiar friendly voice telling of future programmes, the weather, and the time.

Twenty-Three

The tide was unusually low, so it was possible to turn right in front of 'Ahoy' and walk along the stretch of beach that was usually covered, past the tangle of undergrowth and low trees that rose sharply from the usual waterline. A low sun gilded the far-out reaches of the river. The mud seemed alive with a million invisible sucking and squelching creatures, but the river was quiet. The end of the season; people had started to go home.

They unlatched the gate and walked along the beach in silence. Occasionally Tom made a remark and Anna murmured vague assent, glad that was all he required.

There was still the boy, she thought, still the windsurf boy to think about, quite deliberately as before, and yet with some resentment too – that even now he could slip between her mother and herself. They had been humiliated in front of each other, Matthew and she, and yet she could not hate him for that. It was George who was right, and she, Anna, foolish; made foolish by the boy, just as she had been made pathetic when John had left her, and (it suddenly occurred to her) ridiculous, by all her mother's secrets.

She frowned down at the muddy shingle, trying to concentrate. What was it? Where did it come from, this paralysing fear that always made her, yes, a victim – someone to whom things happened, always; or someone who, the rest of the time, fled from what was within her grasp? Perhaps it was, after all, her father's fault, she thought, for he had always protected her, his first girl. Barbara had said so. And there you were, trapped in the body nature gave you, ageing now, and imprisoned within the mind *they* had created, until one day a beautiful boy came and offered escape, and then you were too afraid ('And you don't really like sex, do you', John had said, a few years ago, 'you're afraid of it, Anna,

196

afraid of letting go, of the mess of it.') That night when Matthew came to the cottage, what had he expected? She could have stepped forward and wrapped her arms around him, and let whatever was to happen, happen. If only . . . but that thought was not wistful. Anna's fists, swinging loosely at her sides as she walked, clenched suddenly and she let out an involuntary groan, of passion, of longing, and of grief for all that had gone, all the past, and all the passing present too, with its chances not taken. The boy . . . did Matthew regard her with contempt beneath his composure? Or was it pity? 'Was that what the nurses felt for Barbara?' she wondered – the image of her mother superimposing itself on the vision of Matthew in her mind, so that in the unifying fantasy of that second, it was the face of the boy that aged.

Tom looked up at her. 'Mum, are you crying? I thought I heard you cry.'

'No, I'm not. I just had a bit of tummyache.'

'Guess who I just saw along the beach?' Anna knew; but still asked the question the child expected.

'It was Matthew. He was headed up into that wood place up there. Exploring, I 'spect.'

'On his own?'

'Yes. Shall we go and look for him?'

'No. He'd rather be on his own.'

Just then a gull rose screaming from the scrubby trees Tom had indicated. It startled him, and he took her hand, but Anna had not noticed. Abstracted, she walked on, and he was drawn along with her, resenting suddenly her secret distance from him, and dimly sensing that it came with any mention of that other boy's name. He pulled his hand away.

Anna stared up at the undergrowth, where Matthew was wandering even now, looking through the trees at the river perhaps, or lying in the dappled coolness, on mossy ground – even watching them through the branches. At this thought she smiled up at the trees, but there was no movement. Then something fluttered inside her: an excitement, a sense of daring she had never experienced before. A decision made.

Tom had wandered a short way off and was examining a

clump of seaweed. Ahead, in the distance, she could see the stout, ungainly figure of George Treadle, washing down his ferry boat at the end of the pontoon. It was impossible to keep the urgency from her voice as she strode across to Tom and said, 'I just want to run back and get something, darling. And phone someone. You go on ahead to George and tell him I'm coming to catch you up, so that he doesn't think I've let you out on your own.'

He trotted off obediently, and Anna paused long enough to see that he had no interest in glancing behind him, before she hurried to confront the tangled undergrowth. She chose one of the little choked paths that led from the shore into the tangled shade, walking quietly on the balls of her feet, and glancing around her all the time in case she should miss him. 'Matthew!' she half-whispered, half-called, and again, 'Matthew!' into the rustling trees. The need to find him forced its way into her veins and arteries: Matthew away from the river, and away from other people, just as he had been that night when she had stepped back, rejecting him, as now she would not. 'No, no, no . . .' she muttered, she would not. For soon it would be too late, for everything, as it was too late for Barbara, within her iron bed.

She paused, and stared ahead. The wood was silent, and its peace suddenly permeated her skin, giving her confidence. Midges massed in their aimless patterns over the path. Anna thought she heard a twig crack, just ahead where the massed overhanging trees and shrubs formed a little copse, and suddenly remembered what she knew about this place. It was Richard's den, forgotten until this moment, over there where the peculiarly gnarled branch doubled back upon itself, as if to form a barrier. Even the little heap of stones was there beside the path, tumbled now and covered with moss, where her brother had built a little cairn to mark the place. 'Still here,' Anna murmured, forgetting Matthew for a second in that miraculous loop of time.

In the little circle, where the ground hollowed beneath that tree and the close shrubs made a barrier against the world, Richard had made his pretend-camp, banning his sisters unless by special invitation. Once, though, he had lit a fire and invited them for a picnic, making them carry the battered black frying pan and the sausages. 'We were so happy on that day,' thought Anna, 'just lying around here, not quarrelling for once, drinking from the bottle and feeling adult because our parents had left us alone . . . And yes! I'd had a terrible quarrel with Daddy, just before that. So it was a relief to be away from him. I . . . I hated him.'

Yet those things were forgotten; some filter in the memory had allowed her to remember only what was gilded, ideal, unreal. Until now. Matthew had led her to a truth, just as he had released her, that day in the boat when she had seen the cottage from a distance and known that it was empty. 'Matthew,' she hissed again, wanting to whoop with joy because she had found this place again and because he would be there. She knew. A rustling sound filled her ears, it was all around, and Anna imagined that it was the three of them, as children, echoing softly back in her mind like the dust drifting in pools of light, playing and laughing together. Or perhaps it was him, the boy, waiting there where they could be completely private, knowing that she would come.

She thought she heard his voice, ahead, in Richard's den, and smiled, hurrying forward. He was there, in the sanctum. Reaching the little pile of stones, Anna was about to cry out, loudly this time, 'Matthew!' when she froze. There was indeed a sound, very close to her now, a rustling sound mixed with quiet laughter, and she heard his voice too, talking gently, talking to someone.

'Oh, come on. Don't . . .'

At that minute a trio of gulls whirred overhead, drowning whatever words followed.

Then Matthew's voice again, clearly now and angry too, 'What the hell are you on about? I don't know what you're on about!'

A girl's voice tinkled, 'Oh yes, Matthew Paul, everybody knows about you! You're not really keen on me. You're not really interested in girls at all, because you've already got a girlfriend.'

'Oh yeah! And since I haven't got the foggiest idea, why don't you do me a favour and tell me who?'

Uncontrolled giggling. Anna listened, unable to move, wondering angrily why he stayed to be teased, and dreading what she might hear.

'Go on, then,' she heard him say.

'It's obvious,' said the girl, through her laughter, 'you're always hanging around with her so you must fancy her. It's that lady who lives in the cottage with the mast in the garden. So!'

There was a pause, then Anna heard Matthew's voice, crisp and full of irritation. 'God, I didn't think girls could be so stupid! How can she be my girlfriend when she's about the same age as my mum – hey?'

Anna did not move. She could imagine his face, with that lowering expression and the flash of scarlet in his cheek and his full lower lip thrust out.

She bent her head and looked down at her mud-spattered feet in their dirty sandals, planted upon the path like ugly, alien creatures she did not recognise. Then, as if beyond her control, they moved forward a step, and again, until Anna felt a part of her brain shrink with horror at the humiliation they were leading her to, whilst another part of her welcomed it. That slimy mud between her toes was real – as real as the glittering river which usually covered it.

'I really do like you, you know.'

'Do you mean that?'

'Course I do.' His voice was more gentle, and cajoling, than Anna had ever heard it.

'Well . . . I like you too. But I wish . . . I do wish we didn't have to go home.'

'So do I.'

'It doesn't seem fair.' Her voice sounded close to tears; and no audible words followed, only whispering and rustling that tantalised Anna, just out of reach in the corridor in her mind.

As if to run down that infinite passageway, and chase the unknown that she knew would hurt her – just as a swimmer plunges into an icy pool knowing that the shock will be worse than imagined, but inevitable – Anna found herself moving forward and reaching out to part the leaves before her. She saw them in the tiny clearing, Matthew and Jane, the girl from 'Rose Cottage', dappled in early evening sunlight, and leaning forward to kiss. There was something so clumsy and yet so innocent about their movement towards each other that Anna wanted to cry out with pain – envious of this discovery of tenderness, before real desire, before greed.

But when she saw the boy's hand move across and gently touch the girl's small breast, outside her white tee-shirt, Anna was reminded of him touching her too, on the new sweatshirt with its pretty, miniature sail – and she started to blunder backwards, blinded. A large twig cracked under her foot. The two of them jumped apart, and Matthew looked through the branches at her.

'For Christ's sake, Anna, what . . .?'

'I'm sorry, I was . . . er . . . I mean, I'm looking for Tom.'

'Well he's not here, is he?' said the boy savagely, his face scarlet.

'I had to know.'

'Well, can't you see he's not here?' he shouted, ignoring the girl beside him, who stared at the intruder with blank hostility.

'I had to know. I'm sorry,' said Anna, flatly, and turned on her heel to walk away.

Twenty-Four

'Sandra, Sandra,' Barbara called, not knowing where she was, and forgetting the bell that hung twelve inches from her head 'Sandra! Why don't you come? Why doesn't anybody come? Sandra! Anna! Please . . .'

Waking into full consciousness she heard a rattling all around her, and it was a few seconds before she realised that the bed was shaking because she was shaking, her whole body racked by great shudders. 'Now, come on,' she said to herself, 'just control yourself. You can control yourself, so stop it.' Gritting her teeth she told her body to be still, but at every shake it was as if a million tiny wounds opened up inside her, and tears of panic filled her eyes.

She remembered her dream, and the existence of the bell, at the same time, and groped in the darkness until her finger located the button that would bring somebody running. 'Please,' she whispered into the darkness, her shivers subsiding now, though her nightdress was plastered to her body by sweat.

The opening and shutting of the door, tender crooning noises of concern, gentle hands patting the pillow and switching on the dull red light over the bed . . . and Barbara looked up at the nurse, whispering, 'I'm so glad it's you on tonight, Sandra. I think I had . . . a dream.'

'Looks to me as if you've had a temperature too,' said Sandra Massey, reaching for the thermometer and making as if to put it in Barbara's mouth. But she turned her head to one side, shaking it slowly, and saying, 'No, no, not yet, Sandra. I'm trying to remember . . .'

'What is it, Mrs Lewis? Have you forgotten something?'

'I had a dream, but I can't think what happened. I woke and I was trembling, Sandra, trembling all over but I don't know why. I was hot. I thought I was walking along a beach and going into a house, but I don't know why it was hot . . .'

She sounded confused and near to tears; Nurse Massey made the clucking noises in her throat and murmured, 'Don't worry about your dream, it was nothing. You've had a little temperature, that's all. That's all.' She was taken aback when Barbara suddenly reached for her hand and grasped it tightly.

'I remember, now,' she said, with a sigh that was almost a moan. 'I was walking on and on, and I didn't know where I was going, until I saw a little house in the distance. It was like my house in London, only it wasn't; smaller, squatter, somehow, like a bungalow. And when I saw it I knew that was where I had been heading all along, only I hadn't known why, and still didn't know why. But I felt happy, to see it there.'

'Yes, yes,' Sandra said, disturbed by the brightness in her patient's eyes.

'I had a funny feeling as I hurried along the beach towards it that everything I had ever wanted was inside that house, just waiting for me; but then I found it hard to walk, my feet kept slipping on the stones, and so it always seemed the same distance away. It was an awful feeling, and I started to get hot with the effort of it, because it was summer and the sun was in the sky overhead, beating down on me. No shelter, and anyway I wanted to get there because I knew it would be cool inside. You know how you know things, in dreams?' Sandra nodded, stroking Barbara's head. 'It did get nearer, or rather, I drew nearer to it, with all my hurrying, and I thought I saw someone at the window waving to me, just a shadow, but real, just the same. I waved back, and I started to run, Sandra. I was running in the hot sun, and sweating, but it didn't matter because I was getting nearer and nearer all the time, and waving because I saw him at the window. It was him, just as I had hoped. It really was, and I began to laugh aloud for the joy of it, knowing that something wonderful was just inside that little door, waiting for me, as it had always been waiting.'

She was panting now, and clawing at the nurse's hand. 'I went in through the gate – it was like a fairytale house, you know, with a little wicket gate, like in those pictures we had when we were little – and I could see the door ahead of me, and I thought I heard him calling me. So I pushed the door open, but – Sandra! It was all dark, Sandra, and I walked forward into blackness, as if there were no windows in that house, and no doors, no way in and no way out, just the cold and clammy darkness all around me like a black mist ... There was nothing, Sandra! Nothing!'

Barbara buried her face in the nurse's hand and sobbed, her body shaking again, her hair matted and wet where it brushed Sandra's arm. Confused, but full of pity, Sandra Massey looked down, still stroking that head with her free hand, and murmuring, 'Sssh, sssh,' as she used to do when her children cried in the night. 'There, there, Mrs Lewis, dear, there, there. It's all over now. All gone. It's all right. Don't cry, don't cry, don't cry.'

The sobs subsided. For a long moment Barbara looked up into the nurse's eyes, and then she whispered, 'I'm so afraid.'

'But there's nothing to be afraid of now. I'm here, and I'll see if I can't go and get you something to send you back to sleep.'

'Oh yes, but that's so easy, Sandra, making it all go away as if it had never been there.'

'Well, Mrs Lewis,' the nurse said softly, 'you know I don't think there's anything wrong with that. There's nothing wrong with finding peace the best way you can, is there?'

'No, I suppose not. I'll take whatever you like.'

'Good; that's the spirit, Mrs Lewis. Now I'll just pop down the corridor to the drug cupboard and fetch your usual, then come back and change your nightie, and take your temperature, and generally fix you up. All right now?'

Her voice was gentle, as if relieved to rest upon familiar words, and Barbara nodded. 'Oh yes,' she thought, as Sandra walked across the room, leaving the door ajar behind her, 'I'll do as you suggest, because you're kind, and I know that it is me you see in front of you, not just a patient. Dear Sandra, so kind . . .' She sighed, reached up, and switched off the dull light that irritated her eyes.

Lying alone in the darkness, with just a faint light from the corridor slanting into the room, Barbara thought of her dream and shuddered at the horror of it, the nameless dread that clutched her mind like a hand. 'All gone,' Sandra had said, 'all gone,' as if to console, to offer comfort in the face of chaos, with words that were themselves the substance of the void. All gone. 'Dear Lord,' she murmured, closing her eyes, 'please help me to learn . . . teach me how . . . Dear Lord, I want to pray to you, but I can't, there are no words, God, for me to talk to you with. Not any more. All gone.'

She heard the nurse's footsteps, quick and light, along the corridor, and opened her eyes wide, gazing into the gloom. She tried again, but the words stuck somewhere inside her making her feel that she would choke with the effort, the pain of trying to speak – as it was necessary that she should speak. 'I must. I must. I must be able to,' she thought in desperation, for Sandra's ministrations would make her drowsy once more, and then it would be too late.

Again and again she tried to whisper the name of God. Instead the words, 'Dear William, my dearest Will,' slipped from her lips. When Sandra arrived at the bedside she noticed that the old woman's eyes were closed peacefully, but that the gnarled fingers pulled and kneaded at the bedclothes compulsively. Barbara lay quietly, concentrating upon her litany, on the inward repetition of the one name she was sure of.

And as she lay in bed, restless, Anna stared dry-eyed at her ceiling too, listening to the faint splashes from outside and the pinging of the halyards. 'This is the last night I shall ever hear that sound again in this place,' she thought, and then said it aloud to see if the words would mean more then. But she found it impossible to weep at the thought, because like all sea-changes it would only have meaning much later on in time.

Twenty-Five

The last morning was windy; high fluffy clouds feathered across the sky, making the sun appear then disappear. It was a perfect day for sailing, and soon the boats appeared, though fewer of them now. The trees on the far bank gave the truth away. Their dense green already had that heavy dead look, as if a touch of black had been added to the palette, breaking Impressionist rules. In two or three weeks that green would lighten into russet and yellow, as the leaves had one last fling of beauty before falling to the ground for ever.

Anna worked hard. The cupboard beneath the kitchen sink stank, the floorcloth was solid, but once Tom had returned from the Treadles' shop with fresh supplies, she did not allow herself to rest. The curling notice on the pantry door joined the whole contents of the pantry in the dustbin, and the greasy stove shone. Anna dusted every cheap ornament, every picture frame in the little sitting-room, hauled the old vacuum cleaner out to pick up the accumulated dirt of their stay, and even polished the absurd little coffee table until it shone. Glancing around the room, she noticed the mantelpiece clock, silent as ever. The winder was stiff, but after a few seconds a loud tick filled the room, and Anna threw open all the windows with satisfaction.

She looked sadly at the window seat, sagging in the middle where the wood had splintered. They had made it with so much laughter, that first summer, with William asserting that the pile of orange boxes would hold if they were wedged tightly enough so that all the pressure came from the sides. It had worked, and for twenty-five years the seat, covered in foam and repp by Barbara's skilful hands, had borne the burden of all who lounged on it to stare out at the Syne – until the day when Matthew Paul had lounged there, with Anna watching him. It could not be mended now.

By mid-morning all the cleaning was finished: the bathroom, the lavatory, and even the old linoleum in the hall shone. Anna breathed a new smell in the house. All the windows were open, and she had even taken the mattresses from the bunks in the attic-dormitory, beaten them a little with the old broken doll, and replaced them the other way up. She carried the broken toys down to the dustbin, wiped out their cupboard, and closed the door. Only the old teddy bear in the back room escaped their fate. Anna had found Tom crying two nights earlier, because the teddy would be left alone again. She had promised they would take it back to London. 'Will Aunt Hilda mind?' he had asked.

'She won't mind.'

'Will she be glad I've rescued her teddy?'

'Yes, she'll be glad,' she had said.

As they walked slowly along the pontoon Tom said, 'I think Matthew's getting fed up with his windsurfer.' She asked why he said that. 'He isn't using it today and there's a good wind. I wonder why people get fed up with things?'

Anna shrugged. 'Shall we walk through the village? We could call in at the shop and at "Hacienda", to tell them we're leaving today.'

He nodded. 'You know something, Mum? Half of me is glad we're going home, but half of me wants to stay here. Isn't it funny that you can feel two things at once?'

Mary Treadle opened her shop on a Sunday morning for the convenience, as she was always telling the village, of the village not herself. She stood behind the counter, and George ducked through from their sitting-room when they entered, both the old people making an effort to greet Anna as they used to do. Only a certain angle of their faces showed the strain. George avoided her eyes, as if he were ashamed of his outburst. 'But I don't care,' Anna thought. 'There is no point in caring what these people think of me, because I shall never see them again.'

They chatted for a while, then George asked, 'Will you be down again next year, then, Anna?' as Mary chose a large bar of chocolate from her stock and handed it to Tom.

'I expect so, George.'

'We'll miss the little lad, won't we, mother?' he said, glancing across at his wife, whose face softened.

'Aye, we will,' she said.

'I'll write you a postcard from London,' said Tom.

There was a silence, then Anna and Mary said, 'Well . . .' at the same instant, and smiled. 'We'll see you next year then, Anna. You take care of him, now!' George said, and she nodded, shaking their hands.

There was no reply at 'Hacienda'. 'It's odd that they should go out on a Sunday morning,' said Anna, noticing that the bronze Granada was not under its car port. For a few minutes they stood looking at the varnished door, then Tom kicked at the gravel and asked what they should do. He sounded disconsolate. 'Let's walk around a bit. Maybe they've gone to get newspapers or something, and they'll be back soon. Of course, we could always leave it,' she added hopefully, feeling a sudden nervousness at the thought of meeting one or other of the Pauls. But with the indignant air of an old lady who knows the proprieties he protested that they must say goodbye.

Instead of retracing their steps as usual they continued along the lane in which the incongruous 'Hacienda' was situated, walking slowly, picking a wild flower only to let it fall, and deciding which of the cottages they would choose to live in. Tom was adamant that 'Hacienda' was the most handsome house in the village; he was shocked when Anna, with bitter vehemence in her voice, proclaimed it hideous. 'And corrupting too,' she thought, 'even infecting Tom's sense of what is pretty, with its vulgar assurance!'

At the end of the lane there was a fork, one prong becoming what was known as the High Street, though there were only four cottages in it, and the other leading off to the church and rectory and no farther. On an impulse Anna turned in that direction, pushing open the lych gate and closing it firmly behind her as the notice requested. The mossy path sloped upwards to the plain Norman building, the church standing upon its own small hill within the hilly village. Anna stood still for a moment and looked at it. 'But why have we come here?' Tom asked, with no curiosity in his voice.

A fourteenth-century porch, one interesting window from the same period which showed to good effect the then newly discovered yellow stain, and a medieval stone pulpit, still painted in blues, reds and golds – the church of St John was no different to countless other country churches which are found down quiet lanes, surrounded by the waving grasses of ancient graves. Piscina, rood loft and gilded screen – William had often taken his children to the church and pointed out these things, because, he said, it was a language they should know. At the time it was not the words that spoke to them nor the place; it was the gravity in their father's face.

Anna had a clear picture of William lifting and drawing aside the carpet in the sanctuary to show them the church's one good brass. It was a knight, with lettering in Latin on ribbons around his head and feet. 'In manus tuas, domine, commendo spiritum meum. Redemisti, Domine Deus Veritatis,' said one; and she could still hear William intoning his translations, in a voice they dared not smile at: 'Let all men pray for the soul of Thomas Edwards, who died on the twenty-sixth day of November Anno Domini 1455. May his soul be pleasing unto God.' Once they had attempted to take a rubbing, but it had not been a success. Yet each time they visited that place on an evening walk they asked their father to show them 'poor Mr Edwards', and Anna would trace with her fingers the flowing lines of his robe, hoping that his soul had indeed met with a warm welcome, somewhere up there in the blue sky. Standing still now, and closing her eyes for a second, Anna could visualise the gentle precision with which her father replaced the old worn carpet, telling them always to be careful in such places, 'because it's been here a long time and we want to be sure it's here when we're not' – a piece of advice that was invariably uttered with perfect good cheer.

'It is still here,' she said aloud, looking around at the moss and lichen-covered gravestones around the porch and the path, with their words of hope upon them. Over in the corner, newer graves were in neat lines, oblongs of artificial-looking marble presiding over beds of green-coloured chips of glass. 'George Treadle's sons are over there, and George and Mary will join them soon, and my mother will be dead and I shall be somewhere else, but the tower and the porch and the sanctuary will still be the same, because that is how my father said it would be.' She bent and picked up a few bits of recent confetti from the path, and smiled at it.

'Mum, MUM!' Tom was reading something written on one of the newer graves, and beckoned her frantically, but she motioned him to be quiet. A service was in progress; she had forgotten both the day and the time. Quietly she walked up to the porch and tiptoed inside, standing quite still as the rector's voice came clearly through the studded and felt-covered inner door.

'Almighty and everlasting God, who art always more ready to hear than we are to pray, and art wont to give us more than either we desire or deserve: pour down upon us the abundance of thy mercy; forgiving us those things whereof our conscience is afraid, and giving us those good things which we are not worthy to ask . . .'

It contained no meaning for Anna; what mattered was not the words themselves, she thought, but that they were said. It seemed to her suddenly that the compulsion to name and to praise, and to ask forgiveness, which drew a small group of people she did not know to this place each week, was just a part of something else she knew quite well, but something she had forgotten. It was the vast human need to reach upwards and outwards and to prove by its dying (the illegible stone slab or the sparkling modern marble and the universal tears in the shadow of the churchyard yew) that there was no real ending – not really; simply a continuation of a process that began centuries ago, and would – with the marriages, and births, and maturings – go on for ever.

She read the carefully printed notices, and the flower rota. So, every fourth Sunday Mrs Hastings arranged carnations in the old-fashioned glass vases, and Miss Jackson, Miss Musgrove and Mrs Simpson took their turn, and the same names appeared on the church cleaning rota underneath. Anna smiled. Perhaps it was easier to believe in God if you wielded a duster and a bottle of brass polish, and cleaned his house as if it were your own, paying attention to the corners. 'Pour down upon us the abundance of thy mercy,' it said in the Collect, and yet she could not but smile a little grimly at the idea of that mercy; beauty, yes, the everlasting beauty of the river, but not mercy – not with the Treadle boys under their modern slab, and Barbara lying on her bleak bed, and the oxygen tent, too soon, and somewhere out there by the churchyard path the weeping stone cherub, erected a hundred years ago for the baby who died and was carried out in his doll's coffin . . . No, not mercy, not that, Anna thought, grinding her teeth.

And yet the existence of those names, there in the porch beneath the dogtooth arch, proved something else. 'God of the Flower Rota,' she said, under her breath, without knowing why. It was nothing as grand as mercy; something quite ordinary had the power to give purpose to the lives of Mrs Hastings, Miss Jackson, Miss Musgrove and Mrs Simpson and all the others there inside, and to Barbara, her mother, too. And had it also given William a sense of belonging? Barbara said so. It was impossible to know.

Tom stood in the doorway, in the sunlight, and whispered, 'Mum, why didn't you come? I found a grave with a name like Treadle on it,' but Anna put her finger to her lips. The organ was playing, and the congregation had started to sing one of those old hymns which carry in their cadences an almost unbearable nostalgia, and yet comfort still, because of their familiarity:

'Dear Lord and Father of Mankind . . .'

'Forgive our foolish ways indeed,' Anna said under her breath, and Tom gently pulled her out into the sunlight, saying that he wanted to go.

'I don't like churches,' he said, as they walked down the path.

'Why?'

'Because they're scary. All the dead people around you.'

'But they can't harm you, darling.'

He looked dubious. 'How do you know?'

'I just do. They were nice people when they were alive, so why should they hurt you?'

He looked thoughtful. 'Well . . . er . . . it's because they still want to be alive, and so they get angry and turn themselves into ghosts, and come to haunt all the people who are still alive and whom they're jealous of.' Tom spoke with such conviction that she burst out laughing and asked where he had learned such nonsense. 'It's not nonsense! A boy at school told me. I think that bits of people stay alive after they're dead. I mean, if you can go to heaven, like they say, why can't you turn yourself into a ghost and hang about to frighten people?' He had stopped and was standing with his hands on his hips, like a lawyer earnestly arguing a case.

'I don't know, Tom,' said Anna.

'Well, if you don't know how can you say there's no such thing as ghosts?'

'I can't.'

'Well then,' he said with an air of finality, 'that's why I don't like churches, or empty bedrooms, or attics, or being upstairs on my own awake when you and Daddy are ... I mean, when you're in the kitchen with the door closed. It makes me think of things ...'

'I know what you mean, sweetie,' said Anna, half to herself, 'I think of things too, all sorts of things. This church makes me think of when I was little, and Grandad was alive, and Granny was young, and when I first met your Dad ... All those things are like ghosts, too. Real ghosts.'

'Do they frighten you?'

'No they don't. Not now. They're happy ghosts.'

Comprehension dawned on his face. 'I get it, Mum. You do believe in ghosts really, it's just that you don't think they're all frightening, is that it?'

She nodded, and he added, 'I'll tell you one thing. I bet Matthew doesn't believe in ghosts. He wouldn't be frightened of anything, would he? I bet he'd even come here in the middle of the night, and not be scared.' 'I bet he would,' she said, and something in her voice made him look at her sharply.

'Don't you like him any more?'

'Of course I do, Tom. We'll go and see him now.'

But there was no dread now. 'Drop thy still dews of quietness, Till all our strivings cease,' echoed in Anna's mind as they reached the gate, and she thought calmly that the striving is all there is, and the acceptance of the striving, even the striving for the acceptance that Barbara had achieved. And the still small voice of calm died away, to be replaced by the turbulent birds, as the lych gate clicked shut behind them.

Valerie Paul looked irritable. 'Adrian dragged us all the way to Synemouth at the crack of dawn,' she explained, 'to see a stupid yacht that belongs to someone he knows. They're setting off for the south of France today, lucky devils.'

'Following the sun,' said Adrian, coming to the door behind her. 'Lucky,' Anna agreed, and there was a pause. 'So you're off, then,' Valerie said, 'and I can't say I blame you. We've got a bit longer; but honestly I'd just as soon go home now. I've had my holiday. It gets a bit quiet, doesn't it?'

Anna agreed, and after a few more minutes, in which there was nothing to say, they exchanged telephone numbers. 'Don't forget, if you're ever in Bristol,' said Valerie brightly, and Adrian promised a drink and a meal. 'I'll definitely look you up,' Anna promised, prodding Tom to hold out his hand. As they walked away Adrian called, 'Go down to the river and see if you can see Matthew. He went down as soon as we got back. He'd be a bit miffed if you forgot to say goodbye.'

By waving and calling from the end of the pontoon, Tom attracted his attention, whilst Anna stood wondering how to compose her face. Skilfully Matthew adjusted the wishbone booms and his own body, so that within a few minutes he glided towards them and stood by the pontoon, balancing on the rocking board with the rig dropped in the water, so that the sail floated upon its surface.

Tom said that they were going home, and rattled on, although the older boy said nothing – inviting him to London to see them, and asking if Matthew would teach him to windsurf next summer because there had been no time this year. His chatter flowed over Anna like a wave as she stood silent, finding it painful still to gaze on Matthew's face.

'Not speaking to me, then?' he said.

She made her voice light. 'Of course I am!'

'It'll be boring without you two,' he said, 'though we'll be gone in a week or so. Dad's got to go up in the week anyway, so it'll just be me and Mum.' He made a face.

Anna could not stop herself. 'What about your young friends,' she asked, examining a fingernail. 'The girls, Nicola and Jane, from "Rose Cottage".'

'Gone back this morning,' he said, fiddling with the inhaul line.

'The river is emptying,' said Anna, staring out across the water, then gesturing towards the windsurf board. 'You'll have more room for this.'

'Yeah.'

'Have a good time, anyway. We'd better not keep you; it's a good wind.'

Matthew started to haul up the rig, grunting as he did so. 'Mmmm. And no idiots in their rubber dinghies getting in the way. I like having the place to myself. Oh by the way, make sure you look me up next year, won't you? Will you be down? We will – as usual.'

Anna smiled at him. 'Yes, of course. We'll see you then, and we'll all have a good time again, won't we Tom?'

They watched him draw away with a fluid motion, gathering speed as the wind caught the sail, more graceful, Anna thought, than any bird – for there was no sense of endeavour, only the ease, the flowing outward on the surface of the river, untroubled by its depths.

The car packed, they locked 'Ahoy', and climbed the orchard path. The village was quiet – that end-of-the-season hush that warns the shop and the pub that the lean months are about to begin. Anna took a last look over her shoulder at the still river, catching her breath at the sight, before turning resolutely towards the car. The car park was almost empty; though the Treadles' battered van stood in the corner, taking the space of two. As the car doors clunked shut and Anna started the engine, she sighed to think of all the holidays over for another year. But that was how it was.

'We always used to sing,' she called over her shoulder, as they drove through the shadowed lanes. 'We sang silly songs like Old MacDonald, all of us taking different parts, and we did it all the way home.'

'Why did you?'

'To pass the time, silly,' she said. 'So let's do it now. Shall we try Ten Green Bottles?'

He said nothing, but she started the song, her voice flat, though determinedly loud . . . 'and if one green bottle should accidentally fall . . .' but still he did not join in.

All the way through she took it, piping up the silly words, the *reductio ad absurdum* of mathematics, and existence. 'And if one green bottle should accidentally fall, there'd be *no* green bottles hanging on the wall.'

Tom was silent. Looking in the mirror Anna could see

that he was staring out at the passing hedgerows, his face solemn and his thumb in his mouth. 'Tom?' she said, and felt the word choke in her throat, the single syllable breaking into fragments as tears filled her eyes and began to roll down her cheeks. 'Tom – please talk to me a bit.'

Then he took his thumb from his mouth and looked at her reflection in the driving mirror, blankly, as if he had been living in a dream. He said, 'Mum . . . shall I tell you what I'm thinking? I'm thinking of a sad thing. I'm thinking of the car park, when all the cars have gone.'

Also in Pavanne:

The Anderson Question by Bel Mooney

Bel Mooney was born and brought up in Liverpool. As a philosophy student at London University, she met her future husband, the broadcaster Jonathan Dimbleby. They now live near Bath with their son and daughter. *The Windsurf Boy*, her first novel, reached the *Sunday Times* bestseller list. Bel Mooney has worked as a journalist for a wide variety of publications and has appeared regularly on television and radio. She is now a regular columnist on the *Sunday Times*, and reviews fiction for *Cosmopolitan*.

'A novelist of perceptive strength . . . Bel Mooney plots an authentic, compelling detective story of the soul' COMPANY

Eleanor Anderson's comfortable and well-ordered life is completely shattered when her husband David, the dependable and much respected village doctor, disappears. A few days later he is found dead, apparently the victim of a heart attack, and speculation is stilled as family, friends and patients alike feel a kind of relief at knowing the worst.

But genuine grief at their bereavement gives way to angry bewilderment when a post-mortem reveals that the man they thought they knew so well, the man they all depended on, had taken his own life, for no obvious reason. And Eleanor discovers, in the uneasy company of her ungracious son, that all she had assumed and lived by has been false . . .

'She writes sensitively of a close village life, and tenderly of the anguish and soul-searching in his wife that Anderson's death provokes . . . it marks a real step forward in Bel Mooney's development as a remarkably good novelist' SUSAN HILL, GOOD HOUSEKEEPING

'Beautifully written, compassionate . . . extremely moving . . . one of the best novels I have read for a long time' BOOKS AND BOOKMEN

Also available in Pavanne:

Two important novels by Susan Fromberg Schaeffer—
Anya and *The Madness of a Seduced Woman*

Susan Fromberg Schaeffer is a well-known American author and poet. She was born in Brooklyn, New York. She was educated in New York City public schools and at the University of Chicago where she received her Ph.D degree in 1966 (and where she wrote the first doctoral dissertation on Vladimir Nabokov). She has written many scholarly articles and is a frequent book reviewer for the *Chicago Sun Times*. She is Professor of English at Brooklyn College and a founding member of its Master of Arts Program in Poetry. She lives in Brooklyn and Vermont with her husband and two children.

Anya is one of the most important novels to be written on the horror of survival in the holocaust. The book grew out of a chance remark made to Susan Fromberg Schaeffer by a survivor of the Nazi concentration camps: 'I was so struck by the cruelty she described that I became obsessed with what really went on.' She tracked down survivors and collected all the details she could about life before, during and after the war. The result is a novel of huge scope in the tradition of the great Russian novels, as the *New York Times Book Review* said, 'a triumph of realism in art'.

Anya tells the story of Anya Savikin, a Russian Jewess who grows up in Poland between the wars – a time of piano lessons, elaborate meals, country dachas, fancy dress balls, marriages and deaths. All this is swept away by World War II and the firestorm of the holocaust. Anya loses her mother, her father and her husband – only she and her daughter survive.

Since it was first published in America in 1974, *Anya* has sold over two million copies and the author still receives letters from holocaust survivors who have been moved by the book.

'Anya is a myth, an epic, the creation of darkness and of laughter stopped forever in the open throat. Out of blown-away dust Susan Fromberg Schaeffer has created a world. It is a vision, set down by a fearless, patient poet . . . a writer of remarkable power.' THE WASHINGTON POST

The Madness of a Seduced Woman

'During all those years when everyone wanted me to tell them . . . how I came to fire that shot, I never wanted to talk. Now I think I do . . .'

So begins the story of Agnes Dempster, a beautiful young woman destined to be severely wronged by life and love, whose dreams, thoughts and actions propel her towards a horrific crime of passion she is incapable of preventing.

In her search for an all-consuming, perfect love, Agnes turn her back on an unhappy childhood in Vermont, only to become infatuated with a man who will never make her happy, a betrayer who unwittingly pushes Agnes to the brink of madness, *the madness of a seduced woman* . . .

Set at the turn of the century and inspired by an actual case, *The Madness of a Seduced Woman* is a rich, complex, passionate novel, a powerful evocation of a woman's psyche and the healing and destroying powers of love.

'Fascinating . . . a novel of passion and violence' COMPANY

'The power of this passionate novel lies in the creation of its hero, Agnes. I can't remember a single other character in fiction with whom I have ever identified more' MARGARET FORSTER

'This book asserts the importance of women's feelings, not just this woman's but that of others dedicated to the object of love' FINANCIAL TIMES

'Striking . . . memorable . . . a most remarkable book' FAY WELDON

'A great many women have tried to write *the* feminist novel . . . *this* is the novel they've been trying to write' MARGARET FORSTER

Solstice by Joyce Carol Oates

A departure in theme as well as style for this formidable and compelling author, *Solstice* is a novel of obsession – like *The Madness of a Seduced Woman* or *The French Lieutenant's Woman*, only in this case it is the story of a friendship between two women, a manipulative bond of powerful attraction and its sometimes frightening consequences.

It is about Sheila Trask, a famous painter, widow of an even more famous artist who has left her a big house in rural Pennsylvania – and about a younger woman, Monica, a 'golden girl' with golden hair, who has come to teach at a nearby boys' school, recovering from the break-up of her marriage.

'By the end, the two women have undergone the journey to self-knowledge that is the hero's traditional work. The voyage is not for the faint of heart and neither is this book, written in Miss Oates's highly coloured but firmly controlled prose.

'Miss Oates makes us take Monica's and Sheila's love-hate bond seriously by creating two believable, complicated women and by grounding her story in the universal.

'Almost half a century ago, Virginia Woolf called for a new kind of fiction, one in which women would be described not "only in relation to the other sex". She predicted that when a woman finally wrote a novel in which "two women are represented as friends" she would "light a torch in that vast chamber where nobody has yet been". Joyce Carol Oates, never squeamish about looking into the dark places of the soul, has aimed a powerful beam into that shadowy chamber. *Solstice* should dispel a lot of comforting ideas about the nature of women.' NEW YORK TIMES REVIEW OF BOOKS

'There is no doubt about one's *living through* Joyce Carol Oates's new book, being submerged by it, becoming one with it. It is a tour de force.

'Every subtle nuance of this friendship is chronicled with perception and compassion. The writing is superb, the narrative flow strong and the dialogue memorable.

'But the final touch of genius is the creation of Sheila Trask. Neither Monica nor the reader learns very much about her past or her origins, yet Miss Oates manages to make us feel deeply involved in her strident and disconcerting persona and to accept her – one of the most difficult tasks for a novelist – as a painter of great talent.' THE DAILY TELEGRAPH

Across the Water by Grace Ingoldby

Marking the debut of a remarkable new writer, *Across the Water* is a novel about its characters – a family tragedy set in Co. Fermanagh during the summer drought of 1976. It is about two brothers – Desmond and Boyle Hamilton – who were sent 'across the water' to England to be educated. Desmond escaped from his Northern Irish roots, married an English girl and has become a trendy playwright in London. Boyle, now 40, still lives with his 'Dada' in the dilapidated Georgian family house, isolated in his own world behind huge wrought iron gates . . . Boyle is eccentric, close to madness, and he has maintained a friendship bordering on love with a seventeen-year-old Catholic youth suspected of complicity in the murder of their neighbour.

This murder is investigated by an English army officer who – as it turns out – was at school with Desmond and Boyle when they were 'across the water'. Desmond's wife Aimee arrives to spend the summer – she's bored, conventional, middle-class and very English – and she drifts into an affair with the Englishman. Desmond arrives to make a pretentious film about Irish Celtic twilight and the ancient tradition of a stone which sits on an island in the lake . . . the island where Boyle's disturbed mind will finally crack and where the inevitable tragedy will take place . . .

'A first novel of rare authority, steeped in menace' THE DAILY TELEGRAPH

'A strong, confident and original debut . . . a gripping account of people in whom violence erupts' COSMOPOLITAN

'A strongly imagined and accomplished first novel . . . a horrible family tragedy played out by people exhausted in the heat and made threadbare by old, unresolved conflicts' THE GUARDIAN

'Accomplished and sure in its own right . . . you feel compelled to read on to the horrifying, beautifully described end'
SUSAN HILL, GOOD HOUSEKEEPING

'The wit is accurate and very funny; trenchant, but never dismissive'
COLIN GREENLAND, NEW STATESMAN

Fly Away Home by Marge Piercy

'Ladybird, ladybird
Fly away home.
Your house is on fire
Your children will burn'

It seems to Daria Walker that her husband's behaviour is getting stranger and stranger . . . mysterious phone calls, letters . . . then suddenly he announces he's leaving her – and without a settlement.

Shocked and bewildered, Daria is forced to investigate their finances – and soon she's in for some even greater shocks. Her helplessness turns to rage and terror as she discovers her husband's 'business' dealings include arson – and murder.

Then, one night, Daria awakes to the smell of burning . . .

'Marge Piercy is the political novelist of our time. More: she is the conscience.' MARILYN FRENCH

'Earlier novels by Marge Piercy have been notable for their ferocity about injustices done to women. Here, she works a smaller, more familiar canvas . . . the story moves so vividly, the scenes are so natural that we believe every word of it.' THE GUARDIAN

'Marge Piercy is now established as a top-flight, wider-canvas novelist: a page-turner with class.' DEBORAH MOGGACH, COSMOPOLITAN

'Compelling. A bright, clear piece of fiction.' WASHINGTON POST

'A romance with a social conscience, a tale of love, betrayal and revenge.' NEW YORK TIMES BOOK REVIEW

By the author of *Vida* and *Braided Lives*.